Ibrahim & Reenie

Ibrahim & Reenie

David Llewellyn

SEREN

Seren is the book imprint of
Poetry Wales Press Ltd
57 Nolton Street, Bridgend, Wales, CF31 3AE
www.serenbooks.com
Facebook: facebook.com/SerenBooks
Twitter: @SerenBooks

© David Llewellyn

Print ISBN 978-1-78172-081-3
Ebook ISBN 978-1-78172-083-7

The right of David Llewellyn to be identified as the author of this work
has been asserted in accordance with the Copyright, Designs and
Patents Act, 1988.

This book is a work of fiction. The characters and incidents portrayed
are the work of the author's imagination. Any other resemblance to
actual persons, living or dead, is entirely coincidental.

Typesetting by Elaine Sharples
Printed by TJ International, Padstow

The publisher works with the financial assistance of
The Welsh Books Council

You road I enter upon and look around,

I believe you are not all that is here,

I believe that much unseen is also here.

Walt Whitman, *Song of the Open Road*

1

Until that day, Ibrahim had never seen a pheasant – living or dead. He knew what a pheasant was, had seen innumerable pheasants shotgunned out of grey English skies on TV, but had never seen one, as it were, in the flesh. And its flesh was almost all he could see, spilling out from a tyre-tracked mess of feathers in the middle of the road. The pheasant was the fifth dead creature he had passed, following two hedgehogs, a rabbit and a fox, a dead animal for every two miles walked, and it seemed to him that this road was where all things came when they had outlived their purpose, when they were useless or dead.

At the roadside he had seen a plastic toy car, its bright colours dulled and smudged by dirt; cans and bottles and empty cartons blossoming like garish weeds; three shopping trolleys; a wheelchair with the name of a familiar hospital stencilled onto it in white; the severed, bald, and eyeless head of a doll; and a bunch of fresh flowers, still swaddled in cellophane and placed with mournful deliberation. Now that summer was over, the roadside ferns were beginning to brown and the hedgerows were spattered with angry red berries.

He walked slowly, in some pain, but leaning forward as if braced against a stiff gale. The traffic cut past him in slicing waves – never more than three cars at a time; loud snatches of music blaring from open windows, plastic bags and buckled tin cans and clouds of dust caught up in their wake.

The motorway was near, but it could have been a hundred miles away, because Ibrahim was walking from Cardiff to London, a journey of one hundred and sixty miles, give or take, and he was using the older roads.

He had woken earlier than was usual for a Tuesday, after a night of broken sleep. He ate a light breakfast, packed his things into a rucksack, urinated three times in less than fifteen minutes – the last time coaxing out only a few embarrassed drops – and had left his dusty, mildewed flat four hours earlier. But by late afternoon and the moment when he saw the ovoid puddle of feathers and guts that was once a pheasant, he had covered just ten miles.

It would have been easier to drive or catch a train, but there was never any chance of that. Instead, he walked, resting every half mile or so to take the weight off a leg augmented with titanium pins and rods, but those rest breaks were short, cut brief by his determination and his refusal to admit that he had made a mistake, that he should turn around and go home, that he should reply to his sister's letter and tell her he couldn't come, and ignore every letter she sent from then on. If anything, it was the pain that drove him; that bass note deep inside his leg. The kind of pain that was at once agonising and reassuring, because he would not turn around and he would not give up and the pain could only end when he stopped walking.

Besides, he had spent days planning this journey. What clothes to wear, what food to take. Poring over maps and using the computers in his local library to study online journey planners. Calculating how many miles he should walk each day, and penning Xs on the map to mark each night's resting place. Quickly he began to think of that crooked old road – its arch cresting in the elbow of the Severn Estuary – not as a road but as a cliff-face, with Cardiff as the base camp and London its summit. When resting he drank water and ate chocolate, the Freddo bars he bought – so he told himself – for their cheapness, and not because they were chocolate frogs that reminded him of after-school treats.

Ibrahim was a serious man. Twenty-four years old, but mirthless; his expression many years estranged from a smile or even a grin. Though he lived in one city, and was walking to another, he was ill-suited to the density of other people, as if that place between cities was where he belonged. Some people are made lonely and desperate by distance and isolation, while others thrive and find their peace in it. Ibrahim was the latter. Since leaving the outer edge of Cardiff and the last clusters of newly built show homes, he'd passed only a handful of other people: truck drivers congregating around a layby burger van, and a sweating, red-faced jogger with an iPod strapped to his arm.

If the next hundred and fifty miles were like this, he reasoned, the journey should be easy. Traffic he could handle. It was the idea of people and transport, being surrounded by people and being *inside* any mode of transport, that filled him with dread.

Here's to a hundred and fifty miles of open, empty roads and no people.

But this prayer, this hope, was smashed and ground into the earth when he reached the grass verge between the road and the car park of a chain hotel, and saw the old woman in the deckchair, and the orange tent, and the little table, and the camp stove, and the kettle, and the supermarket trolley crammed full of boxes and bags.

He stopped walking, blinking at the scene before him as if each blink might straighten things out, help it make some kind of sense, but it was no use. She was still there.

There was something marmoreal about her, she and her deckchair carved from the same block and abandoned at the roadside. A permanent memorial to every bag-lady who'd ever lived. Her frame, all but lost beneath a thick all-weather coat, was shrunken, almost no-necked, her chin in her chest, but when he drew nearer she sat upright and craned around to look at him.

He took another step towards her.

'What's wrong with your leg?' she asked. 'You're limping.'

He reached down and massaged the calf of his right leg, wincing as if suddenly reminded of the pain and the cause of it. 'It was an accident,' he said. 'It hurts sometimes.'

Placing her mug on the table, she studied him for a moment, and pointed to her tent. 'If you go in there, I've got another deckchair,' she said. 'Never know when you'll have company. Sit yourself down. You look like you could do with a rest.'

He heard a familiar twang in her accent, an unmistakable trace of East London. Gratefully he nodded, then walked over to her tent and leaned inside. In the filtered, muddy light he saw a deckchair, a sleeping bag and pillow on a thin foam mattress, and in one corner of the tent an ornate, gilded cage housing a tiny grey and yellow bird. The bird shuffled along the bars of its cage, inching towards him using its scaly grey feet and its beak, tilted its head and whistled.

'Don't mind Solomon,' said the old woman. 'He just wants feeding.'

He heaved the chair out from the tent, wrenched it open, and set it down on the other side of the old woman's table.

'Fancy a cuppa?' she asked him. 'I've only just boiled the kettle. I've got tea or coffee.' Then, a minute or so later, passing him his coffee: 'Sorry it's not real milk and sugar. Only got long life and sweeteners, see?'

He thanked her anyway, taking the mug and for a moment holding it in both hands, enjoying the almost painful heat. It was late summer, but already there was a coldness to the air, the incoming creep of autumn. For a week or more, the inner-city evenings had been scented with more bonfires than barbecues.

'I'm Reenie, by the way,' said the old woman. 'Well. My name's Irene. But everyone calls me Reenie.'

'I'm Ibrahim.'

'Ibrahim? That's the same as Abraham, isn't it?'

He nodded.

'Yeah,' said Reenie. 'My dad's name was Avram. That's the same as Abraham. Called himself Albert, though. Thought Avram was a bit old-fashioned, I think. You don't get many Avrams or Abrahams or even Alberts nowadays. But Ibrahim... I bet that's a popular name. I mean with...' She paused, biting at her lower lip as if struggling to seize on a word, the right word. 'Where you from?'

'Cardiff.'

'No, I mean *originally*.'

'Oh. London.'

'No, love, I mean your *family*. Where's your *family* from?'

'Oh. Pakistan. Originally.'

'Right. That's what I meant. I bet Ibrahim's a popular name with *people from Pakistan*.' And she drew those last three words out, as if avoiding other words altogether.

'Yeah, it is,' said Ibrahim. 'And your dad's name was Avram, you said?'

'Yes, love.'

10

'How's that spelt?'

'A-v-r-a-m.'

He felt something in his chest, like the slamming of a door caught in a draft. A heart palpitation? At his age? 'Avram what?' He asked, his mouth drying up.

'Lieberman,' said Reenie. 'He's not famous or anything. Why'd you ask?'

'Nothing.' He avoided her gaze and felt a sudden lurch in his stomach. 'Just wondering.' He smiled at her. 'I've never met anyone called Reenie before.'

'No,' she laughed. 'Probably not. Not so many Irenes about nowadays, I reckon. And Reenie's just a nickname. So. Have you walked all the way from Cardiff?'

'Yeah. It's taken me all day. With my leg, you know.'

'And where you going? Newport? 'Cause, you know, the buses aren't that expensive, and the train'll get you there in ten minutes.'

'No. I'm going to London.'

She said nothing, instead offering an expression he couldn't read, a quizzical combination of frown and smile, and a moment's silence passed between them.

'Well, love,' she said, at last. 'You really should think about getting the train or the coach or something. London's about a hundred and fifty miles *that* way.' And she pointed over her shoulder with a hooked thumb.

'No,' he said. 'I can't get the train. Or the coach. And I don't drive.' He sipped his coffee, hoping she had run out of questions, and stopped himself from wincing at the sickly taste of UHT milk, more overpowering than the charcoal bitterness of her cheap instant coffee. 'How about you?' he asked. 'Where are you going?'

'Me? Oh, I live here. Can't you tell?'

'You... *live* here?'

She laughed. 'No, love. I'm pulling your leg. I'm just resting here for a bit. But it's like they say, wherever I lay my hat...'

'What does that mean?'

'It's a *saying*. Wherever I lay my hat's my home. Not that I've got an hat. I've got an umbrella, but no hat.'

'And the trolley? What's with the shopping trolley?'

'I'm borrowing it,' said Reenie. 'Well. You put a pound in, you get a trolley. And they've got so many of the bloody things; I didn't think they'd miss one of them.'

'But why do you need it?'

'For my things. I needed somewhere for the tent, somewhere for my chairs, somewhere for my camp stove and my kettle and my clothes. Somewhere for Solomon. Course... he gets the back seat. The front end bounces about a bit when I'm pushing it. He'd shake all his feathers out if I put him up front.'

'But isn't that stealing? If you just take the trolley home with you, I mean?'

She leaned forward, her chair's rusted springs squeaking beneath her, and frowned theatrically, as if she already had the answer to his question and knew it before he asked.

'Well, the way I see it is they've got branches all over the country. When I don't need it any more I'll take it to another supermarket and get my pound back. Like I said, I'm not stealing it. I'm *borrowing* it.'

He laughed, or rather he smiled and huffed through his nose, but then his attention was caught by the police car slaloming its way across the car park, towards them.

'Hello,' said Reenie. 'You in trouble with the law, or something?'

He shook his head. 'No. Are you?'

'Not recently, no.'

The police car reached the foot of their embankment in seconds, and two officers – a man and a woman – climbed out and walked towards them. Ibrahim was almost certain he saw the moment when they both studied the terrain, wondering where best to place themselves to assert their authority, and failing when they ended up one higher than the other and both lower than the pair sitting in deckchairs.

'Hello,' said the policewoman, giving each of them in turn a cheery, disarming smile. 'You okay?'

'We're fine, love,' said Reenie, answering quickly, as if she had expected both the arrival of the police, and the question, for some time.

'Right. You see we've had a call from somebody at the hotel. They were a little concerned. They said you're *walking* to London. Is that correct?'

Ibrahim looked from Reenie to the policewoman, his mouth opening and closing. How could anyone in the hotel know he was walking to London?

'Yes, love,' said Reenie. 'Is there a problem?'

The policeman, clearly anxious at standing lower on the verge than his colleague and having to look up at Ibrahim and Reenie, climbed a few steps higher. 'There's no problem, no,' he said, talking to Reenie but staring at Ibrahim. 'It's just they said you've been here a few days, and they were worried about you. Where've you come from? Are you homeless?'

'I'm not homeless. I've got a tent,' said Reenie. 'And I've come from Cardiff, but I'm going to London.'

'Well, you see, London's *very far away*.' The policeman emphasised the last three words as if talking to a child or a foreigner. 'It's too far to walk.'

'I'm not doing it in a day,' said Reenie, sitting up straight. 'I'm taking my time. There's no law against walking to London.'

'No, there isn't. But you've got a lot of things with you. That trolley for one thing, and your tent. Have you got any family in Cardiff? Does anyone know you're out here?'

'I've got no family,' said Reenie, her voice a little quieter. 'No husband, no kids. I'm doing this on my own.'

'And, uh, how about your friend, here?' The policeman looked again at Ibrahim.

'We only just met,' said Reenie. 'But he's walking to London, too.'

'You're *also* walking to London?' The policeman asked.

Ibrahim nodded but said nothing.

'And could I take your name?'

Reenie leaned further forward in her chair. Another squeak of springs.

'I'm sorry, young man,' she said. 'But you didn't take my name, so why are you taking his?'

'It's okay, really,' said the policewoman, rejoining the conversation as if to steer it away from raised voices. 'We're just concerned for your welfare, Mrs...'

'You can call me Reenie. I've been a widow eight years now, so it's a bit late to be calling me Mrs anything.'

'Very well. *Reenie.* We're just a little concerned for your welfare. London's very far away, and you have a lot of things with you. Besides, you're right next to the road here, which isn't safe.'

'Well, I wasn't planning on staying here,' said Reenie. 'I'm just having a bit of a rest.'

'In that case,' said the policeman. 'I think it's probably best we call social services. If you don't have anyone back in Cardiff who we can call, I mean.'

'You don't need to do that,' said Ibrahim, speaking for the first time since their arrival. 'We'll be moving along soon, and I'll be with her.'

'Is that true?' asked the policeman.

'It is now,' said Reenie.

'But you said the two of you only just met.'

'And we did. But if this young man doesn't mind taking it in turns to push my trolley, I won't say no.'

Reenie and Ibrahim exchanged a glance, and smiled as if this had been their plan all along. Turning away from them, the police officers had a moment's conference consisting largely of whispers and shrugs.

'Okay,' said the policeman, when they had come to their decision. 'If you two agree to move on, *today*, we'll leave you to it. But I still think it's a bad idea. Walking to London. You should try getting back to Cardiff, or finding somewhere to stay in Newport. There are homeless shelters. We can get you the details, or…'

'And like I said, I'm not homeless,' said Reenie. 'I've got a tent.'

The policeman nodded and, after a baffled pause, he and his colleague returned to their car and drove back across the car park, pulling up in front of the hotel.

'That'll be the cow I spoke to earlier,' said Reenie. 'Hotel manager. Snooty bint. Came marching out of the hotel. Told me I was on *private property*. Silly mare didn't know what she was talking about. I said to her, I said, "That car park might be private property but this bit of grass here isn't, so you can sling your hook." She wasn't happy about that. Must have called the police.'

'Right,' said Ibrahim. 'So maybe we should pack up and move on, yeah?'

'We?' Reenie laughed. 'Who's this "we", then?'

'Me and you. I thought I was helping you push the trolley.'

'And I thought that was just for *them*,' said Reenie, nodding towards the police car.

'It doesn't have to be,' said Ibrahim. 'Must be hard work, pushing all that. And we're both going the same way. Makes sense.'

'And how do I know you won't rob me blind?'

He laughed. 'Rob you blind? Well, first of all, because I wouldn't. But even if I wanted to, which I don't, have you even got anything worth stealing?'

'Well, there's Solomon.'

'Solomon?'

'My bird.'

'Why would I want to steal a budgie?'

'He's not a budgie. He's a cockatiel.'

'Why would I want to steal a cockatiel?'

She considered this for a moment, staring down at the pale oval of cream in her lukewarm tea. 'Fair enough,' she said, at last. 'You can come, I suppose. But don't think you're sleeping in my tent. I do have *some* standards, you know.'

2

Irene Glickman – Reenie to the friends and family she once had – remembered the first time she felt others seeing her not as a woman, but as an *Old* Woman. It wasn't her first grey hair, her first wrinkle, her first liver spot. It wasn't The Change, or the day her bus pass appeared on the doormat. It was a Thursday, her shopping day, and as she stepped off the bus a young man helped her with her bags. He was only being kind, but there was something in his tone and his smile, something vaguely patronising, or self-satisfied, that said he was proud of himself for *Helping The Old Woman*. It was his Good Deed For The Day. She thanked him, and said something about there not being many gentlemen around nowadays, but as the bus pulled away she felt a kind of sadness as her age, and the reality of it, dawned on her in a way it never had before. It was one thing to notice her body ageing, quite another for others to notice and act on it.

She was grateful, when she began planning the walk to London, that there was nobody to tell, nobody to look at her in *that* way; that patronising, disbelieving way that said, 'Oh, dear. Reenie's lost it.' A friend of hers had spent her last days in sheltered accommodation, every plan questioned by those paid to keep an eye on her; every shopping trip and holiday requiring an unofficial seal of approval. Reenie spent many afternoons in their common room, seeing how they were treated, and she was determined never to end up in such a place. Yes, her house was too big and empty for her; yes, she struggled with the stairs, and she wasn't dusting as often as she should, and the garden had long ago turned into a jungle, but it was all hers. She made her plans alone, with no one there to question them.

The trolley she picked up from a supermarket near her home, and her status as an Old Woman granted her the license to walk away with it, unchallenged. Nobody questioned the sight of an Old Woman pushing a trolley down the street. But in a way, she had wanted someone to stop and question her, if only so that she could throw their question back at them. What was so strange about walking to London? People have been around much longer than cars and trains. Was it so long ago people walked from place to place? Hadn't there been times, in living memory, when people walked great distances, and not always through choice?

The trouble was, it had been a very long time since this had last happened in Britain. In Britain, people had been driven from place to place for generations. If anyone walked a great distance now it was to prove a point, and usually for charity. It was centuries since the last British exodus. Migrations, yes, but these involved cars, and trains, and boats. Photographs of suitcase-laden families walking single file on country lanes, leaving behind them ravaged towns and villages, were of events that had happened Somewhere Else and to Someone Else.

Reenie didn't remember such scenes, but they were as much a part of her as the single hazel fleck in her otherwise blue eyes, a hand-me-down from her father's side. The story of how she came to live in London she remembered like a nursery rhyme, or the bare bones of a fairy tale. Her father spoke rarely of their time in Vienna, and even less of what followed, and her only memory of that time was so vague, so lacking in detail, it could have happened in any city, in any country.

She remembered a vast park, and in that park enclosures filled with exotic animals; zebras and giraffes, elephants and monkeys, a blue-green pond surrounded by flamingos. She remembered a man and a woman, her parents, and mountainous clouds on a dusk horizon, but nothing more.

There were voids in her father's recollections of Vienna and Europe, chapters he'd never shared. They, he and Reenie's mother, had left their home. They were put onto trains. They were taken north. Much of what happened after that remained blank, but her father did once share the story of how he and many other men – there were no women – were made to march west. It was January.

'And Polish Januaries, they are cold,' he said, with a distant understatement.

When she told the young police officers she was walking to London, and they looked at her as if she were insane, she wanted to tell them about her father, and the walk so terrible he never spoke of it again.

Yes, she could have caught the train. That would have been the easy thing to do, and the cost of the fare was unimportant to her. Speed and comfort were unimportant to her. Ease was unimportant to her. It was the journey that mattered. And what about her belongings? They might have allowed her on a train with Solomon inside his cage, and a small suitcase would be enough for her clothes, but Reenie knew she might never return to Cardiff, or the house where she had lived for almost fifty years. If she was leaving, and for good, she would travel as a whole; the parts of her life that still mattered to her crammed into that supermarket trolley.

She hadn't expected to meet another person on the same journey. Perhaps people did this all the time, walking between cities, and it wasn't all that strange. Perhaps there were hundreds of people out there, now, tramping from one end of the country to the other on foot – north to south; east to west. Perhaps, away from the motorways and the train tracks, this was a country full of people walking about like nomads, just walking.

She realised that, had they met under other circumstances, she would have treated Ibrahim differently. If she saw him coming towards her on a dark night she would have crossed the street to avoid him. If he were loitering outside her house, she would hover near the phone, wondering when it was appropriate to dial 999.

Or if she were fifty years younger, how would she look at him then? He was handsome, if a little weighty, but she had always been attracted to bigger, cuddlier men. And there was something exotic in his looks, his short hair and thick beard the darkest black, his skin the lightest shade of brown, but still dark enough to make his almost metallic blue eyes stand out like little coins. He reminded her of a waiter she'd met when in Venice with Jonathan. They were at a restaurant near San Marco, on the Calle Spadaria, and the waiter flirted with her, sparking a jealous row between husband

and wife, not because Reenie had attracted the waiter's attention but because – and only because – she had enjoyed it.

Beneath his scruffy clothes and that shabby bird's nest of a beard, Ibrahim had something of the waiter's beauty; something almost feminine in his long eyelashes, his full lips, his smooth skin; but beyond that something soft and quiet, something gentle. Nothing like the young men she had seen on TV; waving placards and burning flags. Ibrahim was different. She saw no violence in him, no hint of a temper. A sadness, perhaps, but no violence.

As a girl she might have fallen for his looks, for his quietness, for that lack of violence. Liking him, though, was not the same as trusting him. Reenie trusted no one completely, having learnt and relearnt this lesson her whole life.

Ibrahim was not one of the bastards. He hadn't tried persuading her to turn back, or catch the train. He hadn't laughed at her plan, or talked to her as if she was mad. If he wanted to steal from her, he'd already had the opportunity. He was not one of the *bastards*, but still. He'd go soon enough. Get sick of her slowing him down. Hitch a ride or give in and catch the train. Everyone goes away, eventually.

For now, though, it was a relief having someone else push the trolley. It wasn't so much the weight that made it hard work – once you had the whole thing moving it seemed to push itself along with its own momentum. No, it wasn't the weight; it was the wheels that made it a challenge. They had minds of their own, all four of them pulling in different directions, and the whole thing jumping and shuddering with every bump and pothole. But Ibrahim was a young man, and stronger than her, and they made greater progress in the two hours after leaving the hotel than she had made in her first two days from Cardiff.

They entered Newport from the south-west, and all the way across the city centre they were gawped at. Nothing about them – little old woman in raincoat and wellies; stocky, dark young man with shaved head and beard – made sense, and people stared at them as if to say, *They're not a couple, they're not mother and son. What's their story?*

Reenie felt safer outside the cities, where there were fewer people, fewer cars – where there were wide-open spaces and places to camp. The city was noise and commotion, and it was getting late. If they weren't on the other side of Newport by nightfall there would be nowhere to pitch her tent, and she'd have to sleep outdoors, in some cold, hard concrete corner of the city.

Unlike Ibrahim, Reenie hadn't planned her journey with maps. She knew some of the roads she would have to travel along from daytrips taken years ago. Then, she had been the navigator, an RAC road atlas open in her lap while Jonathan drove. She'd hoped some parts of the route would prove familiar, but very few had.

The bridge across the River Usk she remembered, but as a brand new landmark in the city. Now it looked weathered and worn, its concrete pillars the same muddy shade of brown as the river beneath it. The riverbanks were strewn with debris – the half-buried skeletons of shopping trolleys, a discarded bicycle, the rotting carcass of a rowing boat.

Ibrahim said little as they crossed the city. He was slowing, his face flushed and shining with sweat, and while at first he kept a steady pace, always a few yards ahead of her, now they walked side by side; Reenie talking as if to punctuate the prolonged silences between them.

'Haven't been to Newport in years,' she said. 'I remember when they was making that film, *Tiger Bay*. It had the girl in it. What's her name? Hayley Mills. That's her. John Mills's daughter. And it was set in Tiger Bay, down in Butetown, but they filmed some of it in Newport, by the Transporter Bridge. Must have been fifty years ago now.'

'You've... lived in... Cardiff... fifty years?' asked Ibrahim, struggling to catch his breath.

'Yeah. Must be that, at least.'

''Cause, you haven't... got the accent. You still sound... like you're from London.'

'Yeah, well, some people lose their accents, some don't.'

She didn't tell him that as a child her accent, and even the language she'd spoken, were different again, that her accent *had* changed, but that having changed once, and so dramatically, it stayed fixed, as if that one change was enough to last a lifetime.

'And why'd you move to Cardiff?' he asked.

She took a moment to answer him, and in that moment considered the raft of promises that brought her from London to Cardiff and the man – no, the *boy* – who made and broke them all. He'd made this other city, this place away from London, sound like the answer to all their problems, and she believed him. So long ago. She remembered his name, but his face was vague now. Did it happen to her? Wasn't it all just a film she had once seen?

'Just fancied a change of scenery,' she said. 'You know how it is. A change is as good as a rest. Why did *you* move to Cardiff?'

'University.'

'Oh. You're a brainy one, are you?'

He laughed and wiped his forehead with his sleeve. 'No. Not really. Just wanted to go to uni. Got in to Cardiff.'

'What were you studying?'

'History.'

'Did you get a degree?'

He shook his head. 'Didn't finish the course.'

There was something in his expression – as if he was tired of answering that question – that stopped her from asking any more. They carried on in silence until reaching the eastern edge of the city, and by then it was beginning to get dark.

3

Kirsty's phone buzzed its way, sideways, across her desk, nudging itself closer to the edge; the last name she expected to see lit up on its screen. They hadn't spoken in almost a year. Not out of animosity or resentment, rather their clumsy and abortive attempt at dating, an attempt that came close to being 'a relationship' before stalling, had left them with too little to talk about, and nothing in common except the very brief time they shared. So why should he call now?

She picked up her phone and answered it. 'Steve?'

'Hi, Kirsty. You okay to speak?'

'Sure.'

A quick glance around the newsroom. Another researcher thumbing idly at his phone. Rhodri, her producer, soundproofed and pacing in his glass box of an office, talking to someone distant through the speakerphone. Most of the other researchers and production team elsewhere, as the office reached the end of a Tuesday afternoon.

'So. How are you?' asked Steve.

Christ. Where was this heading? Had a year of single life reduced him to rekindling former flames, flicking through the well-thumbed pages of his Little Black Book? That was assuming men even had Little Black Books these days, or that they ever had, outside of films and dodgy sitcoms. Assuming, too, that he had spent the last twelve months single, unable to move on, or frozen in the very last moment she had seen him, in that same way that it's impossible to imagine rivers flowing if you're not around to watch them.

'I'm good, thanks,' said Kirsty. 'How are you?'

'Great. Great. You still with the BBC?'

'Yes.'

'Oh, that's good. That's kind of why I called you, actually.'

She frowned for the benefit of no one. 'Right. Well. Yes. I'm still here.'

'Still working on the news?'

'Yes.'

'Okay. Well, as it happens, I might have a story for you.'

'Really.'

'Yeah.'

'Are you sure? I mean, is that even, you know, *allowed*?'

'Well. Not really. But, you know, as long as I'm not mentioned by name or anything. I mean, anyone could have given you this story. And it's not like we're... you know. And anyway...'

'So what's the story?'

A long pause. Steve was a policeman, at least he had been when they dated, but this was the first time he'd ever called with a story. She leaned back in her chair, waiting for his explanation.

'This old woman and this Asian guy are walking to London,' he said.

She scowled. It sounded like the opening line of a joke.

'They're walking to London?'

'Yeah. We got a call from this hotel, just off the M4. They were complaining about the old woman camping next to their car park, so we went to check it out. Turns out she and this Asian guy are walking to London.'

'What? For charity?'

'No. That's the thing. They're just walking to London. It's not for charity.'

'Right. And... I mean... who are they?'

'Don't know. They weren't breaking any laws or anything. We moved them on. But I just thought... It's *weird*, isn't it? Apparently, they'd only just met.'

'So they don't know each other?'

'Don't think so.'

'But they're walking to London *together*?'

'Yeah.'

'So you thought you'd call me?'

'Well. Yeah. It's the kind of thing you report on the local news, isn't it?'

True. It was September. The last dreary days of Silly Season. Unless war broke out (and even a war was unlikely to impact much on *local* news) or some major crime or accident occurred, they were in the slow news doldrums between party conferences. Paradoxically, a 'slow news' month meant a busy month for researchers, whose job it then became to comb through acres of minor events in the search for something newsworthy.

'So where are they?' she asked.

'Just off the M4. You know the junction with the hotel and the business park?'

'I think so.'

'Well, there. But we moved them on, so they'll be heading towards Newport.'

'Right.'

Another silence that became pointed.

'So, anyway,' said Steve. 'Just thought I'd let you know. You know. In case it was something you could use.'

'Yeah. Well, thanks for that, Steve.'

'Don't mention it. You know. Just thought, we haven't spoken in *ages*, and then this happened, and I thought, "Kirsty might be able to, you know, use this," so I called you.'

'Yeah. That's great, Steve. Thanks.'

'Cool. Well. Maybe see you around, yeah?'

'Yeah.'

'Great.'

'Take care, Steve.'

'Right. Yeah. You too, Kirst.'

'Bye, Steve.'

'Bye.'

She ended the near-interminable call with her thumb, got up from her desk, crossed the office to Rhodri's glass box, and rapped her knuckles three times on the door. Rhodri was still talking at the grey plastic triangle in the centre of his desk, but he gestured for her to come in, and she entered, closing the door quietly behind her. He was talking to somebody in Welsh, a language Kirsty had never spoken. Even after eighteen months of working there she still felt a twinge of resentment in those moments when colleagues jabbered away in this familiar yet foreign tongue as if they were doing it on purpose to exclude the handful of people, a minority, who couldn't.

'Iawn iawn, byddain siarad i chi'n fuan! Wel dwi'n credu bod e di bod yn Barcelona penythnos yma. Yeah… Mae'n alright i some! Iawn, hwyl hwyl.'

Finished, Rhodri clapped his hands together and grinned at her. Or rather, he gave her tits a cursory glance and then grinned at her.

'Kirsty,' he said. 'What can I do you for?'

She smiled falsely, more a grimace than a smile. 'Erm, I think I might have a story. Filler, really. Nothing major. Too late for tonight, obviously, but maybe we could get it done for tomorrow morning.'

'Okay. What's the story?'

'Old woman and some Asian guy walking from Cardiff to London.'

'For charity?'

'Not for charity.'

'Gandhi Asian, or Jackie Chan Asian?'

'I didn't ask.'

'And where'd you get this?'

'A friend. He works for the police.'

'They've been arrested?'

'No. Nothing like that. He just called me, because he's seen them, and…'

'Because if it's police business it could get messy.'

'No. They've not been arrested. I was thinking human interest, filler, like I said, maybe something we could check out…'

He nodded. 'Right. Okay. Tell you what. You drive up there, to wherever they are. Do a recce. If it stands up, give me a ring. We're stretching bugger all very thin tomorrow morning as it is. I mean, we're bloody *leading* with that leisure centre closure. So we might be able to use it. But you go scope it out first, yeah?'

'Okay.'

With that decided Kirsty returned to her desk and picked up her handbag and her car keys. The drive out of Cardiff took an age, her progress slowed by the rush-hour traffic pouring like treacle from the city. She sat in gridlock, drumming an impatient tom-

tom on the steering wheel. The passengers of a coach stared down at her from their windows, an ageing gallery of white perms and dewlaps. The driver of a white van, his beefy arm tattooed with the greening feathers of a Welsh *fleur-de-lys*, leered at her and winked. Three Asian guys, teenagers, sat chicken-winging – elbows dangling from the open windows of a BMW; black bandana-and-baseball-capped heads bobbing in time with thunderous hip-hop.

Then the cars and vans and lorries moved, and she was out of Cardiff and on the motorway, but by the time she reached the hotel near the junction her quarry – the old woman and the Asian man – had gone. Undeterred, she drove on and was within the southern limits of Newport when, finally, she saw them. Sure enough, an old woman and, a few paces ahead of her, a young man pushing a supermarket trolley.

They looked like a story. Never mind what that story might be. There was struggle, pathos, grim determination, the faintest whiff of the eccentric. Exactly the kind of thing the audience for local news laps up. She was thinking like a journalist, because that was what she trained to be. Shame then that she wasn't a journalist, but a researcher; a job only one or two rungs up from runner, though she could barely tell the difference. Still, this was your 'foot in the door', as people told her. Your way in. Knuckle down, look for stories. If you're good, they'll notice. They – the anonymous *They*. The omniscient *They*. The all-seeing *They*. The practically trademarked Powers That Be. Would they notice her this time? Would this be the filler, the piece of fluff, the small dose of whimsy that drew attention to her? Perhaps. She had seen true nonentities promoted for less substantial stories than this.

Though she slowed the car as she passed them by, Kirsty was soon a hundred yards ahead of them. It would have looked strange for her to slow down to their pace, as if kerb crawling, and there were other cars behind her, so she drove on until the next roundabout, performed a U-turn, and came back, driving past them a second time.

Perhaps it was a statement. Some kind of protest. There was something bohemian about the old woman. Didn't seem the cosy, grandmotherly type. Was their journey political? A comment on the struggles of people in a faraway land? But if that was the case, where were their placards and t-shirts printed with slogans? Where was their message?

Or perhaps something theatrical; an oblique work of performance art. No, that was ridiculous. Perhaps there was nothing to the story. Perhaps there was no story. Perhaps she should drive back to Cardiff and tell Rhodri there was nothing worth seeing, let alone reporting.

And yet, as they shrank away, framed in widescreen by her rear view mirror, they looked like a story. So telegenic. This could work. *This could work*.

Presently, she found somewhere to pull in and called the office, waiting briefly on hold before being put through to Rhodri.

'So. What's the story?'

She pictured him staring fixedly at that grey plastic triangle on his desk, the lid of a ballpoint pen tucked in one corner of his mouth where he wished he had a cigarette.

What was the story? They *looked* like a story. But what *was* the story?

'They're on the move,' she said. 'They've left the hotel and they're heading in to Newport.'

'And they're *both* walking to London?'

'I think so. Well. They're definitely walking to Newport.'

'Right.'

She felt the prolonged silence from the other end of the line draw all the air out of her lungs and stop her heart from beating. Her mouth got dry, and she felt she might be blushing. Why had she called him so soon? Why hadn't she taken the initiative to follow them, stop them, ask questions before calling Rhodri? This wouldn't be the day she got noticed. If anything, this would be the day she got unnoticed, reverse-noticed, ignored.

Forget Kirsty. She'll bring you nothing but rubbish. In fact, maybe she'd make a better *runner*…

'Sod it,' said Rhodri. At last. 'Find them. Quiz them. If they're walking to London, call me back and I'll send Angharad and a crew.'

And Kirsty promised him she would do just that.

4

They had reached the Coldra, a large interchange on the far side of Newport, and Ibrahim couldn't remember another time when he had felt so tired.

In the centre of this interchange, in the shadow of the motorway flyover, lay an oasis of grass and trees, the perfect place for them to pitch Reenie's tent. The motorway would provide shelter, should it rain, and the trees could hide them from the road.

He could leave her there, of course. Sure, it was getting late and the sky was beginning to ink over with night, but in the plans he drew up, the notes he scribbled on maps, he ended his first day so much further along the road than this. He had thought he might walk for twelve hours, at least, and in those plans ended his first day in Lydney, on the other side of the English border. He had no idea where he would stay when he got there, perhaps a bus station where he could spend the night, or a park with a bandstand. Somewhere dry, with no people.

Now, as they put up the tent and began unpacking the things from Reenie's trolley, he tried convincing himself he could walk another twelve miles, at least. Maybe even reach the border. He had no obligations. He had helped her get this far, never promising to take her all the way to London. Besides, there was an urgency to his journey. Time was a factor. He could help her set up camp, in the middle of this roundabout, then carry on walking. He could walk well into the night. Eventually the roads would get quieter, and on some he might feel like the only man on Earth. What was keeping him here?

But then he remembered the name she'd said and he felt the thudding pain in his right leg; an ache that was spreading now, through every limb and tingling like pinpricks in the soles of his feet. He was exhausted.

'Shall I put the kettle on?' asked Reenie, unfolding her small table and draping over it the gingham tea towel she used as a tablecloth. 'Nothing like a cuppa after a long walk. We used to walk all the time when I was a girl. We'd walk for miles and miles. All the way up over Hackney Marsh, or out as far as Epping Forest. We'd walk all the way there, all the way back. Nowadays, no one walks anywhere. Too bloody lazy, if you ask me.'

He nodded and smiled but said nothing. He had both hands on his leg, working at the muscle with his thumbs, and each time he applied more pressure a shot of pain pounced through his leg, but it was that good, almost reassuring pain that he could tolerate, though only just.

'You alright?' asked Reenie.

'I'm fine.'

'That leg of yours giving you gip?'

'Yeah.'

'So what happened to it?'

'An accident.'

It came out blunt, colder than intended, and it was strange for Ibrahim to remember a time when he couldn't even call it that, when he'd *refused* to call it an accident. For months and even years he had called it his *injury*, both the physical damage to his body and the event that caused it. Injury seemed the only word for it; 'accident' felt so diluted, so small. An accident was something unintended, random, without reason.

The damage he suffered seemed so precise, so calculated, he often wondered if it was the product of some grand, unseen design. There had to be a reason why his leg was broken in so many places, why his face was smashed beyond recognition, why – microscopic and undetected for two years – there had been one final punchline to his injuries. His faith told him there was a reason for everything, that everything that happened was the will of God, from blessed miracles to deaths and injuries. Even his father had believed this, saying it was a sign, a message from Allah. If his father could suggest that, knowing only what he knew, what would he have said had he known everything?

As it was, the timing was all wrong. Two years earlier Nazir

Siddique may have had a point. Had Ibrahim's accident happened then, there may have been some justice to it, and even then if he was the only one to be injured, but what had the others done? What had Rhys and Caitlin and Aleem done to deserve that?

He refused to believe his accident – *their* accident – was some divine punishment, backdated to earlier actions, as if the heavenly clerics and number crunchers meting out spiritual justice were simply catching up with a backlog. And into this single plughole of doubt he saw his faith begin to vanish, like so much swirling, brackish bathwater. He tried clinging to the vestiges of it, but he might as well have tried clinging on to soapy dregs. If the accident, his *injury*, was not the work of God, what was it? If it was just that, an accident, why do such things happen? If there is no reason why they happen, what then? His doubt, and the absolute terror it gave birth to, was a cancer to his faith, and he began to wonder if he had ever truly believed.

Yes, he had proclaimed that God is great, and done so at the top of his voice, but it was said as a chorus, with a dozen of his friends. They spoke loudly, as if volume added credence, or took away the need to question what was being said. Now that he was left with none of those friends and just the sketches of his faith he realised they could have shouted anything, any choice of words, in any order. It wouldn't have mattered.

Of course, they had never questioned the substance, the character and the mind of Allah. When their discussions were over, and they'd finished poring over another passage, reciting it in their faltering, East London Arabic, Allah remained as faceless and unknowable as He was before they began. His words, so the sheikh told them, were there in the book. There was nothing more to know. It is the word and the law of God. Even thinking about what He might look like, or how His mind might work beyond those pages, was *haraam*.

So in losing God, or his faith in God, he often felt he had lost nothing at all. The God who allowed his accident to happen, or turned a blind eye when it did, was the same unknowable, monolithic God who shrouded Himself in scripture and defied all questions and inquiries, who demanded nothing more substantial than that His name be shouted by a dozen men with a limited command of the chosen language. The God who wasn't there at all was almost indistinguishable from the one he had sworn to fight and die for.

Reenie passed him a mug of coffee and took to her own deckchair. The sky was getting darker still and the lights at the roadside flickered to life with a sickly, peach-coloured glow. Rush hour was ending, the traffic thinning out until the sound of each passing car and van became a pulse, almost metronomic, rather than a constant hiss of white noise.

'It was a car crash,' said Ibrahim.

Reenie peered at him through the steam rising from her tea, and it had been so long since her question, he wondered if she remembered asking it.

'The accident, I mean,' he said. 'It was a car crash.'

She nodded and glanced down at his leg, her expression almost placidly unmoved. 'Broke your leg, did you?'

'Leg. Pelvis. Fractured skull.'

'Were you in hospital long?'

'Six months.'

Reenie drew a sharp breath, as if she'd stubbed her toe, and she slurped her tea noisily.

'Six months,' she said. 'That's a long time to be cooped up. Can't *stand* hospitals. My husband worked in one. Couldn't even bear popping in to see him when he was in work. Can't *stand* them.'

'Me neither.'

'Don't blame you. Six months. And half the time you come out with more wrong than when you went in. All these super bugs they have nowadays and what have you. Can't *stand* hospitals. Full of sick people. And there's no dignity in it. In any of it. I was in, couple of years ago. Overnight stay. One of them mixed wards, so there was me, some old dear in her eighties, some lad who must have been thirty, and this one man. Well. I don't know what the *politically correct* word for it is, but he was a bit funny...' She tapped one finger against the side of her head. 'You know. *Up there*. And the old dear in her eighties, she spent most of the night screaming. And the lad who was a bit... *you know*... in the head... Well, he'd get up and walk about the place with his smock all hitched up so you could see his bits. And there's me just trying to get a good night's sleep.

'By the time the old dear stopped screaming and the funny boy went back to sleep it must have been three o'clock, and then they wake you up at half six to take your blood pressure and stick all those instruments in your ear and what have you. Half six! And let me tell you, I'm not one of those people who can get back to sleep. Once I'm up, I'm up. So they wake you up at half six, and then they don't get round to serving tea and toast till nine. Well, by then I was *starving*. I *hate* hospitals. Can't *stand* them.'

He smiled and took a sip of his coffee. There had been times when he hated the hospital, days when he longed to see something from beyond its car park. Some of the upper wards had views over the city's suburbs, but they were so distant as to be rendered abstract, little more than rooftops and trees.

The hospital was vast, practically a town in its own right, or so he came to think of it. There was a concourse with shops – the usual selection of newsagents and florists – and a self-service café. There was a central quadrangle where patients and visitors could go to smoke, or just to get out of the sterile, bleached air of the wards.

Once he was more mobile, more confident using a wheelchair, Ibrahim spent hours touring the hospital, searching for undiscovered corridors, places he hadn't yet seen, and it was while wheeling himself around the corridors that he saw, on a television suspended in one corner of the day room, the image of a red London bus blasted in half, the street around it littered with debris. He entered the room and asked the only other person there – a burly rugby type with his leg in plaster – to turn up the volume.

'...a scene of carnage at Tavistock Square, where it would appear there has been an explosion on board a bus. The top deck of the bus, as you can see, severely damaged...'

The rugby type looked at Ibrahim with a brief sideways glance – brief but held long enough for Ibrahim to notice – and that one look said enough.

This was your lot.

And on TV there were people with faces covered in blood and there were bodies lying in gutters and people weeping and what Ibrahim saw wasn't a statement or a victory but chaos and blood and smoke and nothingness.

It meant nothing.

He hated the hospital most of all when things were demanded of him; when he was sent for x-rays or told to stay in his ward and wait for the latest in a string of junior doctors to come and assess him. These things were stark reminders that he was damaged. His body had been damaged. It no longer worked as it should. His legs were all but useless, his left arm still feeble. He found it difficult to eat anything with a consistency tougher than soup. His eyesight was still poor, making all the newspapers and magazines brought by visitors little more than colourful waste paper.

And to begin with, once he was well enough, there had been many visitors. His family came from London and Birmingham to see him, sometimes checking into hotels to stay the night and visit again the next day. His Cardiff friends, most of them students, travelled up en masse, and brought odd gifts picked up in second-hand shops and flea markets. Early on, they'd sit around the bed cracking jokes, sharing gossip.

It was during one such visit that he learned they were clearing out his room, in the house he had shared with four others. The academic year was nearing its end; the landlord had new tenants ready to move in over the summer. Ibrahim might have reacted to this angrily, were it not for the painkillers and sedatives that kept him placid most afternoons. Besides, as he had to remind himself, and keep reminding himself, he was lucky. The friends sitting around his bed, telling him these things, were talking to the only friend of theirs to survive the crash.

Eventually the gaps between visits from all but one person became longer. In justifying it, both to Ibrahim and themselves, his family reminded him of the distance and the cost. Neither petrol nor train fares were cheap, they said. You'll understand, won't you, if we don't make it up this weekend, they said. Maybe next weekend? Then the semester was over, and many of his friends went back to their hometowns, and their words came to him as text messages.

Soon enough he stopped hating the hospital in any real sense. He might tell others he hated being there, but all the raw anger had trickled out of him. He even came to find some comfort in the hospital's patterns and routines, in its inherent safety. Nothing terrible could happen to him there. He was surrounded, day and night, by staff whose job it was to keep him safe.

When, after six months of treatment, his doctor announced he was well enough to leave, Ibrahim felt a kind of panic, an anxiousness, a sensation only heightened by his leaving, and one that stayed with him, constantly ringing, like an emotional tinnitus.

The world outside the hospital was, he realised, dangerous; made up of random sequences of events that had no meaning. There was cause and effect, yes, but the spidergram was so vast, so intricate, it made him nauseous to consider it for any length of time. Meeting Reenie, for instance, and learning her father's name. Looking at her from across their small campsite, he wondered if she could be a product of his imagination, if he could be dreaming. But when he dreamt, invariably those dreams were filled with meaningless violence and an acute, unending sense of loss.

While passing through Newport, they had stopped at a supermarket to pick up supplies – bread and cheese, bottles of water, cartons of UHT milk; bananas, apples and clementines – and Reenie made them both a supper of sandwiches, which Ibrahim gobbled down in seconds, leaving a litter of breadcrumbs in his beard and a splatter of ketchup on his t-shirt.

What neither of them noticed, as they washed their plastic plates and cutlery in water, was the small black car orbiting the interchange; a car that had followed them, intermittently, since Newport, and now left the road and came to a halt a short distance from where they'd set up camp. A young woman got out of the car, gingerly crossing the four lanes of traffic and trudging her way across the island of grass beneath the motorway.

'Who's this?' asked Reenie.

He squinted at the young woman and shrugged, and the young woman waved at them and smiled.

'Hi,' she said, short of breath. 'My name's Kirsty. I'm a researcher for the BBC. Do you have a moment?'

5

It was too early to go home. There was a point in the night when, once he was out through the door, Gary knew he wouldn't go back until breakfast.

He'd mastered the art of getting out of bed without waking Emma; learned to take his uniform to the bathroom and get changed there, never once letting a single noise or the slightest bit of light from the landing disturb her. He knew which floorboards creaked, and he avoided them. If, before leaving, he made coffee, he would close the kitchen door to stop the noise of the kettle from travelling up the stairs. He could open, close and lock their front door almost without making a sound.

It took months, maybe years, for him to get used to this – waking in the middle of the night after only a few hours' sleep. It no longer rattled him as it used to, when he began working nights. Back then the sudden noise of his pager caused his body to react as if in shock, as if all his senses were under attack. If the night was warm, he woke up feeling clammy. If it was cold, the room felt like a fridge. The darkness played tricks on him; the bedroom ceiling full of swirling colours and patterns until his eyes adjusted to the dark. The silence of the sleeping world left him feeling alone though Emma still slept beside him. All this happened at once, so that the experience of waking at two or three o'clock in the morning was a near-harrowing, disorientating one, but eventually this passed and now, when work called, he could be out of the room in a minute and out of the house in ten.

The summer months were quieter. People didn't use their boilers so often in summer. Showers, baths, washing the dishes, that was about it. The winter months were much busier. Then he could expect three or four call-outs a night. Maybe more. Another pensioner or young mum who could smell gas. Another family with no hot water or heating. Flats and houses like iceboxes. People in dressing gowns and nighties, arms folded, faces all wrinkled up and sleepy, waiting for him to 'work his magic'.

The summer months weren't so bad, but the nights felt more broken up. A night with no sleep at all was somehow better, less disruptive, than a night chopped in half by a single call-out, and the later that call-out came the less likely he was to go home before breakfast. Emma was a light sleeper. He was amazed she could sleep through the sound of his pager, but she did. Perhaps she was used to it now and knew how to block out its noise, to *unhear* it. It was the irregular sounds that woke her – sirens and car alarms – and, after a certain time, once awake she could never get back to sleep.

At first she had tried sleeping tablets, but these left her sluggish and groggy in the mornings, so Gary decided that if he was ever called out after three he wouldn't go back until she was up and awake, and this often left him stranded in the night with nowhere to go. The call-out might take minutes; an imagined scent of gas, a dead thermocouple replaced before the dressing-gowned customer had a chance to offer him tea. He'd go back to his van, tiredness weighing down every limb, and stare anxiously at the clock, praying for another call before dawn.

That morning his pager had woken him a little before 4am. He reached the customer half an hour later, and was out of there again by five.

For a while he drove and listened to the radio. Gary preferred stations where they talked, having failed to find a music station that didn't, sooner or later, piss him off. One DJ played rock, the next played love ballads. Never any consistency. At least with the stations where people talked he might learn something, or they'd talk about something he found interesting. Sometimes he'd answer back, agreeing loudly with those he agreed with, swearing at those he didn't.

Right now there was only news. Bombs exploding and protestors getting shot somewhere foreign. The economy up the spout. Some politician talking bollocks, as usual. Outside it was getting light, but Gary imagined the presenters on the radio sitting in their dark, windowless studio, a room where it could have been any time of day or night, and he felt sorry for them. He actually felt sorry for them.

He drove back towards the city on near-deserted roads, and veering around the interchange at the Coldra saw a small orange tent pitched on the grass at its centre. He wondered, briefly, who would camp in a place like that, but those thoughts drifted effortlessly to a vision of bacon and fried eggs and beans and sausages and fried bread and *both* sauces.

In the city he went a café he knew would be open. On weekends the place was invariably full of nightclub bouncers and bleary-eyed kids at the tail-end of their nights on the town, but on a Wednesday morning it was mostly drivers – cab drivers, lorry drivers, maintenance men. A greasy spoon place with red plastic gingham on the tables and, for some reason, pictures of sports cars on its walls; the kitchen a racket of clanging pots and pans and the hiss of meat and eggs frying on the hotplate, a catering boiler firing hot jets of water into mugs and stainless steel teapots with a steamy whoosh.

After ordering his breakfast at the counter, Gary sat at a table near the window, where somebody had left behind their newspaper, and he read – or rather *scanned* – it while he waited.

Everyone he knew was asleep. Dreaming, not dreaming. Snoring, not snoring. With someone, alone. Sleeping. And nobody, not even Emma, knew where he was. Most of the people he and Emma knew had regular jobs, Monday to Friday, nine till five. They woke at respectable hours and enjoyed peaceful, unbroken nights of sleep. Their weekends were sacred, their time precious. Whenever there were parties, at Christmas or on birthdays, these friends made a point of sympathising with Gary. Always the first to leave, hardly ever drinking.

'That must be *horrible*,' they'd say, as if they understood, but they didn't.

The achievements and successes of his friends and family were a sore point, but those were thoughts he kept to himself, knowing how bitter it would make him sound. When he congratulated his mates on their promotions, it had that veneer of sincerity, and sometimes it was genuine – he wasn't yet bitter enough to wish for their failure – but behind it lay a shadow of regret.

Gary ate his breakfast quickly, pausing just once to watch as an old man in a heavy, camel-coloured duffel coat shuffled along the street outside, bending down to pick half-smoked cigarette butts from the gutter.

Disgusting. What was the world coming to? He saw these things more often now, but were they always there, or had something changed? Driving around the city in the early mornings, everything looked shabbier, more worn. Paint peeling. Windows boarded up. Graffiti everywhere. Broken glass everywhere. Dog shit everywhere. Things were beginning to slide, as if no one cared about anything any more. He was the only person in the café to notice the old man picking soggy cigarette ends from the gutter. When did people stop seeing these things?

The city was waking up, the traffic getting heavier. Soon it would be time for him to go home, which was just as well, because he wanted nothing more than to leave this place and forget about the old man and his damp, second-hand cigarettes. And his timing was important. Emma hated being woken in the night, but more than that she hated waking in an empty house.

Later that day, when it was time for him to sleep again, Gary contemplated the importance of timing; how time and coincidence play such an important part in anyone's life. It was typical for that kind of thought to pop into his head just as he was trying to get some sleep, and that night he was kept awake by the idea that just a few minutes difference could change somebody's life completely, and that this could in turn begin a chain reaction, influencing others, each minor event triggering another, until the shape of the world was somehow different. The next morning he sat in front of his computer and read about the so-called Butterfly Effect and chaos theory and fractals, but he came away no wiser than when he had sat down.

If he stayed in the café a few minutes longer, or took a different route home, he wouldn't have entered their house just as Emma turned on the television. She was standing in the centre of their living room, still wearing her dressing gown, a steaming mug of tea in one hand and the remote control in the other. He kissed her on the cheek, noticing that she still had that morning smell – stale but not unpleasant – and he said 'Good morning', but then his attention was drawn to the television.

On the screen was the night-time image of an orange tent pitched beneath a concrete flyover.

'The Coldra, Newport,' said the television: a woman's voice, soft but sincere. 'Irene Glickman is seventy-five years old. She's lived in Cardiff more than forty years, but is returning to London, the city where she grew up.'

A pause, as the camera lingered on the image of an old woman in a deckchair, sipping from a white mug.

'What makes Irene's journey remarkable,' the voiceover continued, 'is that she's doing it on foot. Irene is *walking* the one hundred and sixty miles to London, *alone*. She is travelling with all of her belongings in a supermarket trolley, and tonight she will sleep in a tent next to one of the busiest roads in South Wales.'

It cut to a close-up of the old woman. Hard to tell whether she was happy about being filmed. If anything, she looked as if she couldn't care less.

'I've just got so many things,' she said. 'And I wasn't planning on coming back to Cardiff. Thing is, I haven't got a car, and I couldn't take all this stuff on the train. It just made sense.'

Emma dropped herself into an armchair and shook her head. 'Mad old thing,' she said. 'Walking to London? That's the *Coldra*, isn't it? She must have Alzheimer's, or something.'

The image on screen switched to the reporter; beige suit, rigid hair, too frosty and pinched for Gary to find sexy.

'Earlier today, police in Newport moved Mrs Glickman on from a busy roundabout on the other side of the city. A spokesperson for Gwent Police told us that while they were concerned for Mrs Glickman's welfare, she had not committed an offence. They said, "Mrs Glickman is of sound mind, and capable of making her own decisions. This is why we have not taken the matter further or referred her current situation to social services."'

Gary turned to his wife. 'What was that you were saying about Alzheimer's?'

'Meanwhile,' the reporter continued. 'Irene Glickman still has a very long way to walk.'

'Still think she's mad,' said Emma. 'They should put her in a care home, or something. It's not right, leaving her out there. Even if she ain't a danger to the public, she's a danger to her*self*.'

'She seemed alright to me,' said Gary. 'I mean, she only wants to get to London.'

'Well, couldn't somebody have driven her there? I don't know… a neighbour or something?'

'Maybe she hasn't got anyone.'

The news moved on to another story, leaving the old woman where they found her. From what Gary had seen as he drove around the Coldra, she was still there now. And she had no one. This alone bothered him. We think the world will always provide for us, that there'll be friends and family to keep us safe, that we won't be abandoned or ignored, but how many years had the old woman been alone? When had she last had a conversation, a proper conversation, with anyone? He imagined her in a supermarket, chatting away to the staff because they were the only people she ever spoke with. And maybe they knew her by name, but they didn't really *know* her. She had no one.

So many of them. The old woman sleeping under the motorway. The old man picking fag butts from the gutter. One city, and two people that alone, that desperate. Just one city. Not even a big city. Not even that many people. But two of them. Two people like that.

'D'you want a cuppa?' said Emma, but he was on his feet and out of the room before she'd finished the question.

On reaching the landing, the first thing he noticed was an open door, and the bright and colourful light from the room behind it. There, visible through the narrow gap between the door and its frame, he saw the blue and pink border decorated with teddy bears. That door was usually shut, which meant Emma had been in there again, something she only ever did when he was out. He closed the door gently, hoping she wouldn't hear it, and went to their bedroom.

For a moment he sat on the edge of their bed, and caught sight of himself, reflected in the mirror above Emma's dressing table.

He aged the face he saw, adding further creases to the corner of each eye, drawing the hairline a little further up his forehead and peppering the hair with dashes of grey. He imagined his life without Emma, without friends or family, in which his only conversations were with the people on supermarket checkouts.

In the bathroom he brushed away the aftertaste of coffee and cigarettes and splashed cold water on his face to remind himself it was morning. Emma had already sensed something was wrong, or that something was *different*, by the time he came back downstairs and walked out of the house, and she followed him as far as the front door.

'What *are* you doing?' she asked. 'Ain't you going back to bed?'

He didn't answer her at first. Instead, he opened the van and began taken out his equipment – the tool kit; the industrial-strength vacuum cleaner; the different tools and devices for detecting water mains and electrical currents. He stacked as many of those things as he could, and carried them up the short driveway.

'Oh no,' said Emma. 'You are *not* bringing *that* stuff in *this* house. Gary? Gary. I said you're *not* bringing that stuff…'

He was already past her, and carrying everything through to their kitchen.

'Gary? What are you doing?'

Groaning with the weight, he crouched and placed the stack of tools down on the kitchen floor. 'Just making a bit of room,' he said, as if this made perfect sense.

'But *why*?'

'I've got an idea.'

He walked back through the house, and out through the front door, and began taking more things from the van.

'What do you mean? What idea?'

'I'm gonna drive her over the bridge,' said Gary, carrying the last pile through the house, and putting it down next to the first. 'There's room for all her stuff.'

'Who're you on about?'

'The old woman,' he said. 'Off the telly. I've got a couple of hours spare. I can drive her over the bridge.'

'Gary. Have you gone mad?'

'No, love. I'm not mad. I just think… it makes sense.'

'Makes sense? You're gonna drive a complete stranger, a mad old woman, over the Severn Bridge in your van, with her trolley and all her rubbish, and you think that makes sense?'

'Yeah.'

'Listen to yourself. You're tired.'

He laughed. It was a long time since anyone had told him he was tired. Wasn't that what his mum and dad would tell him, when he was a kid? The minute the grizzling began, they'd tell him he was tired, and he remembered perfectly the indignation he felt. He wasn't tired, he was angry, and right now he wasn't tired, he was determined; determined to use his day to shape the world, to be more than just another cog, turning because a bleeping pager commanded him to turn.

'I'm not tired,' he said. 'Anyway. It won't take long. I can be over the bridge and back in an hour and a half. And think of the time it'll save her.'

'But you don't know her,' said Emma. 'Why should you drive her?'

Gary shrugged.

'You know what would make me laugh?' said Emma. 'Is if you get there and they're queuing up. All the white van men who saw her on the news, queuing up to offer her a lift.'

'Yeah,' Gary laughed. 'That would be funny.'

They were in front of the house, Emma holding her dressing gown a little tighter around her thin frame, accentuating her belly, and Gary caught himself glancing down and feeling that dreadful, familiar wave of shame and horror and grief. He gasped, too quietly for her to hear, and he turned away to look inside the van. Plenty of room in there for a trolley, he was sure of that. The old woman could sit up front, assuming she said yes. And maybe Emma was right; maybe he'd get there and they'd be queuing up. He closed the doors with a loud clunk.

'I won't be long,' he said. 'Promise.'

He kissed her, this time on the lips, a kiss that couldn't help but feel like an apology, and he climbed into his van. The engine started with a splutter and cough, and he drove away, leaving Emma on the driveway, watching him until he'd gone.

6

'Must be nothing else happening in the world,' said Reenie. 'I mean, why'd they want to talk to me? Don't make any sense.'

Ibrahim shrugged. Despite his sleeping bag and the cushions Reenie loaned him, he'd woken up cold and tired. The pain in his right leg had subsided, but he knew this couldn't last. It would return as soon as they were walking again, but perhaps the pain might give the day some focus. He had decided that today he would make it over the border and into England.

'And why didn't they talk to you?' asked Reenie, as if he'd said something in reply. 'I thought that was odd.'

'Must be because you're old.'

She responded with a scowl.

'What?' he asked, unsure what he'd said to offend her.

'Who're you calling old?'

'Well you *are*,' said Ibrahim.

'I know that, but no need to be so blooming blunt about it.'

He had been here before; said something, and watched somebody's expression change. Said the wrong thing. Not a lie, not an insult. Just wrong. Used the wrong words. It hadn't always been like this.

'What I mean,' he said, 'is that they took one look at us, and thought you'd look better on TV.'

'Well,' said Reenie. 'I don't mind you saying *that*. Even if you don't mean it in a nice way.'

He knew he was right. The minute the reporter and camera crew arrived, they seemed perplexed, almost put out, by his being there, as if he damaged the story somehow. First, the researcher, Kirsty, had spoken to them both, taking their names – which they gave reluctantly – and making notes. She told them that they – 'they' being the BBC – were interested in the story, about their reasons for walking to London, but as the conversation went on, more and more of her questions were aimed at Reenie. By the time the reporter joined them, with the cameraman and sound technician in tow, it was clear they had no more interest in him.

He found it funny they would never see themselves – or Reenie, at least – on screen. The next leg of their journey would take them further away from the towns and cities, and they were unlikely, even if they wanted to, to find a television before nightfall.

When they'd finished packing the trolley, he took the folded maps from his bag, and showed them to Reenie.

'This is the way we should go,' he said, dragging his finger across the page. 'Up through Chepstow, over the border. We should make it as far as Lydney.'

'And how far's that?'

He paused, gauging the distance between his forefinger and thumb.

'I don't know. Twenty, twenty-five miles?'

'Twenty-five miles?'

'Yeah.'

'How long's that gonna take us?'

'Seven or eight hours?'

'Are you having a laugh? With this?' She gripped the trolley's handlebar, shaking it for emphasis. 'And with me? I'm seventy-flippin-five.'

'Yeah, alright. No need to go on about it.'

'And you've got a gammy leg.'

'What does gammy mean?'

'It means you're almost a cripple, love.'

'A crip–? Look… we'll be *fine*. We'll take breaks. If we set off now we can get to Lydney before it's time to set up camp again.'

'Ibrahim. Listen. Love. I'm seventy-five years old. I can't go as fast as you, even with that leg of yours. Yesterday left me knackered. I can't walk twenty-five… I mean, that's a bloody marathon, that is… I can't walk twenty-five miles in a day.'

'Well, let's just try, yeah?'

She looked at the trolley, and at the birdcage balanced on its plastic child's seat. The traffic rumbled around them like constant thunder, echoing off the underside of the motorway. He wouldn't leave her here, in this nowhere of a place, but neither would he wait much longer for her to make up her mind.

'Alright, then,' she said. 'But let me feed Solomon first.'

They left the Coldra, and came eventually to a stretch of road running parallel with the motorway, flanked on both sides with tall hedgerows. Quietly, Ibrahim dreaded the next crossing, the next interchange. These roads existed solely for cars, their pavements – when there were pavements – put there as an afterthought. Why couldn't there be a single, deserted lane from Cardiff to London?

'So what do your mates call you?' Reenie asked, apropos of nothing.

'What do you mean?'

'Your mates. Your friends. What do they call you? It's just… Ibrahim. It's a bit of a mouthful. You must have a nickname.'

'Right. I see. Well, my family, my dad, calls me Prakash. It's a Punjabi tradition, to give your kids a nickname, so that's my family nickname.'

'Pra…?'

'Kash. Prakash. It means "sunshine".'

'Oh, that's lovely, that is. Sunshine. Like the song.' She started to sing: *'You are my sunshine, my only sunshine…'*

'Yeah,' said Ibrahim, smiling. 'Something like that. But no one's called me Prakash in years. My uni mates used to call me Ib.'

'Ib?'

'Yeah. Short for…'

'I know what it's short for,' said Reenie. 'It's just a bit *too* short. Ib. It's like you haven't finished saying it properly. Like it's half a word.'

'Well, that's how it works, isn't it? Mike's short for Michael. Ed's short for Edward. Ib's short for Ibrahim.'

'Yeah. Just doesn't sound right, somehow.'

'That's only because you've never met another Ibrahim. Besides. What's "Reenie"?'

'Short for *Irene*,' said Reenie.

'How is it short for Irene? It's the same number of syllables. I-rene. Reen-ie. And how'd you spell it?'

'R-e-e-n-i-e.'

'Hang on. That's six letters.'

'Yes. And?'

'Irene's five letters.'

'So what?'

'So your nickname is longer than your real name?'

'Yes.'

'That doesn't make any sense.'

'Well, it doesn't *have* to be shorter,' said Reenie. 'It's just a nickname. When I was little, when I came to London, my foster mum called me Reenie and it stuck.'

'Foster mum? You were adopted?'

'Not adopted. Fostered. My parents were still in Austria.'

'You're Austrian?'

'Was.'

'You don't sound it.'

Reenie laughed. 'Well, no. I was only little at the time.'

'So why did you come to…' he started, freezing halfway through his question. 'What year was that?'

'Thirty-nine.'

'Was it the Kindertransport?'

'How'd you know that?'

'I studied history. Remember?'

He'd never studied the Kindertransport, though. Not in class. Read about it, heard about it. Remembered his friend Yusuf saying, 'That's how cruel they are. First sign of trouble, they abandon their kids. Their *kids*. Pack them off to live with strangers. A Muslim wouldn't do that. Says it all.'

He looked at Reenie. She seemed to have taken his word for it, but she looked different to him now, now it was confirmed, the thing he'd known almost since they met.

'Oh yeah,' said Reenie. 'Well, that was it. It was Quakers took me as far as Holland. They were allowed to travel back and fore, see? And they put me on a ferry with all these other kids, and when we got to the other side we were put in Dovercamp. They made it seem like we was on holiday. And about a month later my foster parents, Mr and Mrs Ostroff, came to pick me up.

'Oh, they were a right pair. They were a lot older than my real mum and dad. Must have been in their late forties, early fifties when they took me in. She was tall and thin, looked a bit like a schoolmarm, but she was lovely. One of those voices that's full of kindness, you know. And Mr Ostroff, well, he was about six inches shorter than his wife, and big and round and cuddly, like a big bear. And if someone said something to make him laugh, he couldn't stop! He'd laugh until there were tears rolling down his cheeks and he was bright red in the face. He was a carpenter, Mr Ostroff, and his hands were huge, like shovels, even though he was so short.

'I was just five when I came over. Just me and my clothes and a piece of string around my neck with my number on it. It's funny. You'd think I'd remember something like that, but I can't. It was my dad who told me most of it. He said when they were sending us off they made us use a railway station outside the city, out in the suburbs. They said the sight of all of us together might upset the Viennese. As if we'd come from somewhere else. Can't remember any of that. I was too young to remember much of anything, I suppose.'

For a while they walked in silence, and more and more it made sense to him that they should both have chosen to make this journey on foot. Born in London, he'd never fled a country, but his grandparents had, and the story of their journey – every overcrowded boat, every lost bit of luggage, every bout of sickness and diarrhoea, from Okara to West Ham – was recycled at family get-togethers. Sometimes they were trotted out to make a point, to illustrate to the youngsters just how easy their lives were, how much they had to be grateful for. Sometimes they were just stories, funny anecdotes, the trauma and heartache stripped out leaving only the slapstick and punchlines.

As a teenager, he'd come to resent their stories, whichever version was being told. At first it was the repetition; the umpteenth retelling of how his dad's older brother, Ibrahim's *Thaya* Ahmed, was seasick when they were only ten minutes out of Karachi, or how his *Bhua* Yasmin, tried to eat a banana with the peel still on it, as if that were the funniest thing any child had ever done. Then, more and more, he began to resent the idea that he should be

47

grateful. Grateful for what? For being looked down on every time he wandered outside a certain, safe little corner of East London? He remembered those school trips, when they had strayed out into the Home Counties, and he remembered the looks they got. Never seen a group of Asian kids before, you'd think. And that look, always the same look. Policemen stopping and searching because you look the type, talking loud and slow before you say a word because they think all *Desis* have a limited command of the Queen's English. And always some posturing twat in the paper saying how if you don't support the cricket team you aren't properly British or bitching because a local council printed something in Urdu. *They come over here, they take our jobs.* Was he meant to be grateful for all that? No. Britain wasn't a sanctuary; it was a place where every *Desi* had just a handful of choices. *Doctor, cabbie, shopkeeper. They're your options. Don't like it here? Well why don't you piss off home?* Britain was cold and it was godless. Full to the brim with cross-of-St-George skinheads, tattoos on their necks, singing 'Lager! Lager! Lager!' But worse than them were the bastards who'd make a joke, take the piss out of you for your colour or your name, and when you didn't laugh say, 'Where's your sense of humour? It was just a bit of banter.' As if their right to laugh at you, to ridicule you, trumped all else. That was Britain. Britannica. A pompous, sneering *gori* bitch with her shield and her lion. If it wasn't for her, his grandparents would never have had to leave their homeland in the first place. Fuck Britain, and fuck his grandparents' grovelling. Why should he be grateful?

But that anger, like so much else, had disappeared in time; so gradually it was difficult, if not impossible, for him to pinpoint the exact moment of its passing. The accident, perhaps, or was it earlier than that? Meeting Amanda? Leaving London? Earlier, still?

There was no point in thinking about all that now, not while he was walking. And walking. How far had his grandparents walked? He had seen the few photographs they took while travelling, and everything looked so old, so long ago. And black and white took the heat and the sunshine out of everything, so that he only knew a certain road in Punjab was dusty because his grandfather, his *dada*, told him it was dusty, and only knew that it was hot because his *dada* told him it was hot. Did they have to walk along the hot and dusty road? How often, on their journey, were they carried along by nothing but their feet?

The details his *dada* remembered seemed so small, so intimate, Ibrahim was sure they must have walked at least some of the way. Travelling by car or by train, he now realised, you see only trees, but on foot, when walking, you see not trees but the individual branches and leaves.

They had walked almost half an hour that morning when the van – light blue, the logo of an energy company emblazoned along its side – pulled in, stopping several yards ahead of them, its passenger side window lowering with three jerky movements.

'If he asks us if we're off the telly,' said Reenie, struggling to keep up, 'tell him he's mistaken us for someone else. Tell him we're just lookalikes. Or that we're eccentric millionaires.'

When he was level with the open window, Ibrahim stopped walking and the trolley jangled to a halt. Inside the van the driver, a youngish man with grey-flecked red hair, leaned across the passenger seats, his chin almost resting on the top third of the windowpane. He looked at Ibrahim with surprise, as if expecting someone else. Only when Reenie caught up with them did he smile.

'Hiya. D'you wanna lift?'

Reenie looked from the driver to Ibrahim and back again. 'What do you mean, "a lift"?'

'I can drive you over the bridge. There's room in the van for all your stuff.'

'Well how do you know I'm going over the bridge?'

'I saw you on telly. This morning. Irene something, they said your name was. They said you're walking to London.'

'Well, maybe I am,' said Reenie. 'But I don't see what that's got to do with you.'

The driver looked stung, and slouched back into the driver's side of the cabin.

'Right,' he said. 'I just thought… It's a long way to London.'

'So everyone keeps telling us.'

'And they said you're travelling alone.'

'Well, that's not true, but then that's the news for you.'

'I just thought it would make things easier if someone drove you over the bridge, dropped you off the other side of Bristol.'

She turned to Ibrahim. 'What do you reckon? Might get us there a bit quicker.'

'I can't,' he replied.

'Why not?'

'I just can't.'

'But he's got a van. We can get my trolley in there. How long would it take us to get to the other side of Bristol if we was walking?'

'A few days. Maybe longer.'

'Exactly. And you're saying you don't want a lift?'

'I just can't. I'm sorry.' He turned to the driver. 'You got any ID on you?'

'Excuse me?'

'ID. Like a card with your face on it, or something?'

'Er, yeah. Sure.'

The driver reached into his shirt pocket and produced a plastic card printed with a company logo, a passport-style photograph, and a name: GARY EVANS.

'Gary Evans,' said Ibrahim, 'Gary Evans Gary Evans Gary Evans.'

'What're you doing?' asked Reenie.

'Memorising his name,' said Ibrahim. 'Just in case. Look. You should go. Think how much time you'll save. Think how much closer you'll be when he drops you off.'

'What about you?'

'I'll manage. I'll get there eventually.'

She looked away from him, her gaze falling to her feet, as if searching the tarmac for her next words. 'Would you have gone all the way to London with me?' she asked.

He chose his answer carefully. Last night he had considered moving on without her. Shortly before falling asleep, a good two hours after she retired to her tent, he decided he would wake early, before her, and move on without saying goodbye. He was sure she would understand. They were making the same journey, yes, but didn't plan it together. They hardly knew each other. But there was something else, a nagging thought, the fragments of a memory, and when eventually he woke, he'd abandoned all thoughts of leaving her behind.

'Not *all* the way,' he said. 'Not if you were slowing me down.'

'I see,' said Reenie. 'Well, that's fair enough. Wouldn't want to slow you down, now, would I?' She stood on tiptoes, peering into the van. 'Alright, love,' she said to the driver. 'It's a deal. You two'll have to get the trolley in there, mind. Might be able to push it, but I can't lift it.'

It took all the strength of both men to hoist the trolley up into the van, and Ibrahim noticed her watching him as they did. She looked so disappointed, and he cursed himself for not telling her everything there and then. Why he couldn't come with her, why he wished he could. Why he was sorry. Why he regretted almost everything he'd ever done. But it had been this way for so long. As if what lay inside his head couldn't be translated into words, the right words. How could he begin to tell her? She would never believe him.

With the trolley loaded, doors shut, driver behind the wheel, and birdcage balanced safely on her lap, Reenie looked down at him from the open passenger-side window. 'Sure you can't come?' she asked. 'There's plenty of room in here.'

'I can't,' said Ibrahim. 'I'm sorry.'

Reenie nodded but said nothing, and the van began to move. She leaned out of the window to look at Ibrahim one last time, but didn't speak, and as they picked up speed, Gary, the driver, beat out a 'goodbye' on its horn.

Later that day Ibrahim would remember how they hadn't said goodbye to one another. Perhaps, he would think, it was because they weren't friends, in any real sense. They were barely acquaintances. They had shared food and a portion of their journey, and a little of their time. They breathed the same air, and walked under the same sky, but what else?

He knew what else.

But maybe that was it. Twenty-four hours, or less, in her company. The kind of coincidence you read about in cheap magazines. Something he would remember, but not a story he would ever share, and yet it didn't feel final, and a part of him was almost certain they would meet again.

7

Sputnik scratched and snuffled at the gap between Casper's bedroom door and the threadbare carpet. A helpless, desperate whimper. Hungry? Thirsty? It couldn't be that he needed a piss. When that dog wanted to piss he pissed, never mind where he was.

Casper sat up. Though he lived at the top of the house, three floors up, his bedroom was cold enough for him to see his own breath, and it wasn't even winter. He heard music coming from Andy's room, drum and bass, and voices laughing. They were still going from the night before. And the house stank.

But then, the house always stank. The kitchen had a stench of takeaway food impregnated into its walls, a smell you'd never get rid of. Elsewhere, the carpets had a mildewy staleness; three years' worth of spilt ashtrays, bongs and beer bottles. From the first floor up the house had the pissy, ammonial tang of strong, home-grown cannabis. The individual bedrooms smelled of damp, forgotten towels and old socks.

When Casper opened his door, Sputnik came bounding in, prancing around his ankles before charging back out onto the landing.

'Okay, okay,' said Casper. 'Chill. We'll get you some food. Hang on.'

He followed the dog downstairs, past the noise coming from Andy's room – music and a bellowing chorus of laughter followed by the bubble and hiss of another bong hit – and went straight to the kitchen. Nothing in the cupboards, nothing in the fridge.

'Shit,' said Casper.

Sputnik whimpered.

Casper ran back to his room, avoiding the step where the carpet came loose, turning their staircase into something from a funhouse, and on reaching the top floor noticed that once again there were small orange mushrooms growing near the bathroom door.

He found his least smelly pair of jeans and the t-shirt he'd worn yesterday, sprayed himself with deodorant, and slipped on the pair of trainers with the greatest degree of structural integrity. On his way out he knocked on Andy's door, and it was answered by a man he'd never seen before with tattooed teardrops on his left cheek.

'Just popping to the shop. Anyone want anything?'

'Ketamine,' grunted the man with the teardrop tattoos. The others in the room laughed.

'No, mate,' said Andy. 'We're fine, thanks.'

Sputnik shadowed Casper as far as the front door, now certain he'd be taken for a walk, and Casper apologised as he edged his way out of the house, closing the door quickly enough to prevent the dog from following.

Casper often thought that if it weren't for the houses on either side of them, theirs would almost certainly collapse. Everything about it felt so ramshackle, the floors so uneven, the walls chipped and peeling. Everything creaked and groaned. All too easy to imagine it caving in on itself one day, leaving a gap between their neighbours like a missing tooth.

He'd never forget his father's expression the only time he ever saw the place. Not exactly sadness, or even disgust, but something placed mysteriously between the two. Gone was any attempt at humouring his son's choices; that was strictly for his university days. An eyebrow raised sardonically, a witty aside to Casper's stepmother, a good-humoured shaking of the head.

'Well, it's certainly very *bohemian*, I'll give you that.'

There were no such comments this time, and Casper hadn't even wanted him to come. Casper's embarrassment – his father's car so new and big and silver and expensive, parked right outside their house; his father wearing an actual suit and an actual tie – was the unstoppable force to the immovable object of his father's shame. Their conversation happened on the pavement; his father never daring to go any further than the front door.

That was two years ago, and though his father had written and Casper had sent birthday cards, they hadn't spoken, hadn't heard one another's voices, in all that time. There was nothing for them to talk about. They had nothing in common, the only thing binding them was a genetic coincidence which was meaningless in the great scheme of things. His friends were his family.

In the shop, the man who lived at number 16 and who always smelled like sherry was buying a two-litre flagon of strong cider, two packs of Lambert & Butler, and a scratch card. The Sikh lad who worked there made a show of waving his hand in front of his nose after the man from number 16 had left.

'He stinks, man. Always in here, always buying that cheap cider shit. What can I get you?'

Casper paid for the dog food and left. As he neared the house he could hear Andy's music again. Had it been that loud when he went out, or had they turned it up? Thank God most of their neighbours were in work, or unlikely to complain about the noise. If he hadn't had to feed Sputnik, he would have kept walking. The park was quiet and clean and smelled of honest things, like dead leaves and wet grass, and he liked to watch the crows peck at worms. He went there, sometimes, when the house was too much, when there was no money, when he had nowhere else to go.

8

On the map Ibrahim's route, represented by a crooked blue line from Cardiff to London, resembled the outline of a mountain; the journey from Cardiff to Chepstow its rambling foothills, with Gloucester as the summit. No matter what the topography of the journey after Gloucester, he could only imagine it feeling as if he were walking downhill, as if the force of gravity pulled south instead of down. To stop at Chepstow would feel like a defeat, as if this imaginary mountain had beaten him.

Ibrahim thought of Reenie and the stranger in the van. Gary Evans. His name was Gary Evans. He had even made a point of writing that name down, along with the first half of the van's registration number – as much as he could remember – after they had driven away. They would be across the bridge by now. Reenie would be somewhere on the far side of Bristol, and maybe she was ploughing on alone with her trolley, or perhaps had set up camp again beside some near-deserted stretch of road.

How much easier his journey could have been if he'd joined them, if he'd climbed into the van with her, allowed himself to be driven over the bridge. It would still have meant walking a hundred miles or more, but when he traced his fingertip along that other route he saw a less eccentric course carve its way across England.

But he had never considered taking up the offer of a lift, not even for a second, and even when he had walked for seven hours and was only then nearing the English border, not once did he consider hitchhiking. He hadn't been in a car, a bus, or a train in four years. In those first few wheelchair-bound months after the crash, and when there were still people willing to drive him, he was driven from place to place, but each journey was an ordeal, his hands becoming clammy, his mouth dry. He felt his stomach lurch with every turn in the road. By the time they reached their destination he was exhausted by panic alone, and from the moment he could walk again he refused to travel anywhere except by foot.

Walking felt safe, his every step a choice, a decision made by him alone. Walking happens at a pace free from chaos; the chance disruptions that can tear a life apart reduced to a minimum. He took care when crossing roads, always waiting until the lights had changed, and even then checking in both directions as he crossed. Just in case. Excursions beyond his front door became few and far between. On the rare occasions when he left his flat – to buy groceries or to sign for his benefits – he knew exactly which routes involved the least number of crossings, and he knew the times of day when he would encounter the fewest pedestrians.

When planning his walk to London, he weighed the anxieties of walking on busy roads against the two or three hours of sheer, suffocating panic he would experience on a coach or train. He knew there would be no moment, if he chose the latter, when that panic would subside. It would escalate, consuming him; his thoughts a maelstrom of derailings, head-on collisions, deafening flames and black, volcanic clouds of smoke.

On the night of the crash, his heart had stopped beating twice, but he had no memory of this, and so he wondered obsessively how the instance of death in another accident might feel. Would it be a sudden going out of the lights, or would that split second be drawn out, an infinite scream of white noise and searing pain; the unending awareness that this was terminal?

He entered England halfway across the bridge spanning the River Wye, and he stopped there, at that halfway point, and looked back the way he'd come. He wasn't sure what he left behind, but it felt as if he'd passed a point of no return, as if to go back now wasn't just an act of surrender, but a physical impossibility.

On the English side of the bridge the road narrowed down from four lanes to two. A dog leashed to the gate of a farmhouse strained against its rope and barked at him as he walked past, and the sheep in an opposite field followed him with their communal, blank-eyed gaze. He passed small towns and villages he'd never heard of, places that sounded almost fictionally quaint, like Wibdon and Stroat, and he entertained himself by imagining the petty rivalries between villages – the flower competitions and lawn bowls tournaments that turned nasty; the cider festivals where local lads became provincial Bloods and Crips.

He wanted to carry on walking, but he was weak. His stomach ached with hunger, and his mouth was sandpaper dry. Lydney, the place he'd hoped to reach the night before, was only a few miles ahead, but they were a few miles too many. Now, out here between the towns and cities, he realised there were few places he would find shelter. There were no guesthouses or bed and breakfasts, and besides, he doubted any guesthouse would take him in. To the owner of a guesthouse in rural Gloucestershire, he imagined he would look as outlandish, as intimidating, as a Viking.

Instead, he left the road and searched for a place where he could hide – from the road, from the locals, from the elements – settling on a barn that stood a hundred metres or more from its farmhouse. There were no cattle inside or nearby, just bales of hay and what might be bats fluttering in the shadowed beams above him. Though he had virtually no sense of smell – hadn't enjoyed a sense of smell since the accident – the air itself tasted sickly sweet, of cow dung and fresh hay.

He found a place to sleep, hidden from the view of anyone passing the barn's open door. The hay was comfortable enough; despite the straws piercing his sleeping bag and clothes and jabbing into his flesh it was better than the previous night's hard bed beneath the motorway.

It was a cloudy night, and once the sun had set the darkness was absolute. Even when he'd been lying in the dark, trying to sleep, for an hour or more, his eyes failed to adjust. Holding his hand before his face, he still couldn't see the outline of his fingers. He heard what sounded like a screaming baby, echoing across the fields: a desperate, chilling scream. A fox. It had to be a fox.

Another scream, and he shuddered.

There were few other noises that night, but in a way he found the absence of a city's constant drone – traffic, helicopters, sirens – more distracting. Any sound, however small, was amplified by the stillness. A wooden beam creaking as it expanded in the damp night air became the mast of a tall ship sailing into a storm. A single bat flying across the barn became a whole colony of leather-winged nightmares. His feet and legs throbbed painfully, and in the seconds before he fell asleep it felt as though he was still walking, his whole body rocking forward with each imaginary footstep.

9

It was no surprise to find herself alone; she hadn't expected any different. Everyone goes away, sooner or later. Stupid to invest even a tiny bit of trust in any one person. If she had learned one thing in her life, it was that you can only ever trust yourself. Never mind. She preferred it on her own, preferred the pace of it.

It took all morning and much of the afternoon for her to cover just five miles, and in that time the landscape changed very little. Sometimes there were hills, real hills, and the effort of pushing the trolley up each incline exhausted her. At the top of these hills the countryside reached out in seas of recently ploughed earth, the black plastic hay bales like humpbacked whales coming up for air pungent with the scent of fresh manure.

Soon she'd have to stop and rest, but more importantly find somewhere tucked away and private that she could use as a toilet. That was the one thing most people didn't consider on a walk like this. They'd forget it's not just food and clean clothes you need. Sooner or later you'll have to answer nature's call. Not a problem in the cities, where there were public toilets, with hot water and soap, but there was no such luxury between cities. There she had to find a bit of privacy, and even then it was a risky, clumsy kind of privacy; behind hedges or in abandoned coal sheds. Dignity is the first thing sacrificed on a long walk, but she didn't mind so much. She wasn't too proud to piss in the open, though she wondered how it might look to a passer-by.

Eventually she found a place, a short distance from the main road, secluded and sheltered behind a small thatch of trees, in the corner of a vast and barren field. At the top of the field was a farmhouse, but even from some distance she could see it was in poor shape. The outer buildings had yawning black holes in their roofs, and she saw the barely visible hulk of a rusting red tractor, consumed by weeds, in what might once have been a farmyard.

Did anyone live there? *Could* anyone live there? Perhaps, if the farmhouse was abandoned and derelict, she might find her way inside and use it as a shelter for the night. It might not be as comfortable as the house she'd left behind in Cardiff, but it would be better than the tent, and she was drawing up a plan to investigate further when a battered, ancient-looking van pulled up in the farmyard.

The people who climbed out – two men and a woman – didn't look much like farmers. The men had long hair, scruffy clothes. The woman wore her hair in straggly, dirty-blonde dreadlocks. Whoever these people were, they hadn't noticed her, and so she carried on setting up her camp. She washed and changed her clothes, and ate a light meal of bread and cheese. She pissed behind a windbreaker that she had found, before setting off from Cardiff, in the cupboard beneath the stairs. The windbreaker had last seen daylight on a blustery Bournemouth weekend maybe thirty years ago, when it was used to save Reenie, Jonathan and their jam sarnies from the wind and sand.

The afternoon and early evening passed quietly. She fed Solomon, read from a spine-creased Jean Plaidy novel she'd read at least half a dozen times before, and rose to the challenge of a crossword she'd been tackling for the last five days. When it became too dark for her to read, she put away the novel and the copy of *Puzzler*, and she and Solomon retired to the warmth of her tent.

The first vans and cars began to arrive shortly after ten, and she heard music – if it could be called that – coming from the farmhouse. There was no discernible melody, just an electronic wail drifting on the night air, and beneath that a ground-shaking drum – pounding, insistent. When this music had been playing for quarter of an hour or more, Reenie crawled out from her tent, and saw in the distant farmyard flashing, multi-coloured lights and a shifting wall of silhouetted, dancing bodies.

She unfolded one of her deckchairs and sat in that dark corner of the field, watching as more and more people arrived. Every so often she heard a whoop or a cheer above the music, whenever it reached a frantic crescendo. They had begun lighting bonfires now, around the outskirts of the farmyard, and the smoke rose up against the electric lights in glowing clouds that tapered out into the darkness.

What were they celebrating? A birthday? Exams? If Reenie knew anything about youngsters, it was that they needed little excuse. There had been dances when she was a girl, dances with no purpose other than meeting and dancing with boys. She knew people, had met people, who seemed to think those times were more innocent, as if meeting a boy was an end in itself, as if nothing more was ever expected after the last dance of the evening.

She still recalled in every detail her first fumbling moments of intimacy with a boy named Harry Green, in Limehouse. Only moments earlier, she and Harry had been inside the old Market Hall, dancing, as Frankie Laine sang 'What Could Be Sweeter?' and she remembered how they laughed as the record jumped and scratched, having been played at almost every other dance that summer. Not many people had a copy, but the lad who'd organised the dance, George Whitlock, had a brother stationed over in Germany who sent home parcels of American cigarettes and LPs.

When the lights came up she and Harry went for a walk, but even at fifteen Reenie wasn't naïve enough to think that was all he wanted. They found an alleyway behind the hall – a dank and shadowed gully the local kids called 'Lovers' Lane' – and they kissed with open mouths. She allowed Harry to put his hand inside her blouse, and touch her breasts, and Harry guided her hand down towards his already-open fly. Little more happened that night. She'd been forewarned by her friends, those more experienced than her, not to give herself up too early, and she took her hand away when she suspected Harry was moments away from losing all control of himself.

She straightened her blouse and fixed her hair, and wiped the cupid's bows of lipstick from Harry's cheek and neck with her handkerchief. Hand in hand, they walked out onto St Paul's Way, and her waiting friends laughed as Harry made one last adjustment, to hide his erection. The boys, Harry and his friends, walked the girls as far as Mile End tube station, jumping the barriers when no one was looking so that they could see them off on the platform with final goodnight kisses.

It was another two years before she gave herself to a man who wasn't Harry Green, but that night in Limehouse, and the realisation of her sex, and all that it entailed, was like an explosion, an air burst, over the last days of her childhood. The next day she could barely stop smiling, and at breakfast wondered if her father and stepmother noticed this change in her. When she left the house, later that day, she walked as if buoyed by her confidence, as if she'd discovered a secret that she, and only she, now knew.

Were the kids dancing in that farmyard any different? Did they have the same desires and aspirations? Were they there to meet boys and girls? If they were, the music they danced to was hardly romantic. Where were the lyrics? Where were the sweeping strings and the crooner's chocolate-smooth voice? When Frankie Laine sang, and she allowed Harry Green's hands to wander, Reenie had drowned in the music and the words being sung, believing every line. Now it sounded like the kids were dancing to hammers and drills.

She listened to the noise and watched the lights and smoke for almost an hour before deciding to investigate. A good night's sleep was out of the question. She wouldn't complain about the noise. Even if they didn't look like farmers, there was every chance they owned the place, and she couldn't imagine they'd take kindly to a trespasser asking them to keep it down. Better, she decided, to introduce herself, satisfy her curiosity.

After navigating her way, clumsily, across the dark field, Reenie entered the farmyard and was hit by a wall of noise and warmth, and by the thick, cloying smell of smoke. Some of the youngsters were dancing, their bodies moving in rough time with the music. Others sat around the fires, smoking what Reenie knew were not cigarettes.

The first to spot her was a boy whose blond beard looked translucent and out-of-place on his boyish features. Like so many of the others his hair was tangled up in muddy dreadlocks, and his skin was almost milk white. He looked at her, first with a frown, then a smile, and as Reenie walked a little further into the farmyard came bounding over to her.

'Hey! Hey! You okay?'

She turned to face him. 'Sorry?'

'Are you a friend of Womble's?'

'Wom…? Excuse me?'

'Did you just get here?'

She pointed to the dark end of the field. 'My tent's down there,' she said. 'I'm just camping for the night. Whose farm is this?'

'Farm?' said the young man, laughing as if her question was silly. 'Womble owns the house. That's why I asked if you were his friend.'

'I don't know anyone called Womble,' said Reenie. 'Wasn't that on the telly? The Wombles?'

'Yeah. That's Womble. Underground, over-ground. I'm Casper, by the way.'

He held out his hand, and Reenie shook it hesitantly.

'I'm Reenie,' she said. 'And this Womble… he owns the place?'

'Yeah.'

'Can I speak to him?'

The young man, Casper, shrugged. 'Sure. Let me see if I can find him.'

He climbed onto an upturned milk crate, standing on tiptoe and scanning the farmyard. When he saw the person he was looking for he waved his arms, and whistled loudly through his fingers, and they were joined by an older, paunchier man – Reenie guessed he was perhaps twenty years younger than her – with long brown hair, and a saggy, once-aquiline face.

'Womble, this is Reenie,' said Casper, jumping down from the milk crate.

The older man, Womble, studied her with a lopsided grin and narrow, stoned-looking eyes. She'd seen that louche expression often enough to know what caused it.

'Hey,' said Womble. 'Cool name. Welcome to the party.'

Reenie nodded, trying not to stare at the others in the farmyard. 'Right,' she said. 'It's just, this young man tells me you own this farm.'

'Farm?' Womble laughed. 'Honey. Farms make things. They breed animals for meat, or they grow crops. There's not much growing here,' he turned to Casper. 'Unless you count the you-know-what in the attic.' He mimed taking a long drag, inhaling sharply, and he and Casper bumped their fists together clumsily.

'Well, anyway,' said Reenie. 'I just wanted to ask you, I've pitched my tent at the bottom of the field. Your field.'

'Honey,' said Womble. The word was already beginning to grate. She'd never been called 'honey' before, and didn't like it. 'This isn't my field. It's nature's field.'

'So does that mean it's okay for me to camp here?'

'Sure thing, honey.'

Inside her wellington boots, Reenie clenched her toes.

'Right,' she said. 'Thank you.'

'As long as you can handle the noise, you're welcome. We're having a bit of a get-together.'

'I can see that.'

'But you should join us!'

'Yeah!' Casper chimed in. 'You should totally join us!'

'Well,' said Reenie. 'I don't know…'

'Oh, come on,' purred Womble. 'I could tell, the minute I saw you. You were meant to be here. You know that, Reenie? I'm talking about meaningful coincidence. Have you read Jung?'

'Young what?'

'Carl Jung. Synchronicity. It'll blow your mind, man. Blow. Your. Mind.'

Reenie didn't particularly want her mind blown, but within minutes found herself sitting on one of the orange plastic milk crates, next to a fire, being introduced to people a third her age and younger. Casper talked about her as if she were some treasure he'd unearthed or an exotic species found far from its natural habitat. One of his friends offered Reenie a joint, another a handful of dried black mushrooms, and she declined both.

'Not with my constitution,' she said. 'A glass of wine's enough to knock me on my arse most days.'

She listened to them talk, following as best she could what they were saying. In between rambling psychedelic observations, she made out that they were self-described 'travellers'. 'Nomads, really,' said Casper, his voice muted as he held in the most recent drag from a joint.

'You mean gypsies?' said Reenie.

'Yeah, I suppose,' said Casper, proudly.

'But you're not gypsies, though,' said Reenie. 'I mean, I've met gypsies. I've known a lot of gypsies. Romanies and Tinkers, I mean. And you're neither.'

'Well, no. I don't mean we're *actual* gypsies.'

'But you live in a caravan?'

He shook his head. 'Well, no. I don't. We've got a squat. In Bath.'

'A squat?'

'Yeah. Just this house. We've been there a few years.'

'Right.'

'I'm homeless, see?'

She studied him over the flames. He may have straggly dreadlocks and a haze of facial hair, but Casper's skin was unblemished and his blue eyes sparkled without the bloodshot look of a drinker, or someone with too many sleepless nights to look properly rested ever again. When he spoke there were no dropped aitches or glottal stops. Even under the influence of whatever he'd taken he spoke well. If he had been dressed any differently – and it was easy to imagine him dressed differently – Reenie would have called him 'posh'.

'You're homeless?' she said.

'Yeah. That's how come I'm in the squat.'

'You ain't got parents?'

Casper shifted uncomfortably, looking down at the joint in his hand and the scruffy trainers on his feet. 'Yeah. Well. My mum's dead, but I've got a dad and a stepmum.'

'Why don't you live with them?'

'They're just…' he allowed the sentence to drift into silence, and shook his head. 'I just don't need them.'

'You're living in a squat, love. I'd say you need them. Do they even know where you are?'

A nervous laugh. 'What's this? Twenty questions?'

'They must be worried about you.'

'Yeah, well, my dad's, like, the CEO of this big company, and my stepmum's a university lecturer, and it's like, well… I'm just this big disappointment to them, so, you know, fuck them. Besides, if they think I'm gonna turn into just another *drone* like them, they've got another think coming.'

Shaking her head, Reenie laughed and turned to the girl next to Casper.

'What about you? Are you homeless?'

'No,' said the girl, not quite as well-spoken as Casper but her voice hardly came from the gutter. 'I'm a traveller. I live in a camp near Keynsham.'

'Another traveller,' said Reenie. 'And you?' She pointed across the fire to a man who resembled nothing so much as a shabby Jesus.

'I'm homeless,' said Shabby Jesus. 'I live in the same squat as Casper.'

'Homeless,' said Reenie, still shaking her head. 'You're homeless, and you're homeless, and you're a traveller. Have any of you ever actually slept rough?'

Casper sat up straight and frowned at her. 'What do you mean?'

'Have you ever slept rough? On a street?'

'Well. Not as such. I mean, my friend Rory and I... we went to London once, for this party, and we ended up sleeping in this churchyard because the guys we were meant to be staying with...'

'How long was that for?' said Reenie. 'A night? Doesn't count. How about you?'

Shabby Jesus shook his head.

'You neither. Neither of you ever had to sleep rough, but you call yourself homeless.'

'Yeah, well that depends on your definition of homeless, doesn't it?' said Casper, indignation creeping into his voice. 'We're in a squat. Bailiffs could come in there any day and turf us out.'

Reenie laughed, leaning back to take her face away from the glow and the heat of the fire.

'Don't tell me you're homeless,' she said. 'Because I know homeless when I see it, and you're not homeless. You can play at being homeless, and you can live in your squat, and it's all good fun, but if those bailiffs do come and boot you out, and there's no other place for you to go, he'd have you back. Your dad. He'd have you back in a second. And here's another thing. If, God forbid, anything ever happened to him, and you lost him, you'd have him back in a second, too.'

A silence fell around the fire, as if her words had been a clap of thunder, allowed to echo and roll for miles, uninterrupted. Before that silence could curdle, the girl next to Casper huffed and said, 'Man, that's brought me right down. Give me a toke on that.'

'Homeless isn't a choice,' said Reenie. 'It's not some lifestyle you pick. It's something that happens to you. Why would anyone *choose* to be homeless?'

'Maybe we don't want to live like everyone else,' said Shabby Jesus. 'Maybe we don't want a semi-detached in the suburbs, growing flowers and playing golf and all that shit. Not everyone wants that.'

'Then fine,' said Reenie. 'Don't grow flowers and don't play golf. Don't buy a semi-detached in the suburbs. But don't you tell me you're homeless, neither, because you're not.'

Casper glowered at her. 'I thought you were cool,' he said, his voice cracking with disappointment. 'I thought you were, like, this really wise old woman. I thought you were one of us.'

'Who said I was wise? I never said I was wise. I'm not saying I'm wise now. But you're right, I *am* old. I've seen a lot of things and met a lot of people. Right now, you're young. You think nothing matters, that nothing you do now will ever have any consequence, but it will. There's no such thing as the past. The present, the here and now, it only exists because of the past. Everything you've said and done before today. And the things you say and do today, they'll decide where you are and who you are a year, ten years, *fifty* years from now. Believe me.'

She wasn't sure if she'd offended them, or given them food for thought, and she didn't care. If she felt anything at all, it wasn't embarrassment, or the awkwardness of the silence that followed, or even their sullen looks – it was guilt. She wondered if they had seen through her. She had made it sound as if she'd never had their opportunities, their choices, but she had.

She'd always had the choice. To leave, to stay. To keep going, to go back. Always a choice. Like now. She could have gone back, could have given up yesterday, the day before, the day before *that*.

Turned around and gone home. She could have done that, but didn't. Kept going. Always going. Never stopping. Because stopping meant it would catch up with her. Everything she'd done, all the lies she had told and the mistakes she'd made would come crashing up behind her until she couldn't move, couldn't breathe. So she kept moving, kept going, and hoped to God or whoever was listening that she could get away with it. And these kids, they had the same look about them, the same stubbornness. They wouldn't give in, and if they did, no matter what she had told them, a part of her would think less of them for it.

She could have told them all this, but she didn't. Nothing she said to them would come out quite how she meant it, and she couldn't resolve those tensions, those inconsistencies, between the many different people she had been. Refugee. Daughter. Runaway. Lover. Wife. Widow. Each word the shorthand for a million others, and none of them slotting together neatly. She couldn't defend one part of her life without condemning another, couldn't extol one virtue without exposing a dozen sins.

If anything, she thought, life was like the Russian dolls, the Matryoshka, Mrs Ostroff kept in a glass cabinet. No matter how many times Reenie had played with them, she would always forget how many there were; there was always one smaller, each dictating the shape of its container. That centre, the smallest doll, informed the shape of all that followed. So what, for her, was the smallest doll?

That first night away from home? Stepping onto the District Line train? Paying her tube fare with pennies? Walking out of the house without a key? Packing a bag with all her things? No. Earlier than that. Much earlier.

Perhaps the day her father came home with a new friend, Vera. The young war widow from down the street. Reenie had recognised her. Younger than Reenie's father, maybe not even old enough to be Reenie's mother. And Vera's handshake was a limp, insipid kind of handshake, though perhaps Reenie thought this because she knew already Vera was more than a friend. She'd heard snatches of gossip in shops, talk of Albert Lieberman 'courting' and 'romancing'.

Romancing? Had they actually met her father? Albert Lieberman didn't wear his heart on his sleeve. If he wanted for company, for intimacy, he'd never said so. If he'd fallen madly in love with this woman, he never said so. If it was purely lust, well, his daughter found that hard enough to consider, let alone believe.

But Vera hardly fitted the fairy-tale mould of Wicked Stepmother, no matter how hard Reenie tried framing her that way. She was only seventeen years her senior, but so quiet, so dowdy, so *goyish*. How was it possible for a woman so young to be so dull? And how was it possible for a woman so dull to exert so much influence over Reenie's father?

From the minute they had moved into their house on Harold Road, just a few doors away from the Ostroffs, Albert Lieberman had kept the one surviving photograph of his wife framed on their living-room mantelpiece. The portrait, soft focus and sepia-tinted, was taken when Reenie's mother, Irina, was just nineteen, and was as stiff and mannered as any other portrait from the time, but it was the only image of her mother Reenie had. From that one, inexpressive picture she tried to imagine how her mother must have looked when she smiled or when she laughed, when she scowled or when she cried.

As a child, Reenie pretended to remember her mother vividly. When her father, in his broken English, told her stories about Vienna she'd say, 'Yes, Papa. I remember that.' And she'd genuinely believe that she remembered, but in those forced memories her mother was forever nineteen years old, and inexpressive, and every memory was sepia-tinted.

On the morning of his marriage to Vera, Albert Lieberman took the photograph of his first wife from the mantelpiece and placed it somewhere far from view, never telling Reenie where he'd hidden it. Though this was done in such an understated way, there was something in her father's expression, some deep, unspeakable agony, that she could never bring herself to ask him why he'd done it, or to even ask him where the photograph now was, and once the second Mrs Lieberman was in their home, the first, Reenie's mother, was never spoken of again. Sometimes, if her father and stepmother were out, or otherwise busy, Reenie would look for the photograph, searching through the few boxes of belongings Albert brought with him to London, but the search was always fruitless.

The only photograph she found was one of her father, taken when he was a young member of the Vienna Maccabi gymnastics team, but even then she barely recognised him. In it, Albert Lieberman was broad-shouldered, athletic, like Johnny Weissmuller or Buster Crabbe. His eyes and his smile hinted at something mischievous and knowing; a happy-go-lucky confidence. On seeing the photograph for the first time, Reenie spent minutes wondering if it was some unknown cousin or uncle. Only the hint of a familiar scar, near his hairline, gave it away. It had to be her father, couldn't be anyone else. But what could have happened to him? And if this was what They – the unnameable 'They' – had done to him, what had they done to her mother?

Had there been uncles and aunts, other members of the family, in London, Reenie might have spoken to them about her mother, asking all the questions she had yet to ask, but Albert was the only one to have made it. Theirs had been a large family – three sisters and a brother on her mother's side, two sisters and three brothers on her father's, and with fifteen cousins in all, but they'd heard nothing of them since the end of the war. Albert and Reenie were, most likely, the last ones left.

By this time, neither Reenie nor her father were observant. While staying with the Ostroffs, she had attended the *cheder* at their synagogue every Sunday until she turned ten, and had picked up a little Yiddish from them but all that stopped when Albert found them a home. There, they were to speak only in English, no matter how hard her father might struggle, and if a neighbour spoke to him in Yiddish, Albert demurred, preferring to battle on in English than default to a language he'd used only rarely back in Vienna. To him, Yiddish was the language of the *Ostjuden*, Jews from the east. He was an Austrian, he spoke German, but even that language was now poisonous to him.

A few months after his arrival in London, the Ostroffs took Albert and Reenie to the Grand Palais, to watch Meier Tzelniker in *The Merchant of Venice*. Perhaps they had thought Albert would enjoy it. Perhaps they thought a night of Shakespeare, in Yiddish, in London would make the perfect initiation to the city. Whatever they'd thought, he hated it, squirming throughout the play. Maybe he could have withstood Shylock's great speech had it been spoken in English, but in that old language it was too much. Or perhaps it was an immigrant's shame. In Vienna he'd been a school teacher. In London, his hesitant English saw him working in a warehouse. Why should he watch plays in Yiddish? How would this help? And so he taught his daughter no more Hebrew and refused to foist any more religion on her. Some had survived Europe with their culture and beliefs intact, reinforced; survival alone the proof of their importance. Albert Lieberman was not one of those people.

He was more than happy to marry Vera at the registry office on Plashet Grove, a subdued day that ended with the three of them – Albert, Vera and Reenie – eating a joyless supper at a West End restaurant. Then, little by little, things began to change. The pictures on the walls, the newspaper they read, the programmes they listened to on the radio. Not all at once, of course. That might have been too much. It took months for this to happen, but finally Vera gathered up the nerve to steer her new husband toward that mysterious grey building of stained-glass windows, creaking pews, and dog-eared Books of Common Prayer, and within a year of their marriage Albert Lieberman was spending his Sunday afternoons in church.

At first the community said nothing. Albert was the survivor of something never discussed, at least not openly, among the grown-ups, not even in gossip, and perhaps this alone shielded him from the criticism any other man would have faced. The only person to say something, to say anything, was Mr Ostroff, and it was the last time he and Reenie's father ever spoke to one another.

'Listen, Avram,' he said, his heavy, kind hands – a workman's hands – gripping the edge of the kitchen table. He always called her father by his Hebrew name, Avram, never Albert. Reenie listened to them from the bottom of the stairs, and caught occasional glimpses of them by poking her head through the gap where one of the balusters had been kicked through long before they moved in.

'It's not that we *disapprove*...'

'Then what would you call it?' said Albert. 'If not disapproval? Hmm? Prying? Is that the word for it?'

'No, it's just… we're concerned.'

'No, no. This is not concern. This is judgement. You prefer I meet a Jewish woman, yes? A nice Jewish widow or some nice young Jewish girl who doesn't mind that I'm old and my hair is grey?'

'We just think, what kind of lesson does this teach to Reenie, to your daughter?'

'Her name is Irene.'

'You know she is going to these dances, with boys?'

'I know this. She goes there with *girls*. With her *friends*.'

'But there are boys at these dances, Avram. And you want one day for her to marry a *goy*?'

Albert laughed dismissively. 'I wouldn't care either way.'

'You don't mean that.'

'I don't? It's the truth. I wouldn't care. You would rather I keep her under lock and key? Like a strict father? You would prefer I be like you, grow a beard, wear black every day, as if I were still in mourning, as if I am *always* in mourning? Or should I go around speaking in Yiddish, like you and your friends? Because let me tell you, if it were to happen again, if it were to happen here, in London, in England, they will come for you first.'

'Avram, what are you talking about?'

'We would have been fine if it wasn't for the *Ostjuden*. The Nazis, they were thugs, but they would have left us alone if it weren't for them, with their way of dressing, their way of looking, talking Yiddish. We were Austrians. My family had lived in Vienna for a hundred and fifty years. Irina's came from Russia in *eighteen ninety-six*. We looked like any other family. But not them. They came down from Galicia and they brought the *shtetl* with them. They had to be different.'

'And what was so very wrong with being different?'

'It got us killed.'

'Avram…'

'You have nothing to say to me. Nothing.'

'Avram.'

'My name is Albert. Now get out. Go.'

His face scarlet, Mr Ostroff stomped out of the kitchen, breathing heavily through his nose. He saw her, Reenie, on the stairs, but said nothing; as if he had lost all right to even speak to her. Reenie stood, her hands gripping the banister, and looked through to the kitchen, waiting for her father to say something, to call out an apology, but he sat in silence, his hands clasped together tight enough to bleach the colour from his knuckles.

'Papa?' Her voice echoed off the hallway's patterned tiles. Her father didn't move.

Reenie bolted from their house, leaving the front door open, and ran after Mr Ostroff. When she caught up with him he stopped walking, looked down at her and sighed. She had never seen him this way before, so defeated.

'I'm sorry, Reenie,' he said. 'I'm not angry with your father. None of us are. We're worried, that's all. We probably won't speak to one another for a while. I'm sorry.'

Reenie returned to the house shuddering with anger, and went straight to her bedroom. How ungrateful her father had been. How dare he speak to Mr Ostroff – kind, lovely Mr Ostroff – like that?

Months later, while walking home from school, Reenie passed the Ostroff's house, and Mrs Ostroff came running out and called her name. She invited Reenie in for tea and cake, and the three of them – Reenie and Mr and Mrs Ostroff – sat together in the front room, the room they only ever used for special guests.

'We're going away,' said Mrs Ostroff. 'To Israel.'

'On holiday?' said Reenie.

Mr Ostroff shook his head. 'No. Not a holiday. We're going there to live. A new country. My brother, from New York? He's there now, with his family. He says the sun shines every day. It hardly ever rains. And the figs… he says the figs are incredible. And Mrs Ostroff and I… we aren't getting any younger. And London is so *cold*.'

It was the last time she saw them, and the three of them wept as they said their goodbyes. A few weeks after they had left, Reenie received a postcard. Blue skies and blue sea. Cream-coloured houses around the harbour at Haifa, and a *Magen David* stamped on its back. A message in Mrs Ostroff's ever-so-neat handwriting, the last exchange of words between them.

It was hard, despite the drabness of the woman, for Reenie not to blame everything on Vera, to imagine that everything was part of some devious scheme of hers. Was it *she* who had suggested they might change their surname, make it more English? Less German. Less Jewish. Her father only broached the subject once, and Reenie's expression was enough to see it never raised again, but he must have drawn the idea from somewhere, or someone. At times Vera Lieberman – and how silly, how *wrong* that name sounded – seemed to Reenie a gentile Jezebel, luring Jewish men into her strange, exotic church.

The decisive, climactic insult was Vera's suggestion, one Sunday morning, that Reenie join them. Until then there'd been some tacit agreement that Reenie would stay at home on Sundays. She was old enough by then to look after herself, and there was invariably last-minute homework to be done for Monday morning. With this invitation, it felt as if Vera was making a final move in her domestic game of chess.

It was impossible, six decades distant, for Reenie to remember precisely how thoughts led to action that afternoon. If she sat there, stewing in her anger, she could no longer remember it. Condensed by time, she remembered everything happening at once. Her father and Vera, dressed in their Sunday Best. The sound of the front door closing, the knocker bouncing against its brass plate. Running upstairs, packing a bag, leaving the house. Did all that take minutes or hours?

A tantrum, that's what it was. Just a tantrum. But she couldn't turn back on it, couldn't back down or give up. She had to keep going. Stopping meant it would catch up with her. And there was nowhere else for her to go now the Ostroffs had gone.

She had no idea, no real plan. While her father and Vera spent their afternoon in church – rising for the tiresome hymns, sitting or kneeling or whatever it was *goyim* did for their dreary prayers – Reenie went about packing her belongings into the small, paisley-patterned case that had been her only companion on the crossing to Harwich. She searched in desperation for her mother's photograph, but still couldn't find it.

By mid-afternoon she was on the District Line, heading west, with only a young girl's notion that something would happen when she reached the bright lights of the West End; something brilliant and magical. Perhaps she'd meet a theatrical agent, and wouldn't you know it? They were looking for a girl just like her to star in the next big show. Or perhaps she'd meet an exiled foreign prince, and they would strike up an unlikely romance. He would rescue her from the grey, bomb-scarred drudgery of East London, from her hand-me-down clothes and ration books, and she'd taste champagne for the first time, and wear dresses by Dior, like Rita Hayworth when she married Prince Aly Khan.

In the event, Reenie found herself in a grubby café just off Piccadilly Circus, making a single cup of tea last more than an hour by taking tiny, bird-like sips until it was tepid. The sky grew dark, and the walls of the buildings outside were lit up in gaudy shades of red, pink and blue by the Circus' electric lights. A man in a cheap, ill-fitting suit propositioned her with words she didn't quite understand, and when she left the café he followed her as far as Charing Cross Road, falling back and vanishing only when she stopped to ask a policeman for directions.

With what little money she had, Reenie checked into a hotel near Covent Garden, and the woman on the reception – large-breasted but haggard, with a towering peroxide blonde bouffant and a rose tattooed on her hand – studied her over the green plastic rims of her cat-eye glasses.

'You're not having company in there, are you?'

'Company?' It took a second or two for Reenie to realise what the older woman meant. 'No. No company.'

By the following night she had almost run out of money, and years later she realised that if there had been an opportunity for her to go back to her father and Vera with a brace of apologies, that was it, that was the night, but she couldn't. Behind her was a force, a momentum, driving her on, further west, further away, and from what? Not just Albert and Vera and the invitation to join them in church. Not just Harold Road and Friday night dances in Bethnal Green and Limehouse. Not just the grim certainty of leaving school to work in an office or – if she didn't do so well in her O Levels – a factory before settling down with a Nice Local Boy and making lots of Nice Children.

No. She ran away from all those things, but above all she ran away from her life's two pillars, the grief and sympathy of others, and in running hoped she might become more than just the young girl on the ferry with the little paisley bag.

'Synchronicity, yeah?' said Womble; eyes bloodshot, eyelids drooping. 'Everything happens for a reason, Reenie. Did you know, when they were making *The Wizard of Oz*, you know… the film… with Judy Garland… the costume department were looking for a coat for the Wizard to wear, and they found this coat in a flea market, and it was perfect. And only when they'd finished making the film did they find out the coat's original owner was L. Frank Baum. The guy who wrote *The Wizard of Oz*. Straight up. True story. He owned the coat. When he died, it got sold on, ended up in a flea market, and then used as a prop in the film based on his book. See what I'm getting at?'

She nodded, humouring him, but viewed through sober eyes the scene around her was depressing. Womble, Casper and their friends acted as if they were on some sort of quest, attacking each new substance – joints and pills and spindly brown bouquets of dried mushrooms – with an almost military intent. Philosophical rambling gave way to unfinished sentences and bouts of giggling. The girl who had described herself as a traveller spent half an hour staring at a pebble in the palm of her hand, while Shabby Jesus closed his eyes and held up his hands as if shaping some massive, floating ball of clay.

Reenie couldn't quite remember what brought her here in the first place. Curiosity, perhaps. Good old-fashioned nosiness. She'd always been a nosey one. Inquisitive, she'd rather call it, remembering how a school teacher once told her that if she carried on like that her nose would grow, like Pinocchio's, and she had replied by telling the teacher Pinocchio's nose grew because he lied, not because he was nosey.

One hundred lines ('I will not answer back') and a slap across the palm of her hand with a wooden ruler.

But it wasn't prying if you needed to know something, and she had needed to know for herself, to know what drove them; what, if anything, inspired them. She had spent so much time indoors, never talking to anyone, and couldn't remember the last time she'd spoken to anyone their age. There was Ibrahim, but he didn't count. He seemed old beyond his years. But these kids… these kids…

And look at them. Hanging on his every word. A man old enough to be their father – their grandfather, some of them – and he calls himself *Womble*. And they sit around him as if he's an oracle, the fount of all knowledge, and when he opens his mouth, what does he say?

'I'm just overcome by the… *thinginess*… of it all.'

Thinginess? *Thinginess?*

And the kids all nodded and hummed as if the Womble's words had illuminated the greatest of life's mysteries.

Reenie had seen and heard enough. She got up without saying goodbye, and went back to her tent, leaving the noise and lights of the party behind her. At first, she worried she might not sleep, but the day's walking had drained her. She passed out to the distant thudding of a synthesized bass drum and the howls and the cheers of those still dancing.

When she woke she could still hear the music. It was getting light, a strawberry-coloured sun creeping up out of the haze, and as it got lighter still a row of electricity pylons drew long shadows across the barren field. Looking up toward the farmhouse, Reenie saw the campfires had died out; a jaundiced kind of smoke drifting from their embers. Everything about the farmyard and the party looked dead, desiccated, used up and burnt out, but there was still music playing, and human shapes staggering around in the dawn, clinging on to straw-prickled blankets and almost-empty bottles of cider and wine. Had no one told them the party was over; that it must have ended hours ago?

Reenie splashed water on her face, made herself a cup of tea, then ate some bread, just enough to take the edge off a rumbling stomach, and began packing away her things. The field was soft and spongy with morning dew, and she had some difficulty steering the trolley back to the road. As she carried on, along the London Road and toward the village of Marshfield, the music from the party grew quieter and quieter until she could no longer hear it at all.

10

When Nigel first took her there, Gemma told him it was the most beautiful sunset she'd ever seen. They'd walked out over the Big Field, to the edge of the copse, and watched the sun set over the channel. Funny how the Severn could look so mucky in the daytime, even on a summer's day, all brown with silt and God knows what else, but get a few sunbeams bouncing off it and it looked quite pretty. He had known this before taking her there. Knew just the right time, when the light would be perfect, just right, when it would be at its most romantic.

Even so, for his money the sunrises were better than the sunsets. There was something magical about the early morning, the day fresh and new. Sometimes the sun would come up blood red and boiling, and there was a stillness and a silence, not like in the evening. In the evening you might hear cars on the nearest road and planes passing overhead, the tractors and haymakers on neighbouring farms, but in the morning it was almost silent. The early morning, when his wife and son were still asleep, was when Nigel did all his thinking.

Or perhaps 'worrying' was a better word for it. And what better time and place for him to worry than when he could be alone, surveying all that was his. Though, of course, it wasn't his, not truly. The fields and the farmhouse, the place where he grew up, they belonged to the bank. He owned some, but not much of it. The cattle were his, more or less. The sugar beet and the barley were his. But the soil, and the space, these belonged to people far away; faceless, nameless men and women he would never meet.

The letters they sent, each one more aggressive than the last, had signatures printed rather than written onto them, and he doubted that the signatory had so much as glanced at each one before it was sent. He knew how these things worked.

Gemma never saw the letters, and so had no idea just how much they stood to lose. He had told her they couldn't take a holiday that year – just as they couldn't the year before – because he was so busy with things. He couldn't afford to take a whole week off. Who would run things while he was away?

He sometimes felt that he was born at the wrong time, in the wrong age. Hadn't there once been a place for men like him? Men who knew and understood the land, and were passionate about nothing else? If he'd been born a hundred years earlier it would have been easier. A hundred years ago he'd have known where he stood, who owned his farm, who would buy what he had to sell. And he'd have been paid a fair price for it all, too. Wouldn't have to rely on handouts. He hated that most of all. His father had never relied on handouts, at least not when he got started. The food on his table and the money in his bank were his, the product of hard graft, as witnessed by the callouses tough as leather on his big hands and the permanent scythes of dirt beneath his fingernails.

Nigel was getting hands like his father, the palms more leathery with each season. In one of his hands something had worked its way loose; a little ball-like nub of bone or gristle floating about near the knuckle of his third finger. Could be a ganglion cyst, Gemma said, but it had been there three months and showed no sign of subsiding. He told her he would get it checked out by the doctor some time, but he hadn't visited a doctor in years.

Near the cowshed, out of view of the house, he lit a cigarette. He'd cut down to just two a day; one in the morning and one last thing at night. Sometimes Gemma would smell it on him, and she'd tut and shake her head, but so long as he didn't smoke around Josh she didn't mind so much. Without his first cigarette he'd spend the morning like a coiled spring, wound tighter and tighter, the tension bunching up in the back of his neck. Stupid things, daft things annoyed him. He'd kick something or throw something, and sometimes would feel as if he was about to cry for no reason at all. Without the last cigarette, smoked just before he went to bed, he couldn't sleep. Instead he would lie there, staring at the ceiling, imagining everything that could happen to them in painstaking detail. The bailiffs and the auctions and the move to a small house somewhere in town. Tiny little garden out the back, probably decked over or covered in paving slabs. Nowhere for Josh to run around. And in the mornings just the sound of traffic rumbling past as their neighbours set off for day jobs in Gloucester or Chepstow. A night spent thinking this way left him exhausted by the time his alarm went off, feeling hollowed out and angry at everything and nothing.

The night before hadn't been so bad – he'd slept heavily enough – but the few dreams he could remember weren't happy ones.

His cigarette finished and crushed under his heel into the mud, Nigel climbed onto his tractor, started the engine, and drove west, across the Big Field, and away from the rising sun.

11

The lowing of cows made an unsettling alarm clock, but if that sound was somehow integrated into the dying moments of his dream, Ibrahim forgot it the second he was awake. Sitting upright he saw, through the barn door, a yellow sky. It was morning, and above the frantic bass notes of the cattle he heard birdsong, and beyond that the puttering engine of a tractor, making its way across a field and getting closer. He brushed his teeth as quickly as he could, spitting the foam of toothpaste and water down onto a carpet of straw, and he splashed two handfuls of bottled water over his face.

The tractor was getting closer still.

The barn wasn't far from the main road, closer to the road than the farmhouse. If he was lucky, he could leave the barn and be back on the road before the driver of that tractor saw him.

Packing everything he had into his bag, Ibrahim crept around the inside wall of the barn and leaned out through the doorway. To his right the gravel track stretched just twenty metres or so to the road; to his left it carried on as far as the farmhouse.

This was it. No better chance than now. Run for it, make it to the lane, then carry on walking as if nothing had happened. No one could say or do anything once he was on the lane.

Ibrahim ran from the barn, out onto the gravel track, his left leg pounding, the cold morning air drawing tears from his eyes, his bag jumping on his back and its straps digging painfully into his shoulders, and he was halfway to the road when he heard a voice behind him shout:

'Oy! You! Stop right there!'

Keep running. Just keep running. If you get to the road he can't do anything. Can't do anything if you're not on his land.

But he thought of outraged farmers and tabloid headlines. Shotgun-brandishing yokels who'd think nothing of shooting the first swarthy stranger they saw. Everything here was so remote. If there was a gunshot, no one but the farmer and his cattle would hear it. And all those acres in which a body could be buried and never found.

He stopped running, his feet skidding and kicking up clouds of dust, and he turned to see the farmer climb down from the tractor, unarmed.

'What were you doing in my barn?'

'I was just sleeping. Sorry.'

'Sleeping?'

The farmer was only a few feet away from him now. A young man – younger than Ibrahim had expected from his gruff West Country burr – broad-shouldered and suntanned.

'What? You homeless?'

Ibrahim shook his head. 'I was just travelling this way, and it was getting late. I needed somewhere to stay the night.'

'You a gypsy?'

'No. I'm going to London, and it was getting late. I…'

'Were you driving?'

'No. Walking.'

The farmer gave him a look Ibrahim was already used to; that incredulous expression, as if he'd said he was going to the moon.

'You're *walking* to *London*?'

'Yes. And it was getting late. I'm really sorry. I didn't mean to trespass or, or anything. I just… it was getting late and I thought it might rain and…'

'You're not in trouble with the police or nothing?'

'No. Not at all. I…'

'Where you from?'

Where you from, boy? You ain't from round these parts, boy…

'Cardiff,' said Ibrahim. 'Well, London. But I live in Cardiff.'

'You walked all the way from Cardiff?'

He nodded.

'That's miles away,' said the farmer. 'You must be mad.'

'No. I just… I have to walk. It's complicated.'

'How long you been walking?'

'Two days. This is day three.'

'And why are you walking this way?'

Ibrahim asked the farmer what he meant.

'I mean why didn't you go over the old Severn Bridge?'

'You're not allowed,' Ibrahim replied.

'Yeah, you are,' said the farmer. 'They opened a footpath on it a couple of years back.'

Ibrahim reached into his rucksack and took out one of the maps he'd printed, holding it up for Nigel to see. 'No, look,' he said. 'It says you should walk via Gloucester.'

'Oh, no,' said Nigel. 'That must be out of date. You could have gone over the bridge and saved yourself no end of time.'

Ibrahim thought for a moment he might either cry or vomit.

'Anyway, no offence,' said Nigel, 'but you look like shit. And you've still got a long old way to go before you get to London.'

'I know.'

The farmer looked out across his fields and took in a sharp breath through the narrow gaps between his teeth. 'And you're *not* in trouble with the police?'

'No. I'm not.'

'Because it's not often I get people sleeping in my barn, and not being funny but you don't look like you're from round here.'

You ain't from round these parts, boy…

'I'm not. I'm from London.'

'When was the last time you ate anything?'

'Yesterday. I had a sandwich.'

The farmer clucked his tongue against the roof of his mouth. 'I reckon you ain't much of a walker, eh? Walking to London on a sandwich. You'll be dead of starvation before you get as far as Gloucester. And I don't suppose you've had an hot bath since you left Cardiff, neither?'

Ibrahim shook his head.

'Right-ho,' said the farmer. 'Well, you can come back to the house. My wife'll put some breakfast on for you, get you a cup of tea, and you can use our shower. But I'm warning you now, don't you go trying nothing funny. We ain't got any money in the house, and there's nothing much worth stealing, but I *have* got a shotgun. My name's Nigel, by the way.'

'Ibrahim.'

'Ibrahim. What's that…? Indian or summit?'

They went to the farmhouse, Nigel driving his tractor with Ibrahim walking beside him, and on pulling up in the farmyard were welcomed by a chorus of angry, hissing geese.

'Don't mind them. Better than guard dogs, geese. We got dogs and all, but these things, they're vicious. But if you're with me, you're alright.'

Inside the house, before the kitchen, was a small lean-to filled with muddy wellington boots and that same, ripe, dung-and-straw taste as the barn. Nigel stamped his feet, tugged off his boots, and slipped on a pair of canvas plimsolls. In the kitchen his wife, who'd been washing dishes, looked at Ibrahim with a mixture of fascination and caution, as if he were a rattlesnake, something simultaneously exotic and potentially dangerous.

'This here's Ibrahim,' said Nigel. 'Found him kipping in the barn. This is my wife, Gemma. Now, Gem… this lad's only had a sandwich since yesterday, so I said we'd do him a spot of grub.'

'And when you say "we", you mean me,' said Gemma. 'Running an hotel now, am I?'

'Alright, love. Now come on. Poor lad's been in that barn all night. He's lucky he ain't covered in bat shit…'

'Nige. Language. Josh is only next door, on the X-Box.'

'Sorry, love. But we can spare the lad a bit of breakfast, though, right?'

Gemma shook her head, flinging the tea towel over her shoulder. 'Al*right*,' she said, and then, to Ibrahim, 'What would you like? I can do you a sausage sarnie, or a bacon sarnie…?'

'Gem,' said Nigel, his voice a conspiratorial stage whisper. 'He's Muslim, ain't he? They don't eat bacon.'

'Sausage sarnie, then?'

'Or saus… I mean pork, love. They don't eat pork.'

'You don't eat pork?' said Gemma, as if personally insulted.

Ibrahim shook his head as apologetically as he could.

'Okay, then,' said Gemma. 'What about eggs? Are eggs okay?'

'Eggs are fine. Thank you.'

'Eggs it is. Scrambled or fried? I ain't doing poached. Poached is *far* too much fuss and bother.'

'Scrambled, please.'

Gemma shot her husband another withering look, and went about finding the eggs and a loaf of bread.

'I said he could use the bathroom, and all,' said Nigel. 'To freshen up. The boy smells like a cowshed.'

'Oh, right,' said Gemma. 'D'you want me to give Michael and Lorraine a ring, too? See if he can use their swimming pool?'

'Gem, love…'

'Well, I'm just saying.'

Nigel turned to Ibrahim. 'Come on,' he said. 'I'll show you up to the bathroom, get you a towel.'

He took him upstairs, pointing out the way while walking behind him. The bathroom was in an older part of the house, with exposed and crooked wooden beams. It was as if they had designed these places, these old houses, for dwarves, and there was something about the lack of geometry – the uneven lines and bulging, misshapen walls – that Ibrahim found appealing. Impossible, just by looking at it, to say how old the house was; to calculate how many families could have lived in it; how many births and deaths its rooms had seen.

As he showered, Ibrahim heard the creak of floorboards from the other side of the bathroom door. Nigel was waiting for him there, not yet trusting enough to leave their guest alone upstairs in his house. Once he'd dried himself, Ibrahim put on his first change of clothes since leaving Cardiff, and though the fresh clothes were creased there was something instantly satisfying about the sensation of cold, clean fabric against his skin.

Back in the kitchen, a small flaxen-haired boy, maybe four years old, sat at the table, eating cereal. The boy was shoulder height with the table, his feet not touching the ground, and he looked up at Ibrahim as if this stranger had appeared in a monstrous puff of green smoke, like a pantomime genie erupting from his lamp.

'This is our son, Josh,' said Nigel. 'Josh, say hello to Ibrahim.'

Josh stared at him but said nothing.

'Josh. Say *hello*,' said Gemma.

'Hello,' said Josh, still frowning at the stranger, his small spoon hovering motionless above the plastic bowl.

'Here you go,' said Gemma, placing a plate of eggs and toast in front of him. 'Hope that's alright for you.'

Ibrahim attacked his breakfast – swallowing without chewing, drinking his tea in quick, near-scalding gulps – and all the while Josh stared at him.

'Is your dad Doctor Bala?' he asked.

Frowning, Ibrahim turned to Nigel and Gemma.

'Our GP,' said Nigel, blushing. 'He's Indian.'

Ibrahim laughed with a mouthful of food, stopping a spray of crumbs and gobbets of egg with the back of his hand, and he caught the exact moment when Nigel closed his eyes, his already-ruddy cheeks turning a deeper shade of red.

'No, son,' said Gemma. 'Doctor Bala isn't Ibrahim's dad.'

Ibrahim looked at the boy, and tried to imagine what the stream of his thoughts might sound like. He recalled being that age, and the violence of each new emotion as it was felt. He remembered the disparities of scale, how vast his school seemed, how tall the grown-ups, how interminable the two-and-a-half hour drive from London to Birmingham. As a very young child there were only three places he was aware of: London, Sparkhill and Pakistan. If Sparkhill was two and a half hours from London, he reasoned that Pakistan must be another two and a half hours from Sparkhill. Maybe one day, if he was very good and ate all his dinner, his dad would drive him and his mum and his baby sister to Pakistan and not just his grandparents' and aunties and uncles' houses in Sparkhill.

It was strange how distant even Sparkhill and London had begun to feel in recent years, as cousins married and moved on, as his grandparents passed away. The family felt atomised, at least to Ibrahim; the ties that bound those places together fragmented, like desiccated vines. Perhaps it would have been different if he'd stayed in London, and if his uncles, aunts and cousins hadn't been there the night the police arrived on Harold Road. If anything had distanced them, or distanced him from them, it was that night. Suddenly the spaces between them all seemed so much greater than before.

And how big was little Josh's world? Did it extend much further than the rambling fields out there? Living in a place like this, even the nearest small town must have felt to him like a metropolis.

'Here, love,' said Nigel. 'Guess what? Ibrahim's walking to London.'

'He's what?' asked Gemma.

'He's walking to London.'

'London?' said Josh. 'But London is miles and miles and miles and miles and miles and *miles* away.'

'Is that for charity?' asked Gemma.

'No. I just have to get to London.'

'Why didn't you get the train?'

'He can't,' said Nigel. 'It's *com-plic-ated*, apparently.'

'Why's that, then? Is it religious reasons?'

'Gem…'

'Well, I don't know, do I? Maybe they can't. It's like Jewish people. They can't do nothing on Saturdays. They can't even answer the phone. I remember learning that in RE.'

'Love. It's Thursday.'

'Well, maybe Thursdays is special to them.' She turned to Ibrahim. 'Are Thursdays special?'

'Not particularly,' said Ibrahim, trying not to laugh.

'Oh.'

When he'd finished his breakfast Ibrahim insisted on doing the washing up.

'If you must,' said Gemma, her tone pitched halfway between grateful and curt. 'But I'll do the drying, mind. You don't know where everything goes.'

He nodded, and began scrubbing the frying pan.

'I still think you're mad if you think you'll make it to London on foot,' said Nigel. 'You're best off going *back* to Chepstow, getting a train to Newport, and then getting *another* train to London. You'll be there in a few hours.'

'I can't,' said Ibrahim passing the pan to Gemma. 'I can't go back. I've walked from Newport. I was *in* Newport on Tuesday.'

'Well Gloucester, then. The trains are regular. There's one an hour goes straight to London, direct, no changes. Me and Gemma take the train if we're going down there, you know, to watch a show or something. Well, we used to.'

'Yeah,' said Gemma, bent down with her head half inside a low cupboard as she put away the pan. 'We went to see that *Blood Brothers*, didn't we, Nige?'

'I can't take the train,' said Ibrahim. 'I just can't.'

Nigel sighed. 'You know, for someone who says he's in no trouble with the police, you don't half sound like somebody in trouble with the police.'

When it was time for him to leave, Ibrahim thanked them both three more times and crouching on his haunches gave Josh a high five. Their goodbyes, in the farmyard between the house and the cowshed, were muted and clumsy. He felt an almost inexplicable fondness for them, and a kind of sorrow that he would never see them again. There was no satisfying way he could repay them, but in those final moments before he left them, Gemma's attitude towards him seemed to change, to soften – perhaps glad that he was leaving, that this unusual morning was over, that nothing had happened while he was there – but her parting 'Take care' sounded heartfelt.

Nigel climbed onto his tractor, and he drove down the lane while Ibrahim walked until they had reached a junction with the field of sugar beet. Nothing more was said, but he saw in Nigel's expression something like a fatherly, or perhaps brotherly concern. The man was too stoic for anything more; there would be no 'take cares' this time, just a nod of the head, a sad kind of smile, and then he drove out across the field, waving once as he went.

Ibrahim carried on, past the barn where he had spent the night, and out onto the main road. There, he opened his bag and took out the map. Gloucester, the summit of his imaginary mountain, was a little over twenty miles away, and he would reach it by nightfall.

12

His mum might say they'd been 'good as gold', but he could tell they'd been mischief. The living room was a mess of toys and his dad, as always, was half-buried in his own armchair, with that look of relief on his face, even when he was fixed on the football pages.

'So, Jackie working late tonight?' his mum asked.

'Not late, no. Only till seven.'

'Seven's late. I never finished work any later than five when you and Stacey was little.'

'Yeah, but sometimes they're open till seven, so she has to work a late shift. But she's home by quarter past.'

'So who'll be cooking the kids' tea?'

'I will.'

His mum laughed. 'You? Cooking? That'll be the day. Hear that, Bri? Our Simon's cooking the kids' tea.'

Simon's dad huffed. 'Him? Cooking? He'd burn soup, he would.'

'If you'd said you was cooking the kids' tea I'd have done them something here,' said his mum.

'No, Mum. Honest. It's fine. I've cooked their tea loads of times.'

'Well, what're they having?'

'Fish fingers, beans and chips.'

'Is that enough for them?'

'Yeah. They'll have bread and butter, and all. Listen, Mum. I've got to go.'

'Well, do you want to take some cakes with you, for afters? I've got some Mr Kipling almond slices here, or…'

'No. Mum. Really. It's fine.'

'Fair enough. Just thought I'd offer.'

'I know. And thanks. But we've got ice cream and stuff back at the house. And I've really got to go. Thanks for having them, though, Mum. Bye, Dad.'

His dad nodded and huffed from behind his newspaper.

In the car the kids began playing up again. Chelsea had the Nintendo DS, and Kyle wanted it. On Eastern Avenue they got stuck in traffic, and Simon wished his mum *had* cooked their tea. Then Jackie could have picked them up at half seven. No bombing around town like a blue-arsed fly at rush hour. Last thing he needed. Half seven, Robbo and the boys said they'd be around. By the time he got home, cooked the kids' tea, had a shower, got dressed...

'Oh, come on...' he said, drumming his hands on the steering wheel. 'Where's this bloody idiot going?'

'Daddy did a swear,' said Kyle.

'That's right,' said Simon, glancing up at his son in the rear-view mirror. 'And that's a naughty word, so don't let me hear you saying it, right?'

At the junction with Barnwood Road another car cut him up. The driver looked at him, saw him, but didn't hold up his hand to say thank you or nothing. Just looked at him, then carried on cutting him up. Wife next to him; headscarf and face covered, so you could only just make out her eyes.

Bloody ridiculous. Him there in a beige coat, her dressed like they were living in Iran or something. Where did they think they were?

Different if it was the other way around. If him and Jackie went over to wherever this bloke and his missus were from, they wouldn't let Jackie go around dressing how she wanted to. She'd have to cover up, like they do. When in Rome and all the rest of it. And typical of them to just cut him up like that.

Bloody Bombay rules when they're on the road.

Simon could make out three kids in the back of the car, but there were probably another two down in the footwell, another two in the boot. Knowing them. What was that joke? How many Indians can you fit in a car? Two in the front, six in the back, and Gandhi in the ashtray. He hadn't heard that joke in ages.

Probably wouldn't now, though, would you? They'd say it was racist.

On getting home he made the kids' tea and ironed his favourite

Ben Sherman shirt and he tried to imagine his dad cooking a meal or ironing a shirt. Never would have happened. When Simon's little sister was born and his mum stayed in the hospital, Simon had to go stay with his nan and grancha. No chance of his dad looking after him. Wouldn't have had a clue.

Kyle ate all his food except the crusts on his bread. Chelsea ate a half of each fish finger, all her chips, and all but three of her baked beans, but finished the meal with a clown's grin of ketchup and bean sauce around her mouth.

The washing up finished and the plates dried and put away, Simon left the kids watching *Ben and Holly's Little Kingdom* on Nick Jr. while he showered and shaved. After showering, and before getting dressed, he took a moment to look at himself in the bedroom mirror. Twenty-seven years old, and he was getting a belly. Not a patch on the old man's, but give it another twenty years. He remembered having a washboard stomach, abs hard as ping pong balls. He remembered Jackie running her hand up and down his stomach, giggling breathlessly as she did. She hadn't done that in ages.

He heard Jackie come in, heard the kids shrieking and laughing. She came up the stairs and into the bedroom, gave him a peck on the cheek.

'You smell nice,' she said.

'Yeah. It's that stuff you got me last Christmas.'

'Is it? It's nice. Have the kids had their tea?'

'Yeah. Course.'

'What did they have?'

'Fish fingers, beans and chips.'

'Oh, Si. They had chips yesterday.'

'And?'

'I don't like them having chips two days in a row.'

'What else was I supposed to do them?'

'There's rice there.'

'Fish fingers, beans and *rice*?'

'Course not. Something else.'

'Well, sorry.'

'No. It's fine. As long as they've eaten something.'

Ten minutes later, Robbo and the boys arrived. They made a fuss over the kids and the kids made a fuss over them.

'Oh yeah, Si,' said Robbo. 'I managed to get those, er, *tickets* you were after.' And he winked and tapped the side of his nose.

'Cheers,' said Simon. 'How much was it?'

'Forty. Not bad.'

'Bargain.'

Jackie was in the kitchen, making herself a cup of tea, but she looked through the open door at him and shook her head. Their rubbish attempt at code had failed miserably, and she knew he wouldn't get home until late. And when he got home she wouldn't ask him what time he thought it was, or where he'd been, and she definitely wouldn't ask him who he'd been with.

13

A narrow lane, cut down its middle by a thick white line. One side for walkers, the other for cyclists. Orange patches of light dotted along its length, but much of it dark. To his left were trees, some overhanging the path; to his right, a long white railing blistered with rust, brambles crawling through the railings, then a steep embankment and the dual carriageway and the night-time traffic of taxis and ambulances and police cars.

His leg was in agony now, every other step he took an ordeal.

If only the guy at the first hotel hadn't been such a prick. Must have had plenty of rooms. The sign in the window said there were vacancies. He saw Ibrahim coming through the door, decided he'd rather turn down business than have him staying under his roof. And it was the delay that gave it away; that couple of seconds pause between Ibrahim saying he'd like a room, and the man behind the desk saying, 'Sorry… we're fully booked.'

Everything was in that pause. The way he blinked. The way he swallowed hard, making a big show of checking that yellowed, antique PC of his. Not even like it was a big hotel, the kind of place where you might lose track of how many rooms were free. There couldn't have been more than ten rooms there, if that. Just a B&B, really. And yet he had to check if there were vacancies.

After a second apology, no more convincing than the first, the man at the B&B pointed him in the direction of a large chain hotel in the town, and Ibrahim began walking again.

The hotel in the centre of the town was also fully booked, but at least that place looked busy enough. Guests milling around. Lots of suits, ties and name badges. Some sort of conference, perhaps. The girl on the reception – she looked Bengali, though he couldn't be sure – told him they had another hotel, on the other side of town, and that there were vacancies there. She offered to book him a cab, but he told her it was okay. He'd walk.

She printed a map, marking their current location with an X and the next hotel with a small circle, and for a moment Ibrahim entertained the idea that she was flirting with him, holding eye contact a second longer than she would if she were just being friendly or helpful. A smile that was more than just good customer service.

Yeah, she was flirting with him. And maybe she would call the other hotel, find out what room he was staying in, and once he'd got there and checked in…

As he left the hotel, Ibrahim turned around, looking back through the glass front of the hotel reception to see if she was still watching him, but she was already talking to one of the guests. One of the suit-tie-and-name-badge men. Smiling, and holding his gaze just as she'd done with Ibrahim.

She was just being polite. And perhaps the man at the B&B wasn't lying. Maybe he *was* fully booked and had simply forgotten to turn the sign around. *Vacancies/No Vacancies.* Easy mistake. Ibrahim just couldn't read people as well as he used to. Couldn't read anything. His eyesight was terrible, small print impossible. And people. People were something else. In trying to read other people, all he saw was himself. The man in the B&B; Ibrahim only knew what he *wanted* him to think.

He wanted him to be scared; wanted him to think about all those newspaper front pages showing blood-spattered pavements and screaming commuters, because then he was a racist and it was none of Ibrahim's fault. And when that girl smiled at him, he thought she would see him as he used to look. Not like this; scruffy and dirty and his beard a mess. He used to be good-looking. Bit heavyset, big-boned, but not ugly. Definitely not ugly. He wished she could have seen him like that. She *would* have flirted with him then, for real. But not like this.

The thoughts and feelings of others were another country to him now, but it hadn't always been this way.

He remembered a teacher, his history teacher Mrs James,

explaining 'empathy' to the class. 'Imagine putting yourself in someone else's shoes.' What would it have been like to watch the Blitz, or the Battle of Hastings, or the Great Fire of London? All that stuff. And he always got good marks for those essays. Mrs James told him he had good *empathy*, and at the time he didn't think it that important. Remembering names and dates, the story of how it all fit together, that stuff was important, but empathy? Fat lot of use empathy would do him in the real world.

Then one day it was gone. He woke in the hospital unable to fathom the emotions of any other person, as if the world was now a picture in monochrome, or a dry scene being acted out before him. They told him it was a side-effect of the accident, his injury. He'd been crippled and the others, all of the others, were dead. Of course he was upset, of course that was going to affect him *e-mo-tion-ally*. He'd have to be inhuman not to be changed by it. If he viewed the world differently, with suspicion and fear, that was understandable.

He went along with this, agreeing with each diagnosis, for almost a year; which was as long as the sympathy of others lasted, as if he was on some kind of clock, counting down to the point when he was expected to 'pull himself together'. From that point on tolerance for his quirks, his idiosyncrasies, wore thin.

When out in public – which, generally, he tried to avoid – he found himself insulting strangers without realising it. Only the appalled expressions of friends suggested he'd said anything wrong, and even then he had to be told. Telephone conversations with his family back in London became stilted and awkward, but he never quite understood why. Sometimes he'd become enthused by a subject, and would talk for several minutes before realising the person he was speaking to understood neither the subject nor the point he was trying to make.

His interests became increasingly obscure. He told people he was thinking of returning to his studies, but as a free agent, away from the constraints of university. He would write a book, he said, about Saladin, or Al-Hakim. Jerusalem fascinated him, this city, this frontier town where everything meets, a constant city refusing to die in the imagination of millions; from Dawud to the Prophet, from the Prophet to Saladin, from Saladin to William Blake. To this end, he filled countless books with scribbled notes and made endless trips – on foot – to every library within three miles of his flat. The weighty hardback volumes he brought home stacked up, unread. His ability to concentrate was not what it had been.

Others worried about him. He learned this in time, but not until it was probably too late, and the person who delivered this message of concern, a message that felt more like a betrayal than sympathy, was Amanda.

For two years she had been his friend and lover. 'Girlfriend' was too trivial a word for what she was, and 'partner' was too passionless, too formal. There had to be a whole new language for how he had felt about her, the existing words had been cheapened by too many love songs.

In those two years, she had met his family only once before the accident, when Ibrahim's father and sister came to visit him in Cardiff. The four of them went for dinner at a Chinese restaurant in the Bay, but while Aisha and Amanda chatted away like old friends, or even sisters, Ibrahim's father ate in silence, tight-lipped, his expression grey. He didn't say anything that day, wouldn't say anything for some time to come, but Ibrahim knew he wasn't pleased. Nothing needed to be said.

Yet it was Amanda who kept visiting when others stopped. It was Amanda who drove him home from hospital when he was discharged, who bought him groceries and kept him company in those long, immobile early days. He knew that she'd been there, in the hospital, after the accident; that she had been driven there straight from the party. He knew that she would never cry in front of him, except for those few helpless tears that escaped when she first saw him conscious. He knew she did most of her crying alone.

A few days after his return from the hospital, it was Amanda who kissed him, and stripped him of his clothes, and made love to him for the first time in more than six months, making every effort not to hurt him. But something had changed. He knew it from the moment he first woke and saw her looking down at him, wiping away her tears with the back of her hand. The memories of their life before the accident – the early dates, the daytrips and dinners, their first kiss – seemed the property of other people now. He felt an imposter, a stranger who'd somehow stepped into the life of this man, this Ibrahim Siddique, taking everything from him – his life, his possessions, Amanda – without wanting them.

To begin with, he made a good show of playing the part, and Amanda was patient. When visiting, she'd tidy up the chaos of his flat, clearing the reams of notes from the floor and stacking them tidily on his desk; moving the unread books from the sofa to a coffee table. She washed the dishes and cups that had been mounting in the sink, and swiped the thin grey layers of dust from his shelves. She tried bringing order to his world, tried encouraging him to go out each day, but she was fighting a losing battle. He saw himself as a victim of chaos, of random chance, and that chaos had spread out from his accident like dry rot, infecting every part of his life.

And the worst thing was he didn't care. He didn't care if the dishes and cups were cleaned, or if the shelves were dusted; if his bed was made or if his clothes had been washed. He didn't care if Amanda visited him at all.

Her visits grew further apart. Where once he would see her daily, now it was every other day, then twice weekly. She had other things to do – she was preparing for her third and final year, her diary to be crammed soon with studying and then the end-of-year parties. She suggested moving in with him – she needed somewhere to stay in the summer between the last semester of her second year and the first semester of her third, and wouldn't leave him alone in Cardiff – but he dismissed the idea outright. His flat was too small for the two of them, he said. They'd get on top of each other. It would be too much. It never occurred to him that this would upset her, but it did, and for the first time since the accident she cried in front of him; not just silent tears but a mess of sniffling sobs and barely coherent anguish.

He'd changed. He wasn't the same person any more. Sometimes it was as if he didn't even love her. As if she didn't even know him.

'Do you still love me?' she asked, her face blotchy and red, her eyes bloodshot. She expected a blunt 'no' or an apologetic 'yes, of course I love you'. She couldn't have expected the answer he gave, almost instantly, with no discernible emotion.

'I don't know.'

'What do you mean?' she said. 'You don't know? How can you not know?'

'I mean I don't know.'

'It's not a hard question, Ib. Do you love me? Yes or no? You either do or you don't.'

'I don't know.'

He wasn't being evasive. Truth was, he didn't know. He thought he could remember loving her, remember the moment when he'd fallen in love with her, but in searching for the emotion itself he felt nothing, as if he had opened the door to a familiar room to find it stripped bare, ransacked.

Then came the recriminations. She told him she wasn't the only one who thought he'd changed. Others had noticed. She listed the things they'd said, without attributing them to any one name, and reminded him that the accident had happened more than a year ago, that they'd both lost friends, that he wasn't the only one hurting. She apologised for the last point within seconds of making it, but by then it was too late.

Through all this he had listened to her, impassive. She wanted a reaction – tears, anger, *anything* to tell her he was still in there, that he cared about *something* – but there was nothing. She'd lost him, just as surely as if he'd died in the car, or on the operating table. In the hours and days after she left him, he waited for a response, for the emotion that would tell him this meant something, but nothing came.

Three weeks later Ibrahim tried to take his own life. It was an act borne neither of melancholy nor desperation, but of an absence of feeling. Amanda's leaving didn't upset him, not as it should have. Rather, it shone a light on how absurd, how utterly without purpose, life was. What was he, but a lump of damaged flesh and bone? What was life but a long and drawn-out death; a process of atrophy and decay? If others wanted to cling to it that was up to them, but to Ibrahim there seemed little point in delaying the inevitable.

He took an overdose of painkillers, knocked back with a hipflask-sized bottle of vodka; the first alcoholic drink he'd ever bought. He drank half the bottle, tipped a handful of pills onto his tongue, and washed these back with the second half. The vodka was horrible; there was something perfumed and noxious about it that made him gag. He drank it so quickly he didn't even begin to feel drunk until a few minutes after he'd drained the bottle. After another minute or so he felt nauseous and his mouth filled up with saliva. He ran from his living room to the bathroom, regurgitating a vile slurry of vodka and half-dissolved pills into the bowl, and he was sick another three times, until all that was left was bile. Then he passed out, waking the next morning with an aching stomach and a thudding headache.

The next day he visited his doctor and told her what had happened. In a calm and quiet voice he told her about the months of apathy, the strange disconnect with others, and she asked him questions, made notes, and when the session was over referred him to a specialist.

Later, there were tests and scans. He was given the address of a charity for those with brain injuries, and encouraged to attend meetings. He walked from one side of Cardiff to the other, a round trip of almost eight miles, and met others who'd been injured. With some, the injuries were clear; their scars unmistakeable. Others had been left with no outside clue to the damage done, but damaged speech, or their personalities dismantled and carelessly reassembled. At first, Ibrahim refused to believe he was like these people, these clearly damaged people, but then the results of many tests came back.

The scar was so small it would be invisible to the naked eye, they said. It was in the right prefrontal cortex of his brain, and just a fraction of a millimetre in length, but into that microscopic abyss his empathy, the very thing that won him so many red ballpoint ticks in school, had vanished.

He spent hours looking at computer simulations of the brain, studying the canyons of the frontal lobes. The experts never mentioned the soul, but Ibrahim was sure that if there was such a thing you'd find it there, buried deep inside that soft grey jelly. Only now he understood that the soul was neither immortal nor indestructible. It was just as mortal, just as fragile, as every other part of a man. You can lose your soul, the thing that makes you human, and yet carry on living.

The next time he saw Amanda was six months after the moment when he had no real answer for her, and even then it was only through chance. Their paths crossed on Ninian Road, as he walked home from the park. She stopped and talked to him, but the conversation stalled more than once, the silences drawn out and uncomfortable. He spent much of it looking at his shoes and the pavement, and Amanda smiled falsely; a crumpled, sad, defeated smile. She told him she was moving away after graduation, to London at first, then maybe Paris for her masters. He remembered dimly how they'd discussed visiting Paris some day – he wanted to see Notre Dame, she wanted to visit the Louvre – but they never did.

She looked so beautiful that day, but in looking at him what could she have seen but something empty, a sketch of what he'd been before?

They parted with a muted, solemn goodbye, and he said 'See you later', though he knew even then he wouldn't.

There had been no one since. By the summer when he should have graduated, his university friends had fanned out into the world, back to their hometowns or on to other cities. Ibrahim came to view the world beyond his flat as one of danger and hostility. He no longer understood other people, and it was clear other people didn't understand him. He lost nothing by shutting out the world.

Walking through Gloucester that night was a stark confirmation of this belief. It was a student night, he guessed. The crowds queuing up to get into bars and pubs looked young; seventeen, eighteen, not much older. Girls in tiny skirts staggering zigzags down the high street, heels like castanets against the paving slabs. Gangs of men in a standardised uniform of checked shirts, jeans and brown shoes bellowing tuneless, incoherent anthems. The gutters filled with polystyrene trays and plastic forks. On a Thursday night in Gloucester they were singing songs made unrecognisable by karaoke microphones and dancing in garish lightning storms of dry ice and disco lights.

This was what he and his friends had hated most of all. The

oblivion. No self-control, no self-respect. Just noise. Acting like beasts and dressing like whores. Pissing and puking in the streets. Poisoning themselves and dirtying themselves with such intent. It was hard to believe they weren't doing it on purpose, a strategic insult to God, who had given them their bodies and their lives, the ultimate gift, only to be repaid in drink, piss and puke. It made sense to them, to Ibrahim and his friends, that these people could rain bombs on foreign cities without compunction.

There were no innocent civilians in a culture like this.

Moving from London had shifted his view. Meeting new friends from outside the community, realising they weren't the mindless, complicit *kuffar* of his East London friends' tirades. They drank, smoked weed and partied like any other teenagers. They were, in many ways, everything he'd been taught to hate. But they were his friends. And with Amanda, she was so different from the girls he'd known before – the veiled, unavailable sisters who helped them campaign; too fervent, too involved to be thought of in *that* way. It didn't take long for him to realise he loved these new friends, loved Amanda, precisely because they weren't like the friends he'd had before.

Even so, after however many years had passed, a high street bustling with drunks still left him feeling an outsider, and an indignant one at that. He was glad to reach the far end of the high street, to leave the music and the noise of pubs and clubs behind him.

With the evening getting darker, he navigated his way across the city, walking around the edges of a vast industrial estate, until he came to the long path running parallel to a dual carriageway. The path cut in two, studded by orange patches of light. Overhanging trees. A white railing blistered with rust.

He heard the five men before he saw them; heard their voices, loud and raucous, laughing and cheering. The sound of an empty can thrown to the ground. He saw their silhouettes coming out of the orange light, five dark shapes; wraiths of smoke trailing behind two of them. Orange cigarette tips floating in the shadows, growing brighter when they inhaled. Another puff of smoke. He heard their footsteps. Hard shoes, formal shoes, the kind of shoes that would get them past surly nightclub doormen. But they were still silhouettes, and they remained silhouettes until they were almost upon him, and he saw their faces, and their eyes were all fixed on him.

He veered to the right, to step out of their way, but the man on the far side of the group moved at the same time and when passing clipped Ibrahim's shoulder with some force. There was no mistaking the intention behind it.

'Oy. Look where you're fucking going.'

But he had looked where he was going, made a conscious effort to look where he was going. He had stepped out of the way, and still found himself in their path.

He looked back at them. 'Sorry.'

The five men stopped walking.

'What you fucking say to me?'

'I'm sorry,' said Ibrahim, this time a little louder.

'You fucking staring at me?'

There was no answer to that. He was *looking* at him, yes, but only because he was being spoken to. What answer was he meant to give?

'He is, Si,' said one of the others. 'Look at the way he's looking at you.'

Ibrahim shook his head and carried on walking.

Drunks. Just drunks. Mouthing off. Confident with their mates around them. Walk away. They'll get bored with this.

'Oy. Don't you fucking turn your back on me.'

Oy. That word again. He hated that word, more a grunt than a word, but he carried on walking. If he carried on walking maybe they'd just shout something – an insult, a vague threat – and go on their way, leave him alone.

'Are you fucking deaf? I said don't turn your fucking back on me, you fucking Paki.'

He bit his lip. They wanted him to turn around, wanted him to react, but he wouldn't. He carried on walking.

'Where you from, anyway?'

The voice was louder, now, and closer. He heard footsteps again, not just one set but the sound of all five men coming towards him.

If he hadn't walked twenty miles that day, if his right leg wasn't throbbing with pain, he would have run. Forget shame. He would run away from them and not stop running until they gave up.

'I *said*… Where. Are. You. From.'

'London.'

'London, eh?' said the man, and Ibrahim could hear the sneer in his voice. 'You don't *look* like you're from London. London's in England, mate. You English?'

There was no right answer to this, but they didn't want an answer, or if they did, they didn't care what it was.

'Look,' he said. 'I'm just trying to get to my hotel, so leave it out.'

'What did you say?'

He stopped walking. He was tired. His heart beat at a gallop so intense he could feel it in his throat, and his mouth was dry. 'I'm not looking for trouble,' he said.

'Look at the way he's looking at you, Si.'

The first man, the one who'd clipped Ibrahim's shoulder, stepped forward.

'Why don't you just fuck off home to Paki-Land,' he said. 'This isn't your fucking country.'

The blow came from nowhere, and a dark kaleidoscope erased his memory of it. It took a second or two for him to realise he'd been punched, and when he felt something trickling down the left side of his face, Ibrahim's first thought was that maybe the man's hand was wet, and there was a split second's dazed revulsion when he thought maybe that hand had been drenched in a drunk man's piss, but when he put his hand to his face his fingers came away red.

The second punch smashed into his nose with a crunch that seemed to echo in his head, like the splintering of a tree being felled, and his limbs were unstrung. He fell to the ground, landing awkwardly on his backpack, and something – the sharp toe of a shoe – hit him in the ribs and in the side of his head. The sound of the other four cheering on their friend grew faint, drowned out by a high-pitched whine and the thunder of his own pulse. Each new blow sounded as if it were being delivered under water.

Ibrahim curled up into a ball, his arms around his head, knees tucked in as close to his chest as he could get them, and he had a single thought as dark and final as any he'd ever had.

Maybe this won't end.

And now the pain was coming through, as the fog of adrenalin began to clear. He felt his body being pummelled from all sides – there was more than one man kicking him now – as if the whole world had closed in and was mauling him.

Maybe this won't end.

The air kicked out of his lungs. The taste of copper on his tongue. Something gritty (bits of broken teeth?) floating around in his spit.

Maybe this won't end.

A final, sharp blow to his back, then a moment of quiet. The ringing in his ears faded, and he heard the traffic on the dual carriageway, and their footsteps getting quieter. When he dared to open his eyes again he saw the five men walking away, and he heard them laughing.

He waited until they were gone before sitting up, and he spat a mouthful of blood onto the path. His body tingled in the aftermath of violence, different morse codes of pain ringing out from his torso and limbs. It took an effort to stand, an even greater one for him to walk. He placed his hand over the ruptured flesh of his eyebrow, and felt fresh blood leaking out between his fingers. The bleeding wouldn't stop.

The path ended where it met with a busy road, and further along he saw the large illuminated sign of the hotel. If he could just get that far. But what then? If he staggered, bleeding, into the hotel, then what? They might call for the police, or an ambulance, and he couldn't go to hospital, or rather he *wouldn't* go to hospital. If he could just stop the bleeding, he'd be fine. Rest a little, carry on. No need for hospital. No need for the nurses' practised sympathy and the doctors' arch concern. And the police. What would he say to the police? They were five *gore*, dressed like every other *gora* he saw tonight. And what was he even doing here? A long way from either city he'd call home, and if he told them he was walking to London they would think him mad.

His left eye was closing up, the flesh around it swelling and pushing his eyelids shut. When he touched his face the skin felt distended and spongy, obliquely numb, as if it weren't his own. He felt a rising nausea and a dizziness, the orange lights at the roadside dancing like sparklers around a bonfire. The weight of his backpack drew him to the ground, pulling him back, and he landed heavily, rolling onto his side. His mouth filled up with more blood and spit, and the congealed blood inside his nose turned every breath into a rattle. Though it was late summer and the day had been warm, he felt a crystal cold creep through his limbs, and he passed out.

14

'*¿A cuántos kilómetros está Madrid?* How many kilometres to Madrid.'

'A cuantos… a cuantos kilometros esta Ma*drid*.'

'*¿Dónde están las tiendas?* Where are the shops.'

'Donde esta… es*tan* las… las tiendas.'

'*Oiga, por favor. ¿Para ir al aeropuerto?* Excuse me. How do I get to the airport.'

'Oy… oiga por favor. Fa*bor*. Para… ir al…'

'*Quiero una habitción con dos camas para tres–*'

Natalie hit the stop button with her thumb and shook her head. That was enough for one night. She was tired, her concentration failing. She could focus on the road, or she could listen to *Spanish Made Simple*, the CD whose tutor spoke with too sensual and soporific a voice for this time of night.

'*¿Dónde están las tiendas?*' She said, to no one but herself, and with a greater degree of confidence than she had when answering the sultry, seductive voice of her faceless tutor.

And what did this woman actually look like? She pictured an olive-skinned beauty with long black hair; raggedy skirt reaching her ankles and a crumpled white blouse tied around her breasts, exposing a smooth brown stomach. The kind of curvy, buxom woman who'd launch into an impromptu flamenco at the single clack of a castanet. Probably looked nothing like that. She might be plain, or even ugly. Perhaps she was pale-skinned, with hair the colour of damp straw; all bony, boyish shoulders and no tits.

The CD was a gift of several Christmases ago, and it had languished at the bottom of a box, half-forgotten, for years. Since then the box had moved around – from cupboard to dark corner beneath bed and back to cupboard, a different cupboard, again – but the CD hadn't left its case until now.

Now it was a part of the new Natalie, one of many ingredients that would go into making a new, improved Natalie; one ready to take on the world, meet new challenges, try new things; such as learning a foreign language.

Was that a cliché, the kind of thing people in her situation did? Reinvent themselves? She reminded herself this wasn't reinvention, it was self-improvement. There was a difference.

And so she took the CD from its case, making sure it was the only CD in her car, and began listening to it during every journey; to and from work, to and from the shops. She'd even tried listening to it during the night, in the belief that some Spanish might seep into her brain via a kind of nocturnal osmosis, but found it simply kept her awake.

A friend told her there were classes, night classes, at a primary school near where she lived. 'They do everything,' this friend said. 'Spanish, French, German…' But Natalie wouldn't go. She pictured herself sitting in a classroom, on the tiny, plastic classroom furniture, and embarrassing herself before a room of adults, people her age, all of them watching her, waiting for her to slip up. Here, in the relative privacy of her car, where other motorists might think she was talking to someone on her phone, hands free, she could repeat each line with a wavering, irregular confidence; invest her all in mimicking the tutor's Iberian purr. In a room full of her peers she knew she would fail, that the words would fall out in that Gloucestershire drawl she'd spent a lifetime trying to mask, that she would sound like yet another sunburned, monoglot Brit on holiday.

'Dondee esta la player, pour favor?'

This shouldn't have been so difficult. Her grandfather was Italian. Picking up another language, just as he had done, should have been second nature, a genetic memory. Why couldn't she just stop being so bloody English?

It had been an ambition of hers for some time, learning a foreign language. She dreamed of walking into a bar or restaurant in Barcelona or Madrid, placing her order in flawless Castilian. Then, all the shame of her upbringing – so very, tediously British and introspective – would evaporate. Many of her colleagues, fellow nurses, were from such interesting places. West Indians, Africans, Filipinos. She was grateful, sometimes, for that quarter of her that wasn't Anglo-Saxon.

And what a story that was. Captured in Sicily. Brought to Britain as a POW. Met a local girl and married. Settled in England. Lived happily – well, pretty much happily – ever after. What did Natalie have to compete with that? Four (disastrous) years in London. A few foreign holidays. She'd once had four numbers on the lottery. Once saw George Clooney standing outside Fortnum & Mason's. At least, she thought it was him. It looked like him.

Those colleagues of hers, they could tell some stories. The kind of things you can't quite imagine, things you've only ever seen on the news. And when they talked about Gloucester it was with a strange fondness that was endearing and sad at the same time. Natalie had spent much of her life thinking it a dead-end town – pretty enough, but provincial, twee and insular; in a way, a microcosm of the whole country.

To hear people who'd survived civil wars and massacres describe Gloucester – grey and dowdy old Gloucester – you'd think it was paradise. The kind of place you'd run to, rather than from. It made her realise just how spoiled she was. Not just spoiled as in affluent, but spoiled for choice, spoiled for offers, for promises. Spoon fed stories of success practically from birth, all those images of celebrity, wealth and glamour. Against all that – all those rooftop bars, indoor swimming pools, gala openings and parties that made the society pages in the paper – Gloucester never quite cut it. If you hadn't come to it from a place of horror, Gloucester was average, nondescript. Famous for nothing but cheese and serial killers.

It hadn't seemed so bad when she was with someone. Then it was easy to look at the city with charitable indifference; neither its biggest fan nor its greatest critic. Now she found herself noticing everything, every flaw, every shortcoming. Time had slowed right down. Days became long. Being with someone, sharing her life with someone, burned time so effectively. Afternoons spent doing little passed quickly. A whole weekend could be structured around the smallest thing, a sunny afternoon's daytrip. Now she was alone, a weekend away from the hospital had become a vast desert of time, bleak as a salt plain beneath an unforgiving sun; something approached with dread and apprehension.

Within the first month of joining her local library she'd read eight novels, culled from a predictable enough list of 'Books to Read Before You Die'. She found *Wuthering Heights* enchanting, *Brideshead Revisited* fun if a little bogged down by all that Catholicism, and she hated Hemingway's *The Sun Also Rises* with a passion. She took up knitting, producing a misshapen scarf and matching, hideous cardigan that no one would ever see, let alone wear. She then took *Spanish Made Simple* from its case.

She'd given up knitting, those first abortive attempts enough to put her off for life, and her reading had slowed – she'd been wrestling with *Midnight's Children* for over a month and was barely a hundred pages in – but she was determined to persevere with Spanish. Just maybe not tonight.

It was as she neared the dual carriageway, taking a left at the crossroads and heading down beneath the gleaming edifice of a chain hotel, that she noticed a dark shape at the roadside. It looked at first like a bundle of rags, or something stolen and abandoned on the cycle path, but then she saw the outline of limbs, a head, and the suggestion of movement, perhaps breathing.

Could be a drunk, another drunk, too paralytic to make it home after a day spent sitting on a bench drinking cheap cider. The kind of person beyond help. She saw enough of them in the hospital, and there and then it was her duty to help, however impatient she might get, however frustrating it was to help someone who just won't help themselves, but here? Out here on the road, at night? What obligation was there? Who would know if she carried on driving?

She sighed, pulling in to the narrow hard shoulder and flicking on her hazard lights. Probably a drunk. Another drunk. Dark stain around his crotch. The musty stink of booze, old sweat and sick. He'd get surly the minute she woke him. They always did.

She hesitated, clenching and unclenching her fingers around the steering wheel. The embankment, and the dark, all-too-human shape at its crest, were lit up by the orange pulse of the hazard lights. Maybe not a drunk. Old man walking his dog, had a heart attack. Dog ran off, yapping, into the bushes. Or someone who'd been mugged.

Natalie stepped out of her car, and with uncertain, clumsy steps made her way up the embankment and towards the body on the path.

15

Reenie was looking at the stars.

Earlier that evening she had eaten a light supper. Her supplies of food and water were running low. She had hoped to pass a supermarket or any kind of shop where she could buy groceries, but there were few villages in this part of the country, and she'd made little progress since leaving the farmhouse that morning, walking only a few miles before tiredness hit her and she was forced to set up camp again. The next large town, and most likely the next place where she would find shops, was Chippenham, but it would take another two or three days for her to reach it.

Along the way she had picked blackberries from the roadside, collecting them in a plastic carrier bag, and as soon as she stopped walking she ate a few, without rinsing off whatever muck might be on them. What little water she had left was for drinking only. Solomon, the lucky sod, had a full supply of food, enough to get him to London and back several times over.

That night was colder than any other on her journey so far. The summer was coming to an end – the evenings getting darker, the night air laced with the scent of dry leaves and burning wood – and what struck her, out here in the country, was the darkness of the night sky. She had lived in cities her whole life, and it was decades since she'd last seen a night untainted by the glow of streetlights. The darkness above her wasn't black, but rather a deep, velvety shade of blue. The stars she saw weren't distant pinpoints but a spray, and she counted dozens of shooting stars. She saw the moon – perhaps a third of it erased by shadow – and if she squinted and strained her eyes enough was sure she made out the craters on its surface.

The sky had been this dark when she was a girl. She remembered rushing, with Mrs Ostroff, to a neighbour's Anderson shelter, and, while they waited for the all-clear, Mrs Ostroff reading her fairy tales and nursery rhymes; *Babele-ber* and that song by Bialik, 'Under the Little Green Trees':

'Unter di grininke beymelekh
Shpiln zikh Moyshelekh, Shloymelekh,
Tsites, kapotkelekh, shtreymelekh,
Yidelekh, frish fun di eyelekh.

Fartrakhtn zikh tif un farkukn zikh
Oyf nekhtige teg un oyf feygelekh,
Oy, mir zol zany, yidishe kinderlekh,
Far ayere koshere eygelekh!'

She recalled, with greater clarity, the final attacks on London, shortly before the war's end, remembering not images or precise moments but noise; when rockets began falling from the sky.

The first of them came with two warnings. First the drone, like a swarm of angry bees, but getting deeper in pitch, singing out with a low, throbbing hum before cutting off, and that sudden silence, the absence of noise, was their second warning. The rocket was now tumbling to earth, and it took eleven seconds to fall. She knew this because Mr Ostroff was an air-raid warden, and had timed their descent with his watch. Eleven seconds of absolute silence between the last monstrous yawn and the heavy thump of the explosion. A thump if the impact was far away, almost like the sound of somebody beating a rug. If it was closer, not one noise but many. Thunder. Breaking glass. Masonry being pulverised. The hiss of sand and dirt raining back to earth. Screaming.

Then came the second wave of rockets, and with these there was no warning. They travelled at such speed you'd only hear their approach after they struck, and it seemed in that moment as if the sky was the enemy; a vengeful force of nature meting out its punishment on the city below. By the time one of those rockets slammed into Green Street, just five minutes' walk from the Ostroff's home, Reenie had reached an age when she could no longer be distracted by fairy tales and nursery rhymes. By now the idea of death was real. She had been surrounded by it too long for it to remain distant and abstract.

She had been playing in the street when a telegram arrived for number fifty-eight, and she saw Mrs Ingram break down, right there on her doorstep, crying for all the world to see. And the boys in school, the O'Leary brothers, who simply weren't there one morning, after the attack on Plaistow, and no one ever mentioned them again.

And when the rocket hit Green Street its explosion rattled every window in their house and shook ornaments from shelves, and Reenie and Mrs Ostroff hid beneath the dining table and watched as a world that had always felt safe, even when the rest of the world was burning, quaked as if it were trembling.

Reenie later learned how these bombs came not from planes, or even cannons, but from space, and that knowledge filled her with a tingling sense of awe. If the Germans had weapons like *this*, weapons that fell almost silently from space, what hope was there of winning the war?

No one seemed to mention that these days. As if no one wanted to admit it was what they had often thought, when the rockets were falling. *What if we lose?* Because they still could have lost, even then. What if the rockets hadn't stopped falling until there was nothing left but brick dust and ashes?

Later still, when she was married, Reenie learned how the men who created those rockets were neither tried nor punished. Watching grainy black and white footage of a man climbing down onto a featureless grey world, Jonathan turned to her and said, bitterly, 'And to think, it was a Nazi who got them there.'

She asked him what he meant. He'd often say something, as if ending a sentence started in his head, and she'd wait for him to expand on it, to fill in the gaps.

'Von Braun,' he said. 'Rocket scientist. A *Nazi*. Member of the SS. Twenty-five years ago he was building rockets that killed thousands. Now he's building them so the Yanks can go to the moon. If it wasn't for that *Nazi* they'd never have beaten the Russians at *this*...' And he punctuated his remark by stabbing the stem of his pipe towards the television screen.

Reenie looked at the screen, then her husband. The windows of a nearby school were filled with crayoned pictures of spaceships, moons and American flags. A neighbour of theirs, Mr Powell, had resisted buying a television until that very week, when she had seen him hoisting its oversized box from the boot of his Austin Westminster. At the hairdressers, on Monday, it had been the only topic of conversation. Incredible. Amazing. Never see another moment like it in our lifetimes. In the week when Neil Armstrong set foot on the moon, Jonathan Glickman was, it seemed, the city's – no, the *world's* – only curmudgeon.

'Well, at least he's done some good,' said Reenie, meaning Von Braun. 'Maybe it's his way of making up for what he did. His way of atoning.'

Her husband laughed and lit his pipe with a match. *Puff puff puff.* 'Atoning? The man never faced up to his crimes. The slave labour he used to run his factories. The thousands killed by his inventions. So he puts a man on the moon. So what? What does a man on the moon mean if we turn a blind eye to murder just to get him there? What kind of progress is that?'

She looked at him from across the sitting room. Could he understand what his words meant to her? Had he forgotten everything about her, everything that happened to her before they met? It was, she supposed, easy for him to forget. He'd never met her father, and nor would he. His family had been British for so many generations, and they'd lost no one in Europe. His outrage at Von Braun and the Nazis was the outrage of a very British Jew; horrified and at the same time distanced from the event. He'd admitted to her, once, that there were members of his own family who, before the war, resented and distrusted European Jews. And to them, to Jonathan and his family, the atrocities were both personal and academic. Personal because German troops could have landed on the Kentish coast. Academic because they hadn't.

Bristling for a moment (how could he *not* know what his words meant to her?) Reenie thought about Von Braun's factories, about his slaves. Had her parents helped to build those rockets, unaware they'd one day fall on the city where their daughter lived? Was history's sense of humour that sick? She could believe it was.

She'd never tell him, Jonathan, how he hurt her that night. He hadn't meant to, she knew that. It would have crushed him, had he known. Perhaps he thought she'd appreciate his outrage, as if he were somehow defending her, or even her parents, so many years after the fact.

She wanted to tell him: but we don't talk about it. We never talked about it, about any of it. Some things, well… it's as if some things are too big to talk about. As if there aren't enough words.

And now, eight years a widow, Reenie saw in the night sky the blinking specks of satellites once carried by rockets, and the world had changed again and again, and the factories and the slaves had been relegated to the status of footnotes. When the rockets stopped falling on London the blackout ended and the night sky was reclaimed by the city's fuzzy orange glow. Its darkness, and the threat that darkness contained, were gone, as if the city was now cocooned safely beneath a dome the colour of rust. Only here, sat beside her tent and her trolley, could she once again feel the terrifying vastness of space above her. There was a beauty to a clear night sky – she couldn't deny that – but with it came a humbling immensity, no more so than in those places where the land was flat and the horizons distant.

Before climbing into her tent Reenie looked east, across the dark fields barely contoured by starlight. She'd thought she might see some hint of the next large town, a dull umber light, but there was nothing; only darkness and stars.

She felt very small and distant from the world that night. For the first time since leaving Cardiff it occurred to her she might never make it to London, that she could become lost between the towns and cities; that the realities and hardships of her age might catch up with her and take her in the night. She doubted there was anyone in the world thinking of her at that moment, wondering where she was, what she was doing, not even Ibrahim, who – so she imagined – was halfway to London by now and never looking back.

16

He was woken, if it could be called waking, by the sensation of movement, a gentle rocking, and by the dull throb of an engine. Only one of his eyes would open properly, and through it he saw orange lights dancing against the black sky. He was inside a moving car for the first time in four years, but even so it took a moment for the gravity of this to hit him. He tried sitting upright, but every part of him was in pain; even the slightest movement was agony.

'Try not to move,' said the driver; female, well-spoken, a slight gravelly quality to her voice. The kind of husky voice he'd heard on countless adverts. He saw long dark hair and, in the rear-view mirror, dark brown eyes.

'Where am I?'

'Don't worry, I'm a nurse. We're on our way to Gloucester Royal.'

'What's that? Is that a hospital?'

'Yes. I work there.'

Easing himself up, Ibrahim gripped the headrest of the front passenger seat for support.

'No hospital,' he croaked. He could taste blood.

'What's that?'

'No hospital. I can't go to the hospital.'

'You've got some really nasty injuries there. You may have broken something. I'm taking you to the hospital.'

'No. Please. Don't.'

Because hospital meant doctors and nurses and examinations and pills and x-rays and everything he had gone through before. It could mean the end of the road and the white flag of surrender, and he couldn't give up, not now. He clenched his fingers into the headrest until he thought the stitches in its upholstery might burst.

'Let me out,' he said.

'What's that?'

'Pull over. Let me out.'

Beyond the car's windows he saw a motorway's orange lights passing overhead as if flying in formation. The glaring white headlights of the cars in the adjacent lane, and the red tail lights of the traffic ahead glowered in single file, curving off towards the horizon. All that traffic, all those people, all that chaos. He felt a tightening in his stomach, and his body seemed to shrink, as if anticipating disaster.

'Please. Let me out.'

'I can't do that. We're on the dual carriageway.'

'Please. I'm serious. Let me out of the car.'

He was leaning forward, between the front seats, and as he drew close the nurse flinched.

'What's wrong?' she asked. 'Are you in trouble? What is it?'

'Please. Stop the car. I'm going to be sick.'

Sighing impatiently, the nurse drove on another hundred yards until they'd reached a stretch of hard shoulder, then pulled over and hit the hazard lights. Though still in pain, Ibrahim launched himself across the back seat, opened the door, and fell out onto the tarmac. Hunched over and kneeling, he dry heaved three times, his insides clenching and unclenching, his entire body breaking out in a cold sweat. Dimly, he heard the driver's door open and close with a loud clunk, and the sound of footsteps on the road.

'You have to go to a hospital,' said the nurse, standing over him. 'I'm not leaving you here. D'you know, I'm *legally obliged* to help you? So I *literally* can't leave you here.'

'What're you talking about?' He mumbled. The nausea was beginning to pass now that he was out of the car and breathing fresh air.

'Like I said, I'm a nurse. And you need treatment. I can't leave you here, on this bloody hard shoulder. Here. Let me help you up.'

He shook his head, waving his hand to fend her off, and he tried to stand, but couldn't. 'I can't go to a hospital,' he said. 'Not again. Please.'

'Well, will you at least get back in the car?'

Could he do it? He wished he could undo the last four years

completely, unravel the threads that brought him here, and make so many different choices. He knew he was being ridiculous; all his choices in the last four years had been ridiculous. A rational, undamaged person would have taken the train to London, would have been there by Tuesday afternoon. Even if that rational, undamaged person found himself in the situation Ibrahim was now in, he would accept help, go to the hospital, but Ibrahim's mind no longer worked that way. His every thought was strewn with boulders and brick walls. Nothing was ever simple.

'I can't go to the hospital,' he said, and he heard his voice breaking and felt the stinging weight of tears in his eyes.

The nurse looked down at him, and he caught her expression; one of equal parts pity and frustration.

'Well, would you let me treat you, if I took you somewhere else?'
'Where?'

'My house. God… what am I thinking?' She sighed. 'I live near here. I could take you to my house. I've got some stuff there. I can take a look at some of your cuts. But if it's anything more serious than cuts and bruises, I'm calling an ambulance.'

He nodded. 'Yeah. Your house. That's fine. I think.'

She reached forward, hooking her arms beneath his, and hoisted him off the ground with a strength that surprised him. When she lifted him into the car he slumped across the back seat with a groan.

'You're strong,' he said.

'Yeah, well, I'm a nurse. Lifting pensioners out of wheelchairs works wonders for your upper body strength. Arms like a bloody navvy, me.'

He closed his eyes again, and heard her walking around the car, getting back behind the wheel, starting the engine.

'I can't believe I'm taking you to my house,' she said. 'I must be insane. I don't even know your name.'

They pulled out from the hard shoulder, but he stayed lying down, his eyes shut.

'It's Ibrahim,' he said. 'Ibrahim Siddique.'

'Nice to meet you, Ibrahim. My name's Natalie. You okay back there?'

He nodded and grunted in reply, and tried to ignore the feeling of motion and the sounds of the road; the tug of gravity each time she accelerated. He heard sirens, growing louder, then quieter as an ambulance or police car sped past them, close enough for him to see the faint blue flicker of light through his eyelids. He remembered night-time car journeys when he was a child, the way the shadows slid up the back of the driver's seat with every street light they passed, and how those sliding shadows would often lull him into sleep.

The relief he felt when the car had stopped and the engine fell silent was overwhelming, like a moment when you don't know if you're about to laugh or cry; your breath arrested at the very line between two different emotions. She helped him out of the car, his right arm slung around her shoulder, her left arm supporting him around the waist, and she walked him to the house.

Natalie lived on a grey, nondescript terrace; the kind of street that could be in any town or city, in any part of the country. She carried him as far as the living room, where a large antique clock above the fireplace struck midnight. How many hours had passed since he was on the lane? How long was he unconscious by the roadside? How long had it taken for someone to notice him?

She lowered him onto her sofa, and turned on a lamp in the corner of the room.

'Are you comfortable?'

He nodded, trying to smile, and felt dried blood cracking in the lines around his mouth.

'I'm just going to get a few things,' said Natalie. 'Then we'll see if we can patch you up.'

While Natalie went to fetch dressings and medicine, Ibrahim looked around the room, searching for clues as to the kind of woman who'd rescued him. Was there a husband or boyfriend, someone who might appear suddenly, and turf him out into the night in a fit of rage? Were there children? He saw school portraits of two boys and a girl on the mantelpiece, but no other evidence of kids; no bright plastic toys cluttering the corners of the room or Disney films amongst the romantic comedies and boxed-set TV shows beside her television.

On returning, Natalie helped him stand and walked him through to the bathroom, which, thankfully, was on the ground floor. There, she sat him on the edge of her bath and asked him to strip down to his underwear. She helped him remove his t-shirt and his trousers, and though he was still dazed and his body still burned with pain, he felt a wave of embarrassment at having this woman see him almost naked, a sensation he hadn't felt since those first, tentative experiences with Amanda. Then, it was not only knowing what they did was *haraam*, sinful and forbidden, but also the shame of his fleshiness – the rolls of fat around his midriff and the flabbiness of his chest – that embarrassed him. Sitting almost naked before Natalie brought back that acute embarrassment, that shame, and beneath the drying blood on his face he blushed.

'Christ,' said Natalie, grimacing. 'You're bruised all over. What *happened*?'

He looked down at his torso, which was covered in angry welts; some of them almost black against his light brown skin. In places the skin was broken and grazed and beginning to scab. He said nothing.

'Okay,' said Natalie. 'Now this might hurt a bit, but I'm just checking to see if anything's broken.'

He nodded and closed his eyes but nothing prepared him for the electric bolt of pain that shot through his whole body when she pressed her fingers against his ribs, and even the shock of that did little to negate the pain when she did it again, this time on the other side of his ribcage.

'It's okay,' she said. 'I don't *think* anything's broken. Of course, I can't tell for sure without an x-ray, but wouldn't you know it, I don't happen to have an x-ray machine in my bathroom.'

Next she began cleaning his wounds, the cuts to his face and the grazes on his back and on his shins. He winced each time the antiseptic touched open flesh, and saw her small expressions of impatience before she carried on with the job. She applied butterfly stitches to the cut in his eyebrow, and brought him a clean tea towel filled with ice cubes that she had him hold against his nose.

'I don't think it's broken,' she said. 'But it is quite swollen. That should help a little. You didn't answer my question. What happened?'

'Some guys jumped me,' said Ibrahim. 'I was on my way to a hotel, walking along this lane, and they jumped me.'

'Bastards,' said Natalie. 'We get it all the time on weekends, in A and E. Of course, most of the time it's blokes who've got themselves into a scrap in a nightclub. You've not been drinking, have you?'

He shook his head.

'Good. I've got some painkillers that might help if you're still aching. I'll just get you a blanket, and I'll put your clothes in the wash. They're covered in blood.'

When she returned, carrying the blanket, he was still perched on the edge of her bath, covering his crotch with his hands. It was embarrassing enough for her to see his body, let alone anything else, even the *suggestion* of anything else. She put the blanket around his shoulders and helped him back to the living room, where he lay flat on her sofa.

Natalie began asking him questions, and it took him a moment to realise she was checking for symptoms. Symptoms of what, he didn't know.

'No hot flushes? You're not feeling clammy, tight-chested?'

'No. None of that.'

'Good,' said Natalie. 'You're not in shock, then. Would you like some tea, or something?'

He told her he'd like that very much, and lay there with his eyes shut until she came back with two mugs of tea and a plate of chocolate biscuits.

The hot tea jangled against his chipped teeth, he found it difficult to chew without hurting his jaw, and he wondered bleakly if there was a part of him they hadn't punched or kicked. From across the room, Natalie studied him, and he thought he noticed a tiny, almost imperceptible moment of doubt, or hesitation. Perhaps distrust. She was entitled to that, even if he was no threat.

'You're not from Gloucester, are you?' she asked.

'No.'

'Let me guess. East London?'

He nodded.

'Yeah. I worked in the Hammersmith. I was there four years. You kind of get to know the accents. North, south. East, west. What are you doing in Gloucester?'

He laughed, but even that hurt. 'If I tell you, you'll try and have me sectioned,' he said.

'Try me,' said Natalie. 'Having someone sectioned is a nightmare. So much paperwork. Half the time it's not worth the bother.'

'Okay. Well. I'm walking to London. I live in Cardiff, and I'm walking to London.'

'Right. Well that *is* mental. Is it for charity?'

'No. Everyone asks me that.'

'It's the only explanation that isn't insane. You know, you're being sponsored, raising money for Oxfam or, I don't know, Battersea Dogs Home or whatever. It was this or jumping out of a plane or running a marathon. That kind of thing.'

'It's not for charity.'

'Then yes, you're insane. But, like I said, I can't be bothered with the paperwork.'

'So you're not going to have me sectioned?'

'Nah. Not tonight.'

'Thanks.'

'But. I do still want to know why. Why are you walking? Is it money? Because, you know, there's always hitchhiking. I think people still do that. We used to do it all the time when I was a student. Not the most sensible thing in the world, I know, but we did.'

He sighed. Once again, there was little he could say that wouldn't sound insane.

'It's cars,' he said. 'I can't ride in cars. Or buses. Or trains.'

Natalie considered this for a moment, then clicked her fingers and pointed to the far end of his blanket.

'It was a car crash,' she said. 'Wasn't it?'

'What? But how could you…'

'You've had a brace fitted to your right leg. I noticed the scars. And underneath all that blood and dirt on your face, there were a few scars there, too. They're not that obvious, but you can see them up close. Am I right? Was it a car crash?'

He nodded.

'I knew it. And now, when you try riding in cars or trains, what? Panic attacks? You get all hot and clammy?'

'Yes.'

'Well. That's not so crazy. I mean, it kind of *is*, but not the sort of crazy worth sectioning you for.' She paused to sip her tea, and though he still couldn't meet her gaze he knew that she was looking straight at him. 'And what's in London?' she asked.

'Family. My family's still in London.'

'Right. But I'm guessing you're not just popping down for a visit and a catch-up.'

'No.'

'Something serious?'

'Yes.'

Natalie nodded, placing her mug down on the wooden floor next to her feet. 'I'll stop asking questions now,' she said. 'Are you comfortable? Sorry. That was another question. But are you?'

'Yes, thank you.'

'Still achy?'

'Yes.'

'Well, I still think you should go to the hospital. It looks like your head took a bit of a bashing. You should get *that* scanned. And x-rays.'

'I'm fine.'

'Well, you're clearly not.'

He eased himself up on the sofa until he was upright, and pulled the blanket up to cover his chest. For the first time in an age his gaze met hers, and he was able to look at her properly. She was beautiful. Yes, there were indelible creases around her eyes and mouth, but her eyes were a deep shade of brown, and there wasn't a trace of grey in her long black hair. She studied him again with that fixed expression, her lips pouted unselfconsciously, as if she was chewing on a thought, and Ibrahim felt the stirring of a nascent desire, a confusing blend of gratitude and lust.

'Why did you help me?' he asked.

'What do you mean?'

'I mean just that. Why did you help me? Why didn't you just keep driving? I must have been lying there for an hour or more. Lots of people drove past me. Why did you stop?'

Natalie shrugged. 'I've been asking myself the same question. But like I said, I'm a nurse. We have certain obligations. We're not allowed to turn and look the other way.'

'But you could have. Nobody would have known.'

'I would have.'

Ibrahim nodded, once again avoiding eye contact, as if by answering his question she'd made him the focus of the room's attention. He pointed to the mantelpiece, and the school portraits of two boys and a girl.

'Those your kids?'

'No. That's my niece and nephews. But those photos are old now. Joshua is… let me see… thirteen. Jacob's eleven. Which means Jessica's almost nine.'

'All Js.'

'What's that?'

'Joshua, Jacob, Jessica. All Js.'

'Yes. Tell me about it. My brother's name is James and he married a Jennifer. They thought it would be cute.'

'So are you married? Got a boyfriend?'

Natalie laughed. 'Hardly. And I hope you're not getting any funny ideas. Just because I've let you into my house and patched you up doesn't mean this is about to go all *American Werewolf In London*.'

'What?'

'The film? Jenny Agutter?'

'Haven't seen it.'

'You haven't seen *Amer*… Doesn't matter. But no. I don't have a boyfriend. I had a partner. We were together five years, but things kind of… I don't know. Fizzled out. Or whatever. She's now living in *Derby*, of all places.'

'She?'

'Sarah. Her name was Sarah. Is Sarah.'

'You're a lesbian?'

The word was blurted out, almost involuntarily, like a cough or a sneeze, and he felt that familiar twitch of revulsion. It was complicated, this time, by a sense of betrayal, of having been misled, as if the world had shifted, changed without his permission. The same feeling of unease he'd had when Reenie told him the story of how she came to London. Once again he was in the study room, in the *halaqah*, with Ismail, Yusuf, Jamal and the others. A low-ceilinged, starkly lit room with posters tacked to its notice-board. Those plastic chairs with writing paddles fixed to their armrests. Ibrahim and his friends scribbling notes.

'What does it say in the *Hadith* of Al-Tirmidhi?' said the sheikh, his voice echoing tinnily off the grey linoleum floor. 'It says, "There is nothing I fear for my *ummah* more than the deed of the people of Lut." And what does it say in the *Hadith* of Abu Dawud? "No man should lie with another man, no woman should lie with another woman. Turn them out of your houses," it says. "Put them to death," it says. These are the sayings of the Prophet, peace be upon him.'

'You have that look on your face,' said Natalie, bringing him back into her living room.

'What look?'

'That look that says, "Well, maybe you just haven't met the right man."'

'Do I?'

'Okay. What were you thinking?'

'Nothing. It was nothing.'

'Are you religious?'

'What?'

'Are you religious?'

Blindsided by her question, he blinked three times while thinking of an answer. He'd never met anyone who could read him like this, but perhaps that came with her job; meeting and dealing with the evasive, the timid and the injured for a living.

'Kind of,' he said. 'Not as much as I used to be. But yeah.'

'Thought so.'

'How can you tell that? Because if it's, you know, about you being a lesbian, it's not, it's…'

'Your beard.'

'What?'

'Your *beard*. There are only three kinds of men with your kind of beard. Guys who are into computer games and heavy metal, the *Amish*, and Muslims.'

He laughed, and another bolt of pain sliced through his ribs. 'Well, that's kind of racist,' he said.

'No, it's not,' said Natalie. 'I'm stereotyping. There's a difference. But at least you're smiling, so that's something.' She leaned forward, pulling the plate of biscuits back towards her and taking one. After eating it in two bites, she said, 'Religions are weird. I mean, I know that goes without saying, but some of them... they don't even leave a dent. Church of England, for example. Sarah, my ex. She was raised Church of England. But the minute you stop believing in God, that's it. You're no longer Church of England, you're an atheist, or agnostic or whatever. But if you're a Catholic, and I was raised Catholic, you say you don't believe in God? You're still a Catholic. It goes deeper than articles of faith. I imagine it's the same if you're a Muslim. Am I right?'

'Kind of.'

'But maybe that's just us accepting the definition of the majority.'

'What do you mean?'

'Well, most of the people in Britain are Church of England, at least by default. If they stop believing, they get to decide who and what they are. But us? We *others*? It gets confusing, for them, for the majority, if we say we're no longer the thing they've labelled us. They don't know what we are. So we're still Catholic. Still Muslim. And we accept that. We go along with it.' She looked at her watch and sighed. 'Anyway,' she said. 'That's all a bit deep for this time of night. It's late, and I'm knackered. Are you okay sleeping there?'

He nodded. 'I'll be fine. Thank you.'

'Don't mention it. I guess you're just my good deed for the day, or something. I'll see you in the morning.'

She turned off the lamp before leaving the room and he listened to her climb the stairs, brush her teeth, and close her bedroom door. The house was silent now, but for the ticking of the clock on her mantelpiece, and with the quiet came memories of what had happened that night.

Worst of all was how wretched, how feeble he felt at not having fought back, but then he had never been much of a fighter. Despite his size, playground brawls had never ended in his favour. If anything, his height and build left him at a disadvantage; the oversized target of bullies, but slow and clumsy with it. He never had the instinct to punch and kick, something that seemed ingrained in those feral-faced kids with narrow, pugilist eyes and mouths curled up in permanent sneers.

Those years of taking hits built something up in him, the residue of an anger never vented. As a kid he would run home after fights, and sob into his pillow. Tell his mother he'd tripped and fallen if there were bruises to show. Hope his dad wouldn't see him crying. And each time he did this a trace of bile was left behind. Not enough to make him swing a punch, the next time he was confronted, but an anger, a resentment, that festered, day upon day, month upon month, year upon year, and when finally he'd mustered the will to hit back the instrument he and his friends chose wasn't the brute physical force of the playground bully but something infinitely more terrible. Their brothers, their *ikhwan*, in Pakistan and Somalia, in Yemen and Saudi Arabia, had already shown them the way, and they saw those men as heroes.

When their heroes made it onto the news, the violence seemed distant, the damage inflicted abstract. They measured the success of their heroes not in the number of dead, but in the hours of airtime they received. The world was paying them attention, and wasn't that the desired effect of every violent act? When those wiry, sneering, mean-faced kids threw punches or hurled abuse it was to get his attention, and the attention of others. It was to force – rather than earn – his respect. They'd taught him an important lesson, a lesson that was reinforced with every history book he read.

Diplomacy was a myth. Window dressing. No individual or nation had ever succeeded through decorum and kind words alone. The peoples of the world understand violence more than they will ever understand rhetoric. The bullies of his school knew this – on a deep, gut level rather than an academic one – and now he and his friends knew it too. Meeting those friends, talking about these ideas, poring over their well-thumbed copies of Qutb and al-Zawahiri, they felt empowered by this discovery.

Violence was power.

But now he saw that violence for what it was and always had been – an acute kind of helplessness, fashioned into an epic fantasy of *jihad*. The imams, sheikhs and amirs – those his friends admired, rather than those at his family's mosque – spoke and appealed to him directly. They were, almost without exception, young men. In the *halaqah* they talked about the modern world, about economics and politics and Keynes and Marxism and Orientalism, and when Ibrahim's friends mocked him for studying history, the sheikh scolded them, because history, he said, was 'vital', history was 'everything'. And when Ibrahim heard the sheikh talk about the struggles of *jihad*, he believed they were *his* struggles; that his life was linked, umbilically, to every other Muslim in the *ummah*. If he felt like a victim, so must they. If he wanted to fight back, so did they. The *halaqah* taught him he had a place in this *jihad*. He could be more than just the graceless, chubby victim of the playground.

Some *Jihadi*. That night, the first punch floored him, and from then on he had curled up in a ball and prayed – yes, prayed – that they would stop. But he was now more than seven years past the days of his schoolboy *jihad*, and the night when all those adolescent daydreams came crashing down around him like so much broken glass.

17

They had a full house that night, the first night of Eid. Both sides of the family gathered in their little house on Harold Road. His father and uncles talking about their businesses in the living room. His cousins in the dining room and hallway, the boys talking football, the girls talking clothes. The women, his mum and aunties, in the kitchen, listening to Ahmed Rushdi on a portable stereo so old it had not one but *two* cassette decks, while in the dining room the table practically creaked beneath the weight of bowls filled with pastries and sweets.

It had always tickled Ibrahim and his sister. Aisha, watching his mother and their aunties compete with one another through the medium of food. Everyone brought what they thought of as their speciality; *Bhua* Yasmin with her *balushahi*, *Tayee* Samira with her *sohan papdi*, and their mother with her *laddu*, and of course they would all claim they'd simply rustled up 'a little something' the night before when days, and perhaps weeks had gone into their preparation.

Even before the sound of the helicopter and police sirens, that night felt different to any other Eid. There seemed to be a silent realisation, among everyone there, that this could be the last time the whole family, on either side, would come together in one house. The cousins were growing up and moving away; Rashida to Canada, Iqbal to Dubai. Marriages would inflate the family further, and Ibrahim's grandmother, his *dadiji*, joked that any future get-together would have to happen at the football stadium on Green Street.

As such, the mood in their house that night was celebratory but seasoned with something wistful. Or perhaps that was how Ibrahim remembered it with hindsight. Perhaps everyone had been having a wonderful night until then, and it was only what happened next that changed everything.

Hearing the noise and commotion from the street Ibrahim's father, Nazir, rose from his chair and padded out into the hall, almost tripping over the piles of shoes on his way to the front door. For a moment he stood there, his short, thin frame silhouetted against the flashing blue lights. The sound of the helicopter grew louder, the downdraft from its blades rustling through the trees lining the street.

'They're outside number fifty-eight,' his father said. 'They've got guns.'

Ibrahim was seventeen, and considered himself streetwise enough to be unimpressed by a few sirens and a helicopter, but with those words he felt a dropping sensation in his chest, as if his heart had fallen, followed by a wave of nausea.

A brief silence fell over the party, then the chattering began again, but more excitedly, and Ibrahim was almost carried to their front door by the sudden surge of houseguests.

'What is it?'

'What's happening?'

'What's going on?'

Elbowing her way past nieces and nephews, Ibrahim's mother joined them on the doorstep, muttering something in Urdu; always her first language when shocked or surprised. Then came Aisha, standing on tiptoes to peer over their father's shoulders and saying, 'Who is it? Mum? Dad? What is it? Who is it?' The aunts and uncles from Sparkhill, his mother's family, were laughing and saying how *this* was why they lived in Birmingham, you never had *this* sort of thing happen in Birmingham, but Ibrahim's parents were silent, expressionless.

Three police cars and two vans sat on the junction of Harold Road and Thorngrove Road, and there were uniformed officers with machine guns, real machine guns, not the stuff of movies or TV shows, but real and potent and made out of the blackest metal, and a cordon of blue and white plastic tape drew a rough semicircle around number fifty-eight.

The house where Jamal lived.

Front doors the length of the street were opening, people stepping out and staring slack-jawed into the flashing blue lights, and now there were officers coming from number fifty-eight, and they were holding someone by the arms; a shoeless young man, dressed in a crisp white shirt and designer jeans. Jamal.

Ibrahim waited for the awful moment when his friend would look at him, when that one glance, witnessed by his parents, by his whole family, would be enough to prove his guilt. He waited for it with his hands clenched into fists and his toes curled and his mouth dry and his heart beating faster than it ever had before, but that look never came. One of the officers put his hand on Jamal's head and pushed him down and forward and into one of the vans, and on the doorstep of number fifty-eight Jamal's mother was wailing, and his younger brothers were crying, and Jamal's father and uncles and cousins were on the doorstep, shouting at the police, but there was nothing they could do. The van doors slammed shut, and the sound of that slam echoed down the street, for a fraction of a second drowning out even the helicopter's drone and the chattering of their neighbours. 'Tonight, of all nights,' said one of his cousins. 'They've got no respect.'

'That was Jamal,' said Ibrahim's mother. 'Why have they taken Jamal?'

And now all eyes were on Ibrahim, because if any of them should know it was him. He and Jamal had been friends for over a year, since he'd joined the sixth-form college. They studied together, attended Friday prayers together.

'I don't know,' he said, his voice little louder than a whisper.

'Let's go back inside,' said his father. 'No point in standing around gawping at them all night.'

Nazir turned and with a sweeping gesture of his arms ushered everyone back into the house, closing the door behind him. The helicopter was flying away now, and they heard the police cars and vans heading toward Stopford Road. As the convoy passed their house, Ibrahim shuddered, half expecting them to stop outside, for armed officers to come crashing in through their windows, but they didn't.

Within minutes he received the first of that night's many text messages, and before reading it thought it might tell him what he already knew – that Jamal had been arrested. Instead, this message

– written in the urgent, garbled argot of textspeak – told him there'd been two more arrests, the first in Beckton, the second Upton Park, and he knew the names of those arrested: Ismail and Yusuf. Whatever moment of relief he felt when the police vans and cars drove past his house and didn't stop, came to an abrupt end.

The police were coming back. They would take Jamal and Ismail and Yusuf to the police station, to Paddington Green, lock them in cells, and come back for him. The blue and white tape would be torn away from the lampposts and trees holding it in place around number fifty-eight, and another cordon made around his parents' house. The police would beat their fists on the door and order them to 'Open up!' and his mother would start crying and yelling at him in a language he barely understood, and his father would look at him in horror and – worst of all – shame.

When he opened his eyes Ibrahim realised he wouldn't have to wait for the police to come back, for them to beat on their door and drag him away, as they had Jamal, for him to see that expression, because he was looking at it already.

'Ibrahim,' said his father. 'I think we need to talk.'

Ibrahim. He'd called him Ibrahim. Not Prakash. Not Sunshine.

Ibrahim nodded nervously and followed his father to the kitchen. After protests from his mother and the aunties, who saw the kitchen as their domain, they were alone.

'Do you know anything about this?' His father asked, his voice hushed. Ibrahim pictured his cousins pressed up against the door, listening in on their conversation.

Ibrahim shook his head. He hadn't had enough time to think of anything to say; some convincing excuse or lie, some way to sidestep any questions.

'Don't lie to me, Ibrahim. You and Jamal are best friends. You're at that *bloody* mosque every single day. We hardly ever see you.'

'Honest, Dad,' he said, unable to look his father in the eye. 'I don't know why he's been arrested.'

'You're lying.'

'No, Dad. Seriously. I'm not.'

'I can tell when you're lying, and you're lying now. Don't think I don't know what goes on in that place, the kind of bloody rubbish they fill your heads with. I've heard all about it. And when I go to Friday prayers now, there are no young people there. There are...'

'When was the last time *you* went to prayers?' Ibrahim snapped, the question erupting out of him, but the moment he said it he stepped back, half expecting his father to strike him across the face.

Instead, dazed by his son's insolence, Nazir asked, 'What's that supposed to mean?'

'You hardly ever *go* to prayers,' said Ibrahim, with greater confidence. 'So what do you mean, "When I go to prayers"?'

'I go when I *can*. And there are no young people there, because they're all in that mosque of yours, and we know what they're telling you.'

'What? What are they telling us, Dad? Go on. If you're the expert. Tell me.'

His father raised his hand, about to hit him, and there was something almost comical about it; such a short man, small-framed all his life, standing up to his taller son. He'd have to go on tiptoes or, funnier still, leap off the ground to reach his son now. Even so, they'd never come this close to blows, and so Ibrahim flinched, and he didn't laugh.

'You ungrateful little *bastard*,' his father said, through clenched teeth, and his emphasis on that last word stung Ibrahim more than any slap. 'Do you know how *hard* we've worked – me, your *mata*, your grandparents – just so you and Aisha could enjoy the life you have? Do you know how much they sacrificed? And your *Dada*. He served in the *British* Army. In the war. And now you and your friends, you sit there and you listen to that *shit*, and why? Why? So you can play at *Mujahideen* in your bedrooms. Oh yes. Big men. *Brave* men. Because that's what this is about, isn't it? That's why they took Jamal tonight, isn't it?'

Ibrahim's puffed up bravado withered, and he felt his spirit deflating by the second. They'd been prepared for these arguments by their mentors, in those post-prayer discussions. They'd been taught to cut off apostate families as they would gangrenous limbs, to face up to them when challenged, to offer *Da'wah*, the chance to submit themselves to the will of Allah, and if they refused to cast them out. They were told that when they turned away from their families, their brothers, their *real* brothers, their *ikhwan*, would be waiting for them and would look after them.

Where were all those arguments now, now that his father was peering up at him, scowling at him, his hand at his side but his fingers still splayed as if ready to strike? Where were the pious sermons he'd rehearsed so many times in his head? Where was the triumphant declaration of his *jihad*? Though he towered over his father, Ibrahim had never felt quite so small.

'Will this come back to us?' his father asked, after a caustic silence. 'Can we expect the police tonight? Tomorrow?'

He shook his head, hoping he was right. His father's expression of disapproval and shame was now refracted through Ibrahim's tears, and he had to swallow hard to stop himself from sobbing. 'I don't know,' he said.

'You don't know?' The question was asked quietly, his father more worried than angry. 'You don't *know*?'

Again, Ibrahim shook his head.

'Ibrahim. Tell me the truth. Is there *anything* here that could get you in trouble? Any books, anything on your computer, *anything* that would bring them here?'

'No, Dad,' he said, honestly. 'There's nothing.'

'And your friends? Will they give the police your name?'

'I don't know.'

For the first time since closing the kitchen door behind them, Nazir Siddique laughed. 'You don't know, you don't know. That's the trouble, Ibrahim. You think you have all the answers, you and your friends, but when I ask you any question you *don't know*. I thought you were meant to be bright. Well… *Chiragh taley undhera*. Let's just hope they won't give them your name, shall we? But if you're lying to me…'

'Dad. I'm not.'

'But if you *are*. Son. I don't know what I'll do. I have worked so *hard*. I run a business, and that *means* something. It actually *means* something. And now *this*. If they come for you, and they find *anything*. I don't know what I'll do.'

But the police didn't come for him; not the next day, or the day after that. Nothing was said to the rest of the family, not even his mother or sister, at least not while he was present, though his mother must have known. Instead, the subject was preserved in the silences and simmering looks between father and son.

Once they were charged, the faces of Jamal, Ismail and Yusuf were shown in newspapers and on television, and Ibrahim noticed that they used only mugshots, photographs that looked nothing like his friends. In these, they looked tired and sullen, every bit the crazed terrorists demanded by the story.

He was forbidden from going back to their mosque, from going anywhere near it. Instead, the following Friday, he was taken to his father's mosque, named after a Sufi saint, the mosque he'd gone to almost every Friday before meeting his 'new friends'. There, the older men looked at him askance, but nothing was said. Everyone knew, it seemed, that he was the unmentioned fourth man; that he'd escaped arrest either through slippery self-preservation or unimaginable good luck.

He wanted to write to the newspapers and news channels and tell them they'd got it all wrong, that they were blowing the story out of all proportion, but he knew it would achieve little more than his own arrest. Besides, a part of him still wanted to believe they'd been right, he and his friends, that they could have achieved something, that they could have made a statement and forced the world to sit up and take notice. He wanted to believe that, and whenever the story was mentioned in the papers thought he *could* believe it, but a horrible truth had begun to eat away at this conviction; a truth grown from just a single thing his father had said, the night Jamal and the others were arrested.

'So you can play at *Mujahideen* in your bedrooms.'

That one sentence stripped away all their talk of *jihad* and the fourteen hundred years of shared history that justified it, and revealed it for what it was: a game. When the case went to court, the newspapers' tone soon became mocking and snide. His friends were made to sound like pathetic daydreamers, schoolboys hatching plots and schemes doomed to failure. By the time of their sentencing, the judge seemed duty bound to describe those plots as 'sinister and threatening', as if both the jury and the audience at home might have forgotten the seriousness of it all. There were no bombs, no weapons of any kind, just books and websites and plenty of big talk, and the sentences reflected this. Had the police linked Ibrahim and his friends to the only thing they ever actually *did* – as opposed to all the things they talked of doing – it might have given a greater, darker weight to the story. As it was, not one of them was jailed for more than two years.

It was his mother's illness that finally drew a line under the matter. The diagnosis, and the tearful but restrained way in which the news was broken to Ibrahim and Aisha, became the narrative of their family; the focus shifting from wayward son to unwell mother. She downplayed it at first, relegating a malignant tumour to a minor inconvenience. When her doctors told her to rest, she worked twice as hard, as if her defiance could cure anything. On losing her hair, she simply took to wearing the kind of headscarf so many other women in the community already wore. It became easy for him, for all of them to underestimate the damage the illness was doing to her. If she refused to have her life shaped by it, dictated by it, why should they?

After the arrests and the trial and his wife's diagnosis, Nazir Siddique began attending Friday prayers every week, taking his son with him. In time it seemed that Ibrahim had been forgiven by most, if not all, of the other men there, and after one sermon he was taken to one side by the Pir; a grey-bearded old man who looked – at least, to Ibrahim's teenaged eyes – a hundred years old, and who even smelled ancient and exotic, like heavily spiced cigar smoke and old books.

'Better here, yes?' said the Pir, and Ibrahim nodded. 'Yes. Better here. Tell me, Ibrahim, have you read the works of Rumi?'

Ibrahim shook his head. 'I don't know who that is.'

A disappointed frown. 'Jalalludin Rumi,' said the Pir. 'A great mystic. He wrote, *'Men do not praise that which is not worthy, they only err in mistaking another for Him. Just as when moonlight falls on a wall, it seems they forget the moon and worship the wall.'* He wrote, *'Because of such idols, mankind is confused, and driven by vain desires they reap sorrow.'* Do you understand?'

He nodded again, though he wasn't sure he did.

'You have been worshipping the wall, Ibrahim. But that is over now, yes?'

'Yes.'

'Good. That is good. You should read Rumi. And Basri. And Attar. "The Conference of the Birds". *"All things are possible, and you may meet | Despair, forgiveness, certainty, deceit. | The Self ignores the secrets of the Way, | The mysteries no mortal speech can say."* Read them all. I have copies, but they are in Arabic, many of them, or Farsi. But find copies. Read them. Better than these other things you were reading. Your *Pita* tells me you are studying history.'

'Yes.'

'That is good. That is a good thing to study. Work hard at your studies.'

It would be another year before Ibrahim read Rumi, or Basri, or Attar. Despite his shamefaced nods and promises, a part of him still looked at men like the Pir as little better than *kuffar*.

Better than these other things you were reading?

They'd read the Qur'an. Was the old man saying these Sufis, these Sufi *poets*, were better than Allah? He knew what the sheikh, what the imam, would have to say about that. Disingenuous of him, really. He knew that wasn't what the Pir meant. The Pir wasn't talking about the Qur'an. He was talking about *Milestones* and *Knights Under The Prophet's Banner*. Those were the books he meant.

When, eventually, he read Rumi, what struck Ibrahim was how beautiful the poems were, how sensual and full of life. Poems written under caliphates, so much closer in history to the Prophet's life than his own, were filled with joy and pleasure; music, wine, sex, romantic love, and all infused with a spirituality so much more profound than a room full of teenagers shouting in Arabic, or a loudhailered *Adhan* echoing through the streets of East London.

But all that came so much later. First he had to do as the Pir ordered, and study, and so Ibrahim imposed upon himself a kind of curfew, or house arrest, and read his way through a precariously leaning tower of textbooks. He passed each exam, and when it came to choosing a university – and there was little chance of his not going – his parents were eager for him to leave London, as if the city still posed a threat to their son. They, or rather his father,

138

ruled out any of the cities in the north – Manchester, Bradford, Leeds – invariably making some remark about distance or the quality of the university, but Ibrahim knew his father simply wanted him far away from the influence of any '*Jihadi haram zada*'. That was how they chose Cardiff.

Ibrahim's mother spent the week before his departure keeping busy, making endless trips to supermarkets and wholesale shops on Green Street, coming back with tinned foods and bags of rice and chilli powder, piling them all up in cardboard boxes.

'I'm not having you live on Pot Noodles and toast like all the other students,' she said, as the box of provisions began to resemble rations prepared before an impending natural disaster or nuclear war.

His mother would tell the family how *well* she was feeling and how much *better* she was feeling, every opportunity she had, even when no one had asked her. Even so, she wasn't well enough to join them on the drive to Cardiff. Besides, as she was quick to point out, there was hardly any room in the car, what with the boxes full of books and food, the bags of clothes, and the duvet and pillows blotting out the rear window. She remained stoic when she hugged and kissed him on the cheek, and gave a cheerful wave as they drove away, but he saw the way she crumpled as he and his father neared the end of Harold Road, and saw his sister help her back in to the house, one arm around her shoulder.

There was little conversation between father and son in the two-hour journey between cities. The flyover at Chiswick launched them up and out of London, like a runway, and the radio filled the silence between them. They reached the halls of residence in Cardiff in the early afternoon, and it took three trips for them to carry all his things from the car park to his room. Already, music came from several open doors – loud, bombastic music, and the unmistakable scent of cannabis smoke – and Ibrahim saw his father's vague expression of disapproval, of apprehension, but it was too late for second thoughts.

It was only when they were in the car park, and he was back behind the wheel of a car that was now empty, that his father showed any kind of emotion at all, and his eyes grew bloodshot and rheumy with the promise of tears. He urged Ibrahim to 'take care', and on any other day, in any other circumstance, it might have been a throwaway sentiment, but on that afternoon, in a city one hundred and sixty miles from London, those two words were heavy with meaning.

The moment his father's car turned a corner and was gone Ibrahim felt a strange rush; part terror, part elation. For the first time in almost a year he felt he was free, that he'd finally escaped; from London, from his friends, from what he'd done. He walked back into the halls, through waves of music coming from each open door – indie, reggae, hip-hop – and he saw a girl leaving the room opposite his. In a single moment he took in everything about her – almond-shaped, green-blue eyes; pale skin; tightly curled black hair. Firm but generous breasts, clad in the thin, revealing fabric of a tight, grey t-shirt. Was he blushing?

'Hey, we're neighbours!' she said, and pointed at the name card slotted into a tiny frame next to her door. 'I'm Amanda.'

They shook hands.

Later, he'd replay their first meeting over and over, marvelling at the small events that brought them to the moment when they met; the student welfare officer making them neighbours, the timing of his arrival in Cardiff and Amanda leaving her room. Was it possible he gave their introduction more significance than it deserved? Were her pleasant smile and the lingering softness of her touch more than just a greeting? He'd wanted her from the moment he saw her, as if his father's farewell was his licence to want her, but it took months for him to muster the courage to so much as speak to her again, and before then he found himself wrenched out of this new life and drawn back to London.

That year, in the second week of November, his mother died. She'd been admitted to the hospital three days earlier, but, when telling him this, his father softened the news, saying it was 'just for tests'. There was no talk of death, or goodbyes. Ibrahim had spoken to her the Friday before, and as usual she'd 'never felt better', was 'right as rain'.

He travelled back to London by train, and as they rolled in to Paddington he felt the overwhelming density of the city crowd in on him. The blocks of flats grew bigger, blotting out more and

140

more sky; the landscape became one of rail yards and sleeper carriages, flyovers and office blocks. Since his father's call the night before, he hadn't cried. A part of him wanted to, and raged against what he saw as his inhumanity. What kind of son doesn't cry at the news of his mother's death? Even when back on familiar turf – the Bakerloo Line to Embankment; the District Line to Upton Park – he felt nothing. It was only as he entered the house on Harold Road and saw the flowers and the cards crowded together on their dining-room table that the tears came, but there was little comfort from his family. His sister was paralysed by grief, and sat pale and silent in the living room. His father too could barely speak, and when he walked from room to room it was with a shuffling, old man's gait. Worst of all was the absence of his mother, the emptiness of the house without her. The staircase and hallways seemed longer, the shadows darker. Though there were Tupperware boxes filled with food – donations from neighbours – stacked up in the kitchen, there was no longer the smell of cooking or the sound of her singing tunelessly along with the radio.

'Ko Ko Koreena… Ko Ko Koreena…'

As a boy her singing had embarrassed him, especially when school friends were there, but in a dark and empty house he'd have given anything to hear it again. Instead, the house was monstrously quiet; the only sound the hourly chiming of the clock in their hallway. His mother had been the centre of gravity in that house, and without her they were weightless and drifting.

The funeral happened, and though he had little time to prepare for it, the day passed quickly enough. He hoped the prayers, the *Janāzah Salāh,* might help him focus on the infinite, on everything beyond the mortal, and that these thoughts might provide some sort of comfort, but they didn't. He mouthed the words of the *niyyah* and *takbeers* silently, but he could have said anything, mouthed any words. The foreignness of those words was suddenly and painfully acute to him; his attempt to draw meaning from them so desperately futile.

On leaving the mosque they followed the hearse out to a cemetery in Ilford, and there, at the graveside, his father recited *Surah Ikhlass* and *Surah Ya-Seen,* speaking softly and without hesitation. Ibrahim had spent so long thinking his father was not a true Muslim, that his was a family of apostates. To witness this act of devotion, his father's perfect recitation, in flawless Arabic, left him speechless and more heartbroken than anything else that day.

As they drove back to East London the distance between the cemetery and his father's house – and already he thought of it as his *father's* house – felt greater than before, as if they'd abandoned his mother, casting her out beyond the edges of the city. The distance between his mother and him was drawn out now in miles and minutes, her body and his memory of her becoming ever more remote. He wondered if he would ever go back to the cemetery and, if he did, whether he would know through instinct alone where she was buried.

There followed two weeks of wandering aimlessly from one room to the next. Conversations with family. Visits from neighbours. More Tupperware and more food. Friday prayers with his father. People telling him what a good, brave woman his mother was. Imran, at the corner shop, asking after his family, and always in Punjabi:

'Kee tuhadaa parvaar theek hai?'

Ibrahim replying in English.

After two weeks of this he returned to Cardiff. Some of his friends knew what had happened, offered their sympathies, but he never chose to talk about it. There were too many words, so he said nothing. He chose to stay there, in Cardiff, during the holidays, and found himself one of only two students still in halls when Christmas Day arrived. The other was Amanda. He told his father and sister there were other things keeping him from coming home to them – his studies, and the fortnight of work he had yet to catch up on – but by the New Year he'd found another reason to stay, to never want to leave.

He never found out why Amanda almost spent that Christmas alone, and sensing it was not through choice he never asked. Later, he suspected there was a mutual sadness they had sensed in one another, that this was what drew them together, and he wondered then if anything built on a foundation of sadness and loss can ever last.

18

From the kitchen, the hard knock of a mug touching down on a work surface, the boiling of a kettle, the percussive chime of a teaspoon against the inside of a mug. And music; there was music, too. Something classical. A sad clarinet, the kind of frantically insistent piano that reminded him of silent movies and damsels in distress, then a violin, intertwined with the clarinet, bringing things to a melancholic close.

'Piece for Clarinet, Viola and Piano by Bruch, composed in 1913,' said the radio.

So it was a viola then, and not a violin, but Ibrahim had never been an expert. He had grown up with the music his parents listened to, songs from films he'd never seen, before graduating to bhangra and hip-hop. At one point, as a teenager, he stopped listening to music altogether. Musical instruments were, as the *Hadith* says, the 'trappings of ignorance'. But he had missed music the whole time. A car would pass him in the street, bass and drums throbbing from its oversized speakers, and he'd feel something, an envy or longing, that he'd try – and fail – to ignore.

Ibrahim eased himself off the sofa, legs first, the blanket wrapped around his midriff. It took an effort to stand, and as he did the bruises on his legs and torso rang like bells.

'How you feeling?'

Natalie was in the doorway to her kitchen, holding a mug of tea in both hands; already dressed and looking as if she'd been awake for some time.

'What time is it?' he asked.

'Seven thirty. I'm a bit of an early bird, sorry. Did I wake you?'

He shook his head. 'I think I was dreaming about something.'

'Do you want a coffee? Or tea?'

'Coffee, please.'

Natalie went back to the kitchen and the music. Once he had dressed, Ibrahim stretched his limbs and rolled his head, hearing and feeling every click as his body righted itself after a night spent scrunched into a foetal ball. He crossed the room and stood in the kitchen doorway, holding to one side a curtain of plastic beads very much like one his *Bhua* Yasmin and *Phupher* Daljit had in their house in Sparkhill.

'You like classical music?' he asked, trying to sound neither sarcastic nor condescending.

'Yes,' said Natalie, as if readying herself for an insult. 'You don't?'

'Dunno. Never really listened to much of it, to be honest.'

'Well, it's this or Radio 4. I don't do TV in the mornings. The people they have on breakfast TV… Christ. I despair. And just the news generally. I don't need to wake up to that shit. Who needs to hear about politics and bloody war when you've got a day in work to look forward to?'

'Are you working today?'

'No. Not today. Thank *God*. I'm always up this early. I'm not really a "lie in" person.' She looked at the radio. 'I can change the station. If you'd like.'

'No,' said Ibrahim. 'It's okay. It's nice.'

She was looking at him in that way again, scrutinising him, and again he couldn't tell if it was distrust or diagnosis.

'We really should get you to a hospital,' she said. 'Get you checked out.'

His dismissed this with a huff and a wave of his hand. 'No hospitals. Seriously. I've spent enough time in hospitals.'

'The police, then. You were *attacked*.'

'No hospitals, no police. Besides, it was dark. I doubt I'd recognise them if they walked in here right now.'

'But there might be CCTV, or…'

'No police.'

'Christ, you really are a stubborn sod, aren't you?'

He laughed, this time bracing himself for the pain. 'Yeah, I've been told that before.'

'I'm not surprised. Anyway. I'm making breakfast. You hungry?'

He nodded.

'Beans on toast?'

'Thank you.'

Natalie's kitchen was a jumble of colours and furniture. The walls were a custardy shade of yellow, while the small table and chairs, tucked behind her dark blue fridge, were a washed-out shade of green. Ibrahim pulled out one of the chairs, its feet scraping noisily against the tiled floor, and sat. As Natalie made breakfast he rested his head in his hands, the palms covering his eyes.

Reenie was out there somewhere. She was out there, alone, and he had left her to it. Left her to climb into a van driven by some stranger who only promised to take her as far as Bristol. Unless a second stranger had picked her up and driven her the rest of the way, she was still out there.

He pushed his hands into his eyes, the bruised and swollen tissue around his left eye throbbing with the pressure, and he reminded himself of the reason for his journey. He had to get to London. Anything could have happened since he left Cardiff, and maybe more letters from his sister had arrived in his absence, letters begging him to see sense and get on a bus or a train, because what kind of stubborn idiot would try and walk that distance? And Reenie was still out there, and his sister was still waiting for him, and London wasn't far away, not by train, but he couldn't catch the train, and these thoughts piled up, each crashing into the next, forming one big, tangled mess.

'How far away is Bristol?' he asked, taking his hands away from his face and looking up at Natalie.

'Bristol? I don't know. Not far. Half an hour, maybe?'

'By car?'

'Yeah. By car. What's in Bristol?'

'A friend.'

Four slices of toast sprang from the toaster with a creaky, metallic cough, and Natalie dropped them onto a pair of mismatched plates – pastel polka dots and the wedding of Prince Charles and Diana Spencer – and covered them with baked beans.

'Here you go,' she said, putting the polka dot plate in front of him. 'So... do you want to go to Bristol?'

'I don't know,' said Ibrahim. 'I might have to.'

She sat facing him, and shovelled a forkful of beans and soggy toast into her mouth.

'You know,' she said, a bolus of food tucked in one cheek. 'I could drive you.'

'No,' he said. 'It's no use. Cars.'

'Oh yes. You're an automobilophobe, or whatever the word is. You should try Valium. That might help. Then you could maybe think about doing the sane thing and catching the bloody train.'

'Tried that,' said Ibrahim. 'Years ago.'

'And did it work?'

'Not much. Took the edge off, but not completely. I didn't get the, you know, panic attacks, but in *here*,' he tapped his forehead. 'In here it was still the same.'

'Well, I could drive you as far as Bristol,' said Natalie. 'And I've got Valium here. Don't ask me why, but I have.'

'What… Are you suggesting I should…'

'Pop a load of Valium and chill out on the back seat of my car while I do you a bloody great big favour? Yes. Christ. I could be struck off for doing this.'

'Struck off?'

'Yes. Struck off.'

'So why are you…'

'Because I must be mad. And because sometimes the *proper* thing to do and the *right* thing to do aren't the same thing. And maybe because I'm a bleeding heart liberal who doesn't want you thinking everyone in Gloucester is a racist thug. I don't know. You tell me.'

He could do it. Maybe not London; London was too far. No amount of pills would get him to London. But Bristol. He could get to Bristol. And then what? She, Reenie, could be anywhere. Perhaps that guy dropped her off and she stayed where she was. Perhaps she moved on, took the wrong road, got herself lost. She could be anywhere.

He thought back to Reenie's expression when he had lied to her, telling her he would leave her behind if she slowed him down. She hadn't seemed so feisty then. It was the first and only time she had seemed dependent on another human being.

Ibrahim had spent so long considering himself apart from the world, distant from other people, that to think someone might need him was unsettling, irritating, but beyond that there was a comfort in it.

'Okay,' he said. 'You can take me to Bristol.'

'Right,' said Natalie. 'And you're sure about that? You'll be okay?'

He shrugged, sure of nothing.

'Okay,' said Natalie. 'Well, I'll go and get the Valium. We can be out of here in ten, if that suits you.'

Ibrahim nodded and asked if he could use her phone, and Natalie took him through to the hallway where, at the foot of the stairs an orange Bakelite phone sat on a small wooden table.

'Bit old fashioned, I know,' she said. 'Takes ages to dial anything these days.'

With Natalie upstairs, Ibrahim sat on the bottom step, the telephone resting in his lap. It took an age to dial his sister's number – waiting for the dial to grind its way back from all eleven digits – but then he heard the dialling tone, and he waited.

'Hello?' She sounded sleepy. It was still early.

'Aish?'

A long silence, nothing but burbling dead air between them, until his sister spoke again.

'Ib? Is that you?'

'Yeah, it's me.'

'Fucking hell. I mean… *Fucking hell*. Ib. Where are you?'

'I'm in Gloucester.'

'What are you doing in Gloucester?'

'I'm coming to London.'

'Via fucking Gloucester?'

'Yeah.'

'How? I mean… Gloucester? Are you getting the train or something? Has it been… I wrote to you a week ago. It's Friday.'

'I know, Aish. Listen. I *am* coming. It's just. It's taking me a while. But I *am* coming.'

'Cardiff's two hours away, Ib. What the fuck are you doing?'

'Please, Aish. Just listen to me. I'm coming, okay?'

A sigh and the line grew quiet as she placed her hand over the mouthpiece, but swore loud enough for him to hear.

Taking her hand away again, she said, 'Ib. I can't do this on my own. He's in there on his own, and I'm doing this on my own, and you're not here.'

'How is he?'

'How do you think? He's ill. Really ill. And he tries asking where you are, but what can I tell him?'

'Tell him I'm coming, Aish. Tell him I'll be there soon.'

'Really? And how soon is that? Next week? Next month?'

'I'll be there soon.'

'Please, Ib. Just hurry, okay?'

'Okay.'

He said goodbye to her, and his sister muttered something too fast and angry for him to understand before hanging up. Ibrahim placed the phone back on its table just as Natalie came down the stairs, a blister pack of tablets in her hand. It wasn't clear whether she had been waiting at the top, listening to the call, and if she had what she could have gleaned from it.

'Shall we?' she said.

Ten minutes later they were in her car, but Natalie took her time – fiddling with the rear-view mirror and her seatbelt, allowing him time to settle, to get used to it. He sat up front with her, back straight and hands cupping his knees to stop them from fidgeting. When she turned the key and the engine stirred into life he felt an icy sweat break out on his shoulders and he held his breath.

'Relax,' said Natalie. 'I won't drive fast, I promise.'

She turned on the radio and the car was filled with the latter half of a piece that had been playing in the kitchen, in the final moments before they left her house.

'What is this?' asked Ibrahim.

'This? Vaughan Williams. The 'Tallis Fantasia'. Why? Do you like it?'

'I don't know. I think so.'

He closed his eyes and focused on the music, allowing it to drown out the sounds of the car. What began so understatedly, something quiet and serene, the kind of music he had heard in countless TV adverts, built up, minute by minute, as if in layers, into something so incredibly rich it overwhelmed him. The strings breathed, loud then quiet, and swept into the air. With his eyes shut he saw wintry, leaf-bearing spirals, vast clouds of migrating starlings, like black smoke, the crashing silver foam of impossible waterfalls, great cobalt glaciers stretching out to the horizon, until the music reached a climax of almost unbearable poignancy; a moment of such emotion that it stole his breath, and this moment was sustained, so that each time he thought it might end it came back, like short, ecstatic gasps, or shallow waves at low tide, and these waves ebbed and flowed, and he felt the weight of every season that had passed, and as the climax began to fade and subside Ibrahim breathed out, and this breath was given voice by a sudden chord that came from nowhere, acting almost as an exclamation point before giving way to strings as delicate as cobwebs.

There was a soul to this music, something inside it, something between the notes, greater than the man who wrote them down or the musicians playing them. This wasn't music; this was something else, like a voice communicating something, telling him something that couldn't be said in words. No, not telling him something; quite the opposite. This music had found something in him, something he could never describe, and translated it into the only medium that made sense. Anyone could hear this, listen to this, and know what it meant to be him, what it had always meant to be him.

'Don't look now,' said Natalie. 'But you're in a moving car.'

He opened his eyes and stared out through the windscreen at the road ahead, and yes, she was right; he was in a moving car. Ibrahim took another deep breath and held it. He stretched out his arms and braced himself against the dashboard, his fingers digging a little into its soft, foamy plastic.

'You okay?' asked Natalie.

'I think so,' he said, honestly. Perhaps it was the Valium. Perhaps all this was the Valium; from the slight pleasure of feeling the dashboard submit to his touch to the waves of emotion the music stirred in him. Perhaps without the Valium he'd feel none of this.

'If you want me to stop and turn around at any point, just say.'

Hadn't Amanda said something like that, once? Towards the end. He had, by that point, told her about his panic attacks, and they were driving somewhere, some party, and she had used those very words. They were driving and she told him if he wanted her to stop and turn the car around she would, and minutes later he did just that and realised she was only being nice, that she'd had no intention of turning the car around, not when they'd come this far, and it ended in an argument, because by this point he'd scorched away all her patience and sympathy with his silences and his inattention and, yes, his lack of libido, and in that argument he reminded her again that she hadn't been there, in the car, that she couldn't understand, but as usual he felt a fraud, because for him the most terrifying thing of all was that he remembered nothing of the crash.

He remembered everything before it, with a clarity that was almost disturbingly banal. There was a house party in Cathays, and the hosts borrowed lighting gels so that each room was lit a different colour – the kitchen a sub-aquatic blue, the hallway and stairs a coniferous green, the lounge a promiscuous shade of red – and the furniture in this last room had been pushed up against the walls, and people were dancing to Northern Soul.

They ran out of ice. That was it. The clock hadn't yet turned ten, and they had run out of ice. The big Tesco on Western Avenue would still be open, but it was miles away. They needed someone sober, who could drive, and that was when Aleem stepped in and volunteered his services; Aleem Saïd, with his practically-new VW Golf.

A rich kid from what he called West London but what everyone else called Middlesex, Aleem was the nearest thing Ibrahim had to a best friend in those days. More swaggeringly confident than Ibrahim, and always dressed more like a *gora*, with his rock band tour t-shirts, skater jeans, and his wallet on a chain. The first time he ever visited Ibrahim in halls, he took one look at the volumes of Sufi poetry on his bookshelf and laughed, saying, 'From one extreme to the other'. It was one of the only conversations they ever had about religion, their friendship based instead upon a mutual love of hip-hop – Aleem introducing Ibrahim to all the tracks and albums he'd missed these last two years – and afternoons spent playing *Grand Theft Auto*.

With Aleem driving, it was inevitable Caitlin Corby would tag along; the pair of them had been caught in a maddening routine of flirtation and mutual rejection practically since Freshers' Week. Rhys ap Hywel, meanwhile, was of a type found in every university; the small town boy from somewhere rural, remote – in Rhys's case, Anglesey – who, let loose in the city, had smoked, downed and snorted every drug available, usually on the same night. To Rhys the very idea of 'going shopping' this late was hilarious, and he was quick to volunteer.

Then there was Ibrahim. He'd spent much of the night out in the garden, smoking weed – there were no *Surahs* or *Hadiths* against cannabis, so it had become his only real vice – but this in turn made him paranoid, and it was this paranoia that took him from the party to the back seat of Aleem Saïd's car.

Stupid, really. Amanda was talking to an exchange student from Baltimore. Tall black kid. One of those black American names, like Tyrone or Tyrese. They were both studying English and Philosophy. She'd introduced them, Ibrahim and Tyrone-or-Tyrese-or-Whatever, but Ibrahim slipped away from them and stood out in the garden with the other smokers, and looked in through the kitchen window at Amanda and Tyrone-Tyrese-Whatever, and simmered as he analysed each smile, each blink, each reciprocal laugh.

Out in the garden, Aleem Saïd said, 'Me and Caitlin are going to Tesco. Anyone else want to come?'

Caitlin – big-boned Caitlin with the streak of purple in her hair and her raggedy dress and Dr Martin boots – looked devastated. Why did anyone else have to join them?

'Fuck it,' said Rhys ap Hywel. 'I'll come. Might be a laugh.'

'Yeah, I'll come,' said Ibrahim, waiting for Amanda to look at him, as if she was psychic and knew he was about to leave, but she didn't.

The journey to the supermarket took them past crowds all dressed up for a Friday night, staggering in and out of pubs and clubs through a cacophony of police sirens and dance music. The whole world was a carnival that night. Spring was giving way to summer, and even at this hour there were still the last watery traces of sunlight in the west.

'We should do this more often,' said Rhys ap Hywel.

'Do what?' asked Caitlin Corby.

'Go out. I don't mean clubs or anything. I mean just go *out*. Go for night drives. I mean, think about it, while we've been getting stoned and, you know, dancing and stuff, there were people doing their shopping. How mad is that?'

Shopping for ice cubes and beer became a field trip that night, the four of them stumbling and laughing helplessly down each aisle in the supermarket's harsh fluorescent light. They created elaborate, often cruel backstories for the other customers – loners and serial killers, most of them – and took detours through the aisles filled with toys for no other reason than to play with things they had no intention of buying. Away from the party, away from that dark mood, Ibrahim laughed until tears streamed from his eyes and he could hardly breathe.

Back in the car Ibrahim and Rhys did exactly as they'd done when they first left the party; they both tried their seatbelts and found the buckle ends missing, tucked beneath the seats.

'What's the point of having seatbelts,' said Rhys, 'if there's nowhere to put them?'

For some reason that line, or perhaps the way it was said – in Rhys's throaty, sing-song accent – made Ibrahim, Caitlin and Aleem erupt into laughter once more, and they were still laughing as they drove out of the car park and back onto Western Avenue.

'Hey,' said Rhys, leaning between the front seats. 'Fuck the party. Let's go to Barry Island.'

'What?' said Aleem.

'We've got beer,' said Rhys. 'We've got weed. I've got a fuckload of pills. Why don't we go to the beach instead?'

Aleem smiled, and Caitlin looked at him, smiling but with her eyes communicating something else; hesitation or concern that he might go along with Rhys's idea. Ibrahim was thinking about Amanda, and how she was still at the party, and how maybe she was still talking to Tyrone or Tyrese or whatever his name was.

Then there was light.

That was the last thing he remembered. Later he learned how another driver on the road that night, a seventeen year old named

Jason Bevan, had begun drinking earlier that afternoon. The car was Jason's – a Citroen Saxo he'd customised himself – and after draining several cans of lager and the best part of a bottle of vodka, Jason and two friends took to the roads. Nobody would ever know how or why he came to be on that side of the avenue – whether it was somebody's idea of a joke or dare, or a drunken lapse in judgement – but when he collided with Aleem Saïd's car Jason Bevan was driving at sixty miles an hour.

It was thought Aleem hadn't expected an oncoming car on his side of the road; the four lanes of the avenue were separated by a metal barrier. Others posited that he and Jason were engaged in a foolhardy, disastrous game of 'chicken'. Certainly, Aleem's family – prosperous, and therefore deemed newsworthy – weren't spared the publishing of their dead son's toxicity report, the mere mention of cannabis hinting at something reckless on his part.

When eventually the police interviewed Ibrahim he could only tell them he remembered nothing, and it was the truth. The details of the crash he learned second hand, as if it was something he hadn't experienced personally.

Rhys was flung through the windshield, and died of head injuries.

Aleem and Caitlin were crushed to death in the front of the car, which buckled like a tin can.

In the Saxo, Jason Bevan and his two friends were killed instantly, and again bodies were flung through the windshield, so that in Ibrahim's mind the moment of collision became a violent exchange, the two cars merging and swapping passengers in one bloody instant. Robbed of any memory of it, he couldn't help but imagine the crash played out in balletic slow motion; shattered glass filling the air around their tumbling, weightless bodies in a blizzard of gemstones. In these mental re-enactments the event became almost beautiful, but the players remained faceless. He couldn't bear to put the faces of his friends on those flailing bodies, and so their features were lost in a shadowy blur. And as for him, he wasn't there at all.

Acknowledging his presence in the car as it crashed meant facing up to the damage done, to the impossible way in which his body was tested and broken within the mangled wreck. The crash had done its best to change the shape of his body, twisting his leg into a dozen fractures, staving in one side of his face, shattering so many other bones. In the moment of the crash he stopped being the functioning, corporeal form that carried his thoughts around each day, and became something malleable, to be moulded cruelly by the car's imploding frame. More than this, the crash created an abyss, splitting his life in two, into everything before and after it. Though he'd forgotten the event itself, he would carry on feeling the insane forces of the crash on an almost physical level, as if he was forever lurching forward, as if his whole world was now imploding and bending him out of shape.

He felt this more than ever when sitting in a car, a bus, or a train, but now Natalie was driving, and there was music, a different piece, and the soft fuzzy glow of the Valium, and his fingers still digging into the dashboard's spongy plastic, and country lanes, and an unblemished blue sky, and he thought about Aleem's humouring smile, and Caitlin's look of apprehension, and Rhys's gormless, stoned grin, and the sudden white light that ended it all.

'You okay?' asked Natalie.

Ibrahim closed his eyes and nodded.

'You're looking a little pale. Do you want me to pull over?'

'No. No. I'm fine.'

Because he had to get through this. He was back at the abyss, standing on the edges of the great black gulf, and if he could hold his breath and bear it he might reach the other side through force of will alone. And he thought about Aleem's smile, a smile that said 'Yeah, sure,' but didn't mean it, and Caitlin's look of apprehension because driving to Barry Island was *exactly* the kind of thing Aleem might do on a whim, and Rhys's gormless grin because he knew this too, and the white light on the other side of the windshield that meant nothing at the time because there really shouldn't be anything oncoming that side of the avenue, and he tried to remember what happened next but there was nothing.

Ibrahim screwed his eyes shut and shook his head and dug his fingertips a little deeper into the dashboard, and when he opened his eyes again he saw the same country lane and the same boundless blue sky, only now he was calm and the world was coming into focus. He took his hands away from the dashboard, his fingertips leaving behind two dimpled arches, and he watched these indentations vanish slowly until there was no trace of them at all.

19

Mrs Ostroff could make dishes from next to nothing, whole meals cobbled together from the contents of a larder kept half empty by the ration book. Reenie's foster mother was a miracle worker that way and Mr Ostroff would joke that his wife could stretch a penny into copper wire.

Nothing went to waste. Chicken soup with lokshen or kneidlach; kreplach and varnitshkes. A piping-hot English roast dinner. Sumptuous toffee puddings, the toffee made by boiling a can of condensed milk on the stove. Moist and delicate Victoria sponges. The best, most delicious, most mouth-watering home-made chips Reenie had ever eaten, showered and drenched with salt and vinegar. Mrs Ostroff made them all with so very little.

Reenie would have given anything for a meal like that now. Her mouth watered and her stomach issued burbles of complaint. If she had thought she could sustain herself on birdseed, she would have helped herself to Solomon's rations without a shred of guilt.

Looking at him, through the gilt bars of his cage, she wondered how the world must look through his eyes. When she fed him she liked to think he recognised her, but there was no way to prove it. She was the only person Solomon ever saw. If he seemed to perk up at feeding time, flapping from the floor of his cage to his perch, or scuttling along the bars, clinging on with his tiny grey feet and his beak, it might have nothing to do with her. Any other person might get the same response.

Solomon wasn't her first cockatiel, nor was he the first to be called Solomon. In all, she had owned three such birds, all with that name. At the house in Penylan the different Solomons were often let out of their cages – in fact, the same cage, now practically an antique – and allowed to fly around the sitting room or Jonathan's study. If Reenie regretted one thing about bringing the present Solomon on this journey, it was that he had to stay in that cage, viewing with envy or longing the trees and fields through its bars.

The first Solomon was a wedding gift from husband to wife, back in the days when people kept things simple; none of this getting married abroad and weddings costing tens of thousands. The newlywed Mr and Mrs Glickman were affluent enough, but their wedding was modest. Jonathan had little in the way of close family – no brothers and sisters, his parents had died young – and Reenie hadn't seen her father in over ten years. What's more, there was still a faint whiff of scandal around them. Cardiff's Jewish community was sizeable, but closely knit, and some disapproved of Dr Glickman settling down with a woman they still thought of as a waif, and one of rumoured ill repute at that.

The way in which they met hadn't helped. Though never Jonathan's patient, Reenie was being treated at Cardiff's Royal Infirmary, the hospital where he worked. A cold and unforgiving winter and the damp conditions of a Tiger Bay boarding house had given her an agonising bout of pneumonia – not her first, but certainly her most severe – and even then it took three days for her landlady to call a doctor.

Through the haze of her fever Reenie saw the doctor's expression as he entered her small, dank bedroom, and realised for the first time the utter squalor of it. She'd grown accustomed to it in the ten years since East London, these rancid bedsits, and had slept in places far worse, but the doctor took one look at the room – the mildew-shadowed corners and woodworm-riddled skirting boards – with such disgust that she now saw the room through his eyes and to her fever was added shame and regret.

She spent her first day in hospital in a daze. Doctors and nurses came and went, but she was only vaguely aware of them. She was in a room with seven other women, and across the corridor from them was a children's ward. It was a week before Christmas, the corridors decorated with garish tinsel and cardboard stars patchy with glitter, and on the third day the children in the neighbouring ward were more boisterous than usual. They were expecting a visit from Father Christmas and, despite their illnesses and ailments, shrieked and hollered for much of the morning.

In the early afternoon a doctor and nurse came into Reenie's ward, closing the door behind them. The doctor was young, no older than thirty, but stout, almost burly; pale-skinned with dark hair in tight curls and his eyes a deep blue, almost indigo. With the door closed he turned to the nurse and smiled, and there was something about the smile, something conspiratorial and mischievous, that Reenie found appealing. She made a show of pretending to read a newspaper, all the while listening to their conversation.

'So, how can I help you?'

'Well,' said the nurse, bashfully. 'You know how we were expecting a certain visitor this afternoon...'

The doctor laughed. 'It's okay, Nurse Gait. I think we can say his name in here. The ladies are a little old to still believe in Father Christmas, don't you think?'

'Right. Yes. Well, the thing is... our Father Christmas is stuck.'

The doctor doubled over, letting out a long, helpless wheeze, and Reenie thought for a moment he was having some sort of seizure. Only when he was upright again, face red, his whole body shaking, did it become clear he was laughing.

'Don't tell me,' he roared. 'Up the chimney?'

The nurse shook her head, smirking. 'Very funny, doctor,' she said. 'But no. He's in Merthyr. His car's broken down. He just rang us from the garage.'

Thumbing the tears from his eyes, the doctor stopped laughing and frowned. 'Right. And?'

'Well. Sorry. This is embarrassing. We were just wondering... we were... What we were wondering. We were trying to think of a replacement. You see, there's a Father Christmas costume in one of the stock cupboards up on B12...'

'Why is there a Father Christmas costume in the stock cupboard on B12?'

'It's from last year, I think. It has the beard and everything. So, we were wondering...'

'If I'd try it on for size?'

An awkward pause. The nurse closed her eyes and nodded, expecting the worst.

'Well,' said Dr Glickman. 'You do realise that as a Jew I don't celebrate Christmas, and that to dress as Father Christmas would, therefore, be highly offensive to me, on a very deep and personal level…'

'Oh, I'm sorry,' said the nurse. 'I am so, so sorry. I didn't mean… we just…'

Dr Glickman laughed. 'I'm joking! I'm joking! If it fits,' he patted his belly, 'I'd be more than happy to play Father Christmas. A Jewish Father Christmas. First time for everything, I suppose.'

It was then he saw Reenie watching them, and he smiled at her, a smile that made her blush, and Reenie looked down at the open newspaper in her lap. Later, many months later, Jonathan told her he'd asked the nurse for Reenie's name the moment they left the ward.

'I knew you needed something,' he said. 'A helping hand. A chance. Don't ask me how. I just knew.'

Within weeks of the New Year he had found her a job, working in the offices of the solicitors, Leo Abse & Cohen. Nothing fancy – tea and filing, mostly – but it was a job and money at the end of each week, and soon enough she was sharing a flat with two other women on Cathedral Road. Much posher than her old digs down on Loudoun Square. A million miles away from all that. And it was there Jonathan first paid her a visit, a proper visit, bringing with him a bunch of flowers and the offer of dinner.

So that was it. Oh, he was a crafty one; she had to give him that. Some men would have tried their luck the minute she was back on her feet. Taken her to the pictures and tried getting frisky. But this, this took determination and patience. Finding her a job. Finding her a flat. Making himself seem all charitable and respectable. But no different to those crafty buggers who try groping you in the back row before the Pathé newsreel is over.

'What's the worst that could happen?' asked her flatmate, Cynthia.

'Lots of things,' said Reenie.

'Worst thing that could happen,' said Cynthia, 'is you'll have nothing to talk about. And if that's the case, you'll have still had a free dinner. And I bet he'll take you somewhere posh, and all, if he's a doctor.'

'No such thing as a free dinner,' said Reenie, but ultimately she gave in, and agreed to dinner. Not a *date*. Just dinner.

That meal, at a Chinese restaurant, was a disaster. She was on edge, he was coy. Reenie had never before eaten Chinese food, and she fumbled with her chopsticks before asking, bluntly, for a knife and fork, and spent an age staring at the beansprouts in disgust.

'They look like worms.'

Even so, she agreed to a second date. After all, she was attracted to him, or to the idea of him. He was so unlike the lovers she'd had in London and Cardiff, all of them so pale-skinned and weasel thin; xylophone ribcages and artless tattoos. Everything about them colourless and malnourished from head to toe. Jonathan was everything they weren't. He was well-fed and fleshy in a way that made her feel safe, protected in his company. He had a ruddy complexion and eyes that weren't bloodshot, and a smile that promised a cheeky sense of humour, if he could only defeat his shyness. And yes, she was in some way attracted to his Jewishness. Admitting that to herself was embarrassing, like admitting she was attracted to his hairstyle, or his choice of tie, but there it was. He wore his Jewishness with ease, without anxiety, without having to prove or defend a thing.

For their second date – and this time she referred to it as a *date* – he took her to the Capitol Cinema, where they watched *My Fair Lady*, and where he *didn't* grope her. Later they ate supper at an Italian restaurant on Churchill Way, and he was much less awkward, and she was less reserved. There were few lulls in their conversation – she spoke at an almost frantic pace, filling every pause with a joke – and he laughed until his face grew redder and there were tear tracks running down his cheeks.

'I think,' he said, dabbing at his eyes with a napkin, and still laughing, 'you are the funniest person I have ever met.'

Reenie raised an eyebrow. 'Funny ha-ha or funny peculiar?'

He hesitated. 'Both,' he said, and when Reenie scowled at him, 'Funny ha-ha! Funny ha-ha!' He looked serious now, still flushed, but his expression more pensive. 'I wonder where you find it.'

'What do you mean?'

'Your sense of humour. I've known people go through less, far less, and lose their smile altogether. But you? How do you do it?'

'Well,' she said. 'If I didn't laugh I'd cry.'

He nodded sympathetically, his eyes downcast. 'Yes. But you know it's okay sometimes, not to smile? You do know that, don't you?'

'What? Are you saying you don't like my smile?'

'No, no. God, no. No. I *love* your smile…' Another pause, as if that one short word was a china plate dropped onto a stone floor. He closed his eyes, choosing his next words carefully. 'What I mean to say is, if you're worried that the truth of whatever's happened to you will frighten me off, it won't.'

She nodded, and in that moment felt something lifted, or taken out of her, as if she'd coughed out a lungful of something toxic, and on breathing in again inhaled nothing but fresh air. 'Thank you,' she said, and she felt his hand on hers, his grip gentle but firm. As if he would never let go.

By the end of the night they'd emptied two bottles of red wine, and the waiter brought complimentary glasses of some aniseed liquor, which he set alight with a dramatic flourish. It was a mild spring evening, and though he lived on the other side of the city Jonathan walked her home, the pair of them staggering tipsily the whole way. If anything, Jonathan was more inebriated than her.

'You really know how to drink,' he hiccupped, half alarmed, half impressed.

If he expected anything more that evening he didn't show or demand it, but they kissed before saying goodnight, and from her living room window Reenie watched him walk away with an unmistakable swagger, whistling one of the songs from *My Fair Lady* as he went.

Her introduction to his friends and the community was staggered, and her progress made in baby steps. She found them intimidating, sometimes irritating, always suspecting that as polite as they were they looked down on her, with her dropped aitches and her accent still rooted firmly east of the River Lea. They talked about politics and art, and books she hadn't read, places she hadn't been, plays she'd never heard of. They had bid good riddance to Macmillan, but were equally scathing of Douglas-Home. They spoke about the escalating situations in Biafra and Vietnam with genuine concern, when Reenie couldn't have pointed out either country on a map of the world.

Only Jonathan never condescended to her. There were things she'd learned, experiences she'd had, in the years since leaving London that amazed him, but it was only when they first made love, in her flat on Cathedral Road, on a night when all her flatmates were at a dance, that Jonathan saw the physical scars from that time. They weren't many – the most prominent were a jagged white seam on her shoulder, and the triangular patch of milk-white flesh corresponding in shape with the tip of a knife – but each one made him shudder.

He introduced her to the music he loved, playing her old vinyl recordings of Count Basie, Horace Silver, Ella Fitzgerald and Billie Holiday. He said Reenie reminded him of the latter; not in looks, obviously, but because they were both all the more beautiful for having endured. That was the word he used: *endured*. But Jonathan fell in love with her not out of pity, or a sense of obligation. He fell in love with her because she never demanded his love.

Even in the absence of a doting, match-making mother, he'd often found himself nudged – by aunts, great aunts, great-great aunts – towards desperate husband hunters. This was still a time and a world which frowned on single women in their late twenties, even more so those in their thirties, and this created a kind of wild-eyed panic in the women he met at parties and functions. Every introduction was followed by a moment when he felt himself being scrutinised, his prospects and his *edelkayt* weighed and balanced against every other available man in the room. He understood that men could be just as superficial, except for them it wasn't prospects and social standing, but rather those vital, hour-glass statistics and a pretty face. Reenie had neither of those things – her slight frame was vaguely boyish and her face a little hardened beyond her years – but nor did she look at him with cartoonish pound signs in her eyes. In her mind, at least, she'd done perfectly well – pneumonia notwithstanding – without him, and would go on doing well without him if he were to do as so many before him had done and toss her aside. She didn't say this in so many words, of course, but he understood it perfectly.

When he asked about her family Reenie answered with the only lie she would ever tell him, and go on telling him. In this version of her story she was picked up at Dovercamp by the Ostroffs, and they took her to a new home in East London. When the war came to an end they waited for news from Europe, but nothing came. Both her parents were dead. Though it was a lie with some basis in truth, she never quite forgave herself for telling it. Even so, she understood for the first time what had driven her father to hide her mother's portrait the day he married Vera. Occasionally life offers us the chance to close a door, and keep it closed. Hiding the portrait was his, telling Jonathan her father had died was Reenie's, and, more than that, this lie made them both orphans, the two of them against the world.

She almost slipped up a few weeks before the wedding, when she and Jonathan were strolling past the pet shop on the upper level of Cardiff's indoor market. There, in one of many cages, she saw a cockatiel, and pointing at the tiny bird, with its yellow and grey plumage and blushing orange cheeks, she said, 'My dad had one of those.'

Jonathan looked at her and frowned. She'd already told him she remembered nothing of Vienna, very little of her parents.

Reenie felt her heart plummet and she shook her head. 'I mean my foster father,' she said. 'Mr Ostroff. He had one of those.' She'd never once referred to Mr Ostroff as her father before, never called him anything but 'Mr Ostroff'.

From then on, any story involving her father would be changed, with his part now played by the blameless Mr Ostroff. For Jonathan this only made her situation before they'd met all the more despicable. How could Mr and Mrs Ostroff leave her, a girl of sixteen, to fend for herself in London? Why hadn't they taken her with her? ('Though God knows you can count your lucky stars they didn't, the way *that* place is turning out...') What kind of people were they? And by now she couldn't tell him they were two of the kindest people she had ever met, that they treated her very much like a daughter, while still having the respect never to insist on being 'Mummy' and 'Daddy', or 'Mama' and 'Papa', or 'Mammy' and 'Tatsy'. She knew it broke their hearts when Albert

Lieberman came for her, and when she left their house carrying the same paisley-patterned bag she was clutching when they first her met at Dovercamp. She knew, or rather she believed this loss may have been the thing, or one of the things, that sent them to Jerusalem. And now she had turned them into these neglectful, uncaring wretches. Her lie was like a weed, in that respect, taking root and spoiling everything around it.

Whatever Jonathan thought of her foster parents, he sensed her fondness for the bird and when they crossed the threshold of his house, their house, on their wedding night she found waiting for her a cockatiel in an ornate, gilded cage.

'But what should I call him?' she asked. 'I can't think of a name.' She remembered the name of her father's bird – Coco – quite clearly, but to have called it that would have been too much.

'Solomon,' said Jonathan, without hesitation.

'Solomon? Why Solomon?'

'King Solomon? The Language of Birds?'

'What're you talking about?'

'The Talmud,' Jonathan said, hesitantly. 'The story of how we lost the language of birds when we were cast out of the Garden of Eden. And how Solomon got it back.'

'Jon, I'm not bloody Memnonides.'

'Maimonides?'

'Yeah, him and all.'

'No. Of course. Well, anyway. That's how the story goes. I just thought it made a nice name.'

Reenie nodded, peering into the cage. 'You're right,' she said, smiling. 'It does.'

Typical of him to pick a name like that. A lovely name, no question about it, but so bookish. Jonathan had a vast collection of books, most of them inherited, so many that even he hadn't read them all, and as soon as they were living together she began reading as often as she could.

As a young girl, reading had been her passion. She may have played in the streets, like other girls, and run around in a gang, like other girls, but she was happiest when rainy afternoons kept her inside with a book. The Brontë sisters, Frances Hodgson Burnett,

Anna Sewell, Charles and Mary Lamb's *Tales from Shakespeare*. All that had changed with the discovery of music and boys but, now married, she began reading again. While ploughing through Dickens she would read the dialogue aloud so she could hear it, and Jonathan laughed as she became Pecksniff, or Magwitch, or Noddy Boffin, the Golden Dustman. When, in *Vanity Fair*, George died at Waterloo, Reenie gasped, causing her husband to look up over the top of his *Sunday Times*.

'Everything alright?' he asked, grinning.

Reenie nodded, shaken, and turned the page.

Reading wasn't just entertainment to her. It was ammunition. Dinner parties were when Jonathan's circle might judge her most of all, and she wouldn't go in unarmed. Let them sneer behind her back. She'd surprise them, and she did, many times, and each time she relished the stunned look of the person she'd put in their place. This was her life now. Dinner parties and functions. Shaking hands with the wives of Jonathan's friends and colleagues.

They knew early on there wouldn't be children, that having children was an impossibility. Discussed adopting just the once – so many parentless children in the world – but they couldn't do it. If they couldn't see their own child, reflecting something of themselves – same eyes, same nose, same mouth – back at them, they'd have no children at all. Besides, in time they became too selfish, too jealous of their time, and of the life they'd built, to consider sharing it with anyone else, let alone someone as demanding as a child.

They had settled into a routine; Jonathan working at the hospital, Reenie taking care of the house. Many of the other doctors' wives hired cleaners, elderly women who came around two or three times a week, but Reenie wouldn't hear of it. The very thought of it. Getting someone else to clean up after you. What did these women do with their time if they weren't running their own households? So there was no need for Reenie to work, not that there were many jobs for married women, and when not cooking or cleaning she filled her time by reading books and forgetting about the time before.

Occasionally she'd see a face she knew from those years spent in hostels and boarding houses; a fellow resident, a former lover, and it wasn't exactly contempt she felt when she saw them, but neither was it pity. Rather, whenever a familiar face appeared in the crowd she became anxious that they might look her in the eye and say her name, but they never did. She had left them anaemic and half-starved, her clothes little more than rags. Now she wore cashmere and pearls.

She thought about her father less and less; the part of her life spent with him now overshadowed greatly by her time without him. There was no chance of her going back, or even writing. Too much to repair, too much to atone for. Every day, week, month and year that passed made it more impossible for her to even try.

Time brought with it calm, a contentment, which she could never have predicted before meeting Jonathan. Then, everything had been fury and desire. She'd told herself it was only by living this way, never knowing where her next meal came from, or if she'd have a roof over her head the following night, that she could feel truly alive. She had seen others destroy themselves by clinging to this belief, even when things improved, when they were settled, when they should have been happy, as if danger and uncertainty were addictive.

Reenie missed none of it. Jonathan made her feel safe in a way that no one but the Ostroffs ever had, and through him the world became beautiful again, and it remained that way for as long as they were together.

He died at their home in Penylan, in the winter of 2001, three days after his seventy-first birthday. Despite the patients he'd coerced into giving up tobacco he was an inveterate smoker his whole life, starting with cigarettes at fourteen and adding a cigarette a day for every year until he turned forty. Then, in middle age, he graduated to cigars and a pipe.

Emphysema left him fragile and breathless. His appetite went, and with it the bulk of his frame, shrinking him down into a frail old man. Even the colour in his eyes faded to a watery shade of blue. After months of an existence divided between home and hospital, he spent his last few days at home, drifting in and out of consciousness, his moments of lucidity punctuated with incoherent rambling. At times she'd find him talking to an empty room, convinced he was chatting with a long-departed friend or relative, but his last words were as beautiful to her as they would have been meaningless to anyone else.

He'd been asleep for much of the afternoon, an electric fan whirring on the bedside table next to him despite the bitter cold outside, and she was sat beside him reading, when he opened his eyes and said, 'Billie Holliday'.

She closed her book and looked down at him. 'What's that, love?'

'Billie Holliday,' he whispered. 'She had a beautiful voice.'

'Yes, love,' said Reenie. 'Yes she did.'

She held his hand between both of hers, and Jonathan closed his eyes again and breathed out; a long, final breath that seemed to last forever, as if he was letting go of so much more than air. For another half an hour or more she sat beside him, his hand in hers, only letting go when his touch became cold and unfamiliar.

The days before had seen blizzards fall over the city. The buses stopped running, the shops sold out of bread and milk, and Reenie wondered, obliquely, if the gravediggers would make a dent in the frozen topsoil of her husband's plot. She wondered, too, if any of Jonathan's friends, cousins, second cousins, and doddering, now octo-and-nonagenarian aunts would make it to Western Cemetery, on the far side of the city, but when the day came the clouds broke and the sun shone. The cemetery was beautiful, the snow glistening not white but gold in the morning light, and the tall dark trees that surrounded it looked suitably black. At Jonathan's graveside she recited *Kaddish*, dropped a shovelful of soil onto the coffin lid, and silently said her goodbye to him.

When, some months later, the second Solomon died she chose not to replace him. Perhaps she couldn't bear to watch another living thing, however small, die. The garden, once tamed and cared for by Jonathan, now grew upwards and outwards in an explosion of life, as if rebelling against his absence. She had no wish to see something grow old and weak – to watch it atrophy, diminish – and so she placed the birdcage in the cupboard beneath the stairs, and scattered the leftover birdseed for the ducks, geese and swans in Roath Park.

It was five years before she got herself another bird, and she did so at the same stall on the upper tier of the indoor market where they'd bought the first two Solomons. The owner of the stall was different now, not even a descendent of the old man from whom Jonathan bought the first, but other than that the place hadn't changed. There was something timeless about the market, something forever old-fashioned. The city around it was ever-changing, but in the market the ground floor still smelled of fish, fruit and vegetables, while upstairs the birds sang in their cages, and in the café across the way labourers in heavy boots and heavy coats ate dripping bacon sandwiches over their newspapers.

She never asked herself why she had needed to buy another bird, she simply had, but the moment she was home and Solomon the Third was safely inside his cage she felt an odd sense of relief, as if something faulty had been repaired. The sound of his wings rattling the bars, or his insistent trilling, put things right, as did the routine of keeping him fed and watered.

Solomon was a young bird, his predecessors had lived for fifteen and eighteen years respectively, but Reenie wondered if he would make it to London. Already there was a cold snap to the air, and the nights and mornings were getting steadily darker. On balance, she thought his chances better than her own, though she didn't like to dwell on it. She had begun to wonder, though, and for the first time, what would happen if she didn't make it. There was no chance of her simply giving in, handing herself over to authorities who might shovel her into some sheltered accommodation, either out here in the country or back in Cardiff. But her supplies were low, and the distance left to walk still great. She had lost none of her stubbornness, but she no longer had the strength.

What would Jonathan have said, if he could have seen her? Most likely he'd say nothing; it would have been a look, an expression. He'd roll his eyes and shake his head, and he'd laugh, or rather he would laugh and sigh at the same time. Never condescending. If anything, he marvelled at her obstinacy. But then, if he could see her *now*? No, maybe he wouldn't shake his head and laugh and sigh. Perhaps now he would offer her that same crooked, sympathetic smile he first gave her when she was lying in her hospital bed.

She missed him properly for the first time in years; Jonathan – the only one who could ever tell her she was wrong, the only one she'd listen to. She missed his company. The helpless, almost feminine squeal that escaped him when he laughed. The glance and smile across a room that needed no accompanying words, because that single glance said everything she needed to know. *I'm here*. She missed that most of all.

Reenie looked around – at her sagging tent, the mud-flecked trolley, the single carrier bag of scraps and berries – and she gasped helplessly, wanting to be anywhere but in this cold and dirty field.

When first she heard the sound of a car coming to a halt in the lane, she wondered if it might be the farmer, or whoever owned this field; somebody to send her on her way or call the police. Or perhaps it was somebody from that other farm, from the party – Womble, or Casper, or any one of their friends – though why they would follow her, she had no idea.

She had already begun packing her things back into the trolley when she heard a familiar voice shout, 'There she is!' And she saw Ibrahim at the gate, his face bruised and swollen. Standing beside him was a woman, older than him but not old; olive skin and long dark hair.

'There you are!' said Ibrahim, breathlessly. 'We've been looking for you for *hours*.' And he braced himself against the gate, as if to let go would mean collapsing to the ground.

20

Between them they decided not to move on until the next morning. Ibrahim's bruises had ripened in the night and now provided a near constant pain. His trainers were beginning to fall apart from the inside out, and he had blisters on the balls of each foot. And Reenie hadn't the strength to move on. Two days of dwindling rations had left her lethargic, with no enthusiasm at all for an afternoon and evening's trek.

Earlier that day, as he and Natalie drove the lanes searching for Reenie, Ibrahim had had an idea. No one on these lanes was driving to London, and even if they were it was doubtful they'd have room for Reenie's possessions, but on the motorway there would be trucks – flatbed trucks and delivery trucks – many of them heading for the capital.

He could do it. The search for Reenie took hours; hours spent in a moving car. Natalie had given him a blister pack of Valium before she left them. He could do this.

When he told Reenie his plan she laughed at him.

'You want us to hitchhike?' she said. 'On the motorway?'

Ibrahim nodded.

'You're mad.'

'I'm not mad. What's mad is walking to London. On country lanes. Out here, it's all Land Rovers and tractors. Nobody's going to London. We go to the motorway, we stand a much better chance of getting picked up.'

'Yes. By the *police*.'

She still hadn't agreed to it. All they had agreed upon was that the next morning they would start moving again. As daylight drained away over the fields to the west they built a campfire, or rather Ibrahim built it, with Reenie talking him through each step, and before long they were warming themselves next to the flames and making toast, using damp sticks as skewers.

Shortly after they'd found Reenie, Natalie had left them with a wad of cash and a scribbled shopping list, and she returned with five bags full of supplies. Ibrahim had never seen somebody attack a sandwich with as much gusto as Reenie did that afternoon.

He was sad to see Natalie go. Sad they could do nothing more to thank her than insist she keep the measly change. Ibrahim imagined the world as a series of near-touching carousels in an infinite fairground, its people riding painted horses, coming into proximity with one another briefly before being swept away again to the incessant waltz of a pipe organ. The only thing that ever changed was the speed of the carousel, but sooner or later everyone he knew had been taken away.

Sitting beside their fire, Reenie told him about the party she had stumbled upon, and the people she met there, but Ibrahim shared very little in return. He told her he slept in a barn and that the farmer's wife made him breakfast the next morning, but nothing else.

Ibrahim threw the last wood onto the fire, and it hissed and crackled and coughed up a shower of orange sparks. He looked at his watch, then out across the dark field, and driven by something instinctive kicked off his shoes, took a bottle of water from the trolley, and poured some of it on his hands and feet.

'Oy,' said Reenie. 'That's for drinking. What you playing at?'

'I'm praying,' he said.

'You haven't prayed before. Not while I've been around, anyway.'

'I know, but this is different. It's Friday.'

Ibrahim sighed. This would have to do. He was in a damp and muddy field, but it would have to do. He raised his hands, and under his breath said, *'Allahu Akbar...',* God is great, and he wondered if he would ever truly mean those words again. He performed each *rak'a*, each cycle of the prayer with solemn determination, mindless of whether Reenie was still watching him, staring at him. He dropped down onto his knees, facing away from their fire and out toward the darkness of the lane, and he imagined his words drifting on a westerly wind, growing quieter with distance but carried over fields and hills, across the channel and the continent, over the rooftops of cities, between skyscrapers, above forests and mountains, across night-blackened waters and into Asia until their last whispery traces, inaudible to any human ear, came finally to rest in Makkah. When he'd finished he came back to their campfire and slipped his damp socks and damp trainers back on.

'That's an awful lot of standing up and sitting down again,' said Reenie. 'Didn't even think you were all that religious.'

Ibrahim shrugged. 'I don't know. Sometimes I'm not. But… it's Friday. And to be honest, I thought maybe we could do with the help.'

'Well, there's optimism,' said Reenie. 'Mind you. I'm glad I'm not a Muslim. I wouldn't be able to do all that standing and kneeling. Not with my knees. Hey… here's one for you…'

'What's that?'

'A joke. There's this Rabbi, right. What'll we call him? Rabbi Goldman. So Rabbi Goldman's booked himself an holiday. He's had a busy couple of months of it; bar mitzvahs, weddings, he's knackered. So he books himself an holiday down in Brighton, far away from his synagogue. And on his first night there, he thinks to himself, "D'you know what? I deserve a treat. Just this once I'm gonna try pork." So he goes to this restaurant down on the seafront, and he says to the waiter, he says, "Bring me the biggest, finest, juiciest suckling pig you've got."

'So, anyway, he's sat there, he's got his napkin tucked in his collar like a bib, he's got his knife and fork in his hands, like this, see? And he's waiting for them to bring him this suckling pig, when who should walk in but two people from his congregation. Mr and Mrs, I don't know… Schwartz. So Mr and Mrs Schwartz come over to him. "Oh, hello Rabbi Goldman. What brings you to Brighton?" And the Rabbi's getting a bit hot under the collar because he knows his food's coming any minute. "Oh, you know," he says. "Just thought I'd come down, catch the sea air." And Mrs Schwartz says, "Oh, that's nice. Our daughter Esther has moved here with her husband, the lawyer. Have you met our son-in-law?"

'Just then, wouldn't you know it, the waiter comes out with this great big silver platter, it's on a trolley it's that big, and when he's right next to Rabbi Goldman's table he takes off the lid, "Ta-daa!", and there it is, this suckling pig. Large as life, with an apple stuffed in its mouth.

'"Rabbi Goldman!" says Mrs Schwartz. "What is the meaning of this?"

'"Oy gevalt," says Rabbi Goldman. "This place is terrible. You order a baked apple, and look what they bring you!"'

Ibrahim looked at Reenie, wondering if that was the punchline, if the joke was over. It took a moment for him to get the joke at all, as if a sense of humour took practice, a practice he'd been lacking for too long. He felt his mouth twitch almost involuntarily into a smile, and heard himself laugh, and the more he thought about the joke – the unlikely set-up, its punchline, Reenie's delivery of the whole thing – the funnier it became, until his chest hurt and his eyes were glassy with tears.

'Thought you'd like that one,' said Reenie. 'I know another one, but it's a bit rude. Mind you. Talking about pork, I could murder a bacon sarnie right now. Couldn't you?'

'What?'

'A bacon sarnie. Bacon burnt to a frazzle. Lots of brown sauce.'

'I thought you were Jewish.'

'Yes. And? Don't tell me you've never eaten bacon.'

'Never.'

'What? No bacon? No pork? No sausages?'

'Okay,' he said, blushing. 'You've got me there.'

'Knew it. I bloody knew it.'

Staring into the fire he told her about a time when his father, who sold used cars, had taken him to the car auctions in Beckton. His mother and sister were away, he said, visiting their family in Birmingham, so his father took him to the auction, at an old warehouse out past the gasworks. There the cars lined up, the air thick with exhaust fumes, and his father met and spoke with friends, white guys, other traders, and it was the first time Ibrahim had ever heard his father swear.

To either side of the warehouse were stands, rows of seating, and the auctioneer talked so quickly, his voice rattling through the PA like rapid gunfire, that Ibrahim couldn't understand a single word he said.

'Fourninefivefourninefivedoihearfivehunnerdoihearfivehunnerdanyo nefourninefivethenitsfourninefivetothegennlemanintheredjacketgoanonc egoantwiceSOLD.'

Ibrahim's father took notes, and kept a watchful eye on the procession of cars coming in through the wide open warehouse doors, but Ibrahim was transfixed by the burger van in the far corner; the painted sign above it reading *Bob's Buns* in tacky red and yellow. Even from that distance he could smell the burgers and fried onions.

'Da-ad, Dad. I'm hungry.'

'Not now, Prakash. Dad's busy.'

'Da-ad…'

'Son, please.'

'*Dad.*'

The plan had been that they would pick something up on their way home, maybe even a McDonalds, but Nazir Siddique could see he would have no peace until his son had eaten something, and so he walked him over to Bob's Buns.

'Burger, please,' he said.

The man – perhaps Bob himself – shrugged apologetically. 'Sorry, mate,' he said. 'Just sold my last burger. I've still got hot dogs, if you want an hot dog.'

Nazir looked down at his son. 'Sorry, son,' he said. 'We'll get something later.'

'But I'm *hungry*…'

'Prakash. The man only has sausages…'

'Please, Dad. *Please.*' As if 'please' really was a magic word.

'Okay. Listen. You can have a hotdog. But don't tell your mother!'

He could still remember that hotdog; the sausage black on the outside but juicy in the middle, the ketchup cheap and tangy with too much vinegar, the cheap bread sticking to the roof of his mouth and in the gaps between his teeth in doughy clumps. Ibrahim loved every bite of it, and he loved even more that his father and he had a secret that neither his mother nor Aisha would ever know about.

They left the auction late, later than planned, and Ibrahim sat in the back of his dad's car, watching the shadows slide down the driver's seat with every streetlight they drove past. By the time they reached their home in Harold Road he was fast asleep, and though seven years old and a big boy had to be carried from the car to his bed.

'So anyway,' said Ibrahim. 'That was only once. I've never had one since.'

Reenie smiled. 'Yeah. I'm a bugger for those hot dogs you get at fairgrounds and that. Used to drive my husband, Jonathan, up the wall. He was always better at keeping things kosher than me. Strict upbringing as a kid, see? His mum wouldn't even mix meat and dairy. Even my foster mother wasn't *that* strict. And my dad, well. He wasn't all that bothered about that sort of thing.' She sighed, looking not at him but the fire. 'You got any kids?'

'Kids?' he said, wondering how they could have come this far without her knowing. 'No. No kids.'

'Do you want them?'

He shook his head. 'I'm not so good with other people. I've been on my own a long time. So maybe not.'

'Not good with other people?' said Reenie. 'What does that make me, if I'm not "other people"?'

'No, I just mean generally. Generally I'm not good with other people. Most of the time.'

'So you never married? Never had a girlfriend?'

'I had a girlfriend.'

'And what happened?'

'Me,' said Ibrahim. 'I happened. But this was years ago.'

'And you've not seen her since?'

'No.'

'Well,' said Reenie. 'It wouldn't be too hard to find her. I mean, if you wanted to.'

'It's too late for that.'

'No it's not. Not with the internet and the, what's it called? That Face thing everyone's always going on about.'

'Facebook?'

'That's the one. You can find anyone on there, they reckon. I heard them talking about it on the wireless. Anyway. How about that girl? The one who brought you here. Natalie. She seemed nice.'

'What about her?' Asked Ibrahim.

'Well. Did the two of you…?'

'Did we what?'

'You know.'

'No. I don't. What?'

'Get up to any hanky panky?'

'She's a lesbian.'

'She's a what, love? You'll have to speak up. I'm a bit mutton in this ear.'

'She's a lesbian.'

'Lebanese? She didn't look it. I'd have said Spanish, maybe, but never…'

'Lesbian,' said Ibrahim. 'She's a lesbian. A lesbian.'

'No need to shout, love,' said Reenie. 'I heard you the first time.' And she winked at him, and took a bite from a slice of toast coated liberally with marmalade. 'So, I was thinking,' she said. 'This plan of yours…'

'Yes?'

'I think you're probably right. I think we should go to the motorway and try our luck there.'

'Good,' said Ibrahim. 'That's good. Thank you.'

He studied her from his side of the fire, wondering how someone her age could even begin to agree to a plan like his. He had no idea if it would work, he knew only that in the time they had spent looking for Reenie, Natalie could have driven him to London. There must have been a reason he came here instead. A part of him, still quiet of voice and hidden in shadows, knew precisely what that reason was. When Reenie looked at him again, still smiling softly, he avoided her gaze, and instead stoked the fire, watching the last fragments of wood begin to blacken and crumble.

21

The view was unremarkable – the six lanes of motorway a grey strip vanishing distantly between a low hill and a dark cluster of trees – and between them and the horizon lay nothing but greenery and pylons. Nothing exceptional about the view – no landmarks, no natural features worth noting – but all the same it overwhelmed him.

Perhaps, now that they were standing over the motorway, he had, in some small, illogical way, expected to see London in the distance, like a mirage; the faint grey silhouettes of the BT Tower, the Gherkin, or St Paul's.

'What are you looking at?' asked Reenie.

'Just looking at the motorway,' he said.

'Daunting, ain't it?'

He nodded without taking his eyes off the road.

'But we're getting there,' she added, placing her hand on his shoulder. 'So come on, slowcoach. Stop dawdling and start pushing.'

He laughed, out of relief as much as anything else. She still had a sense of humour, at least. They had already trekked four miles that morning, and crossed one busy slip road, narrowly dodging an articulated truck as they did. He thought for a moment she might pack it all in, there and then, tell him to turn her trolley around and head back to the country lanes, but she didn't.

He pushed on to the far side of the bridge, where the tarmac came to an abrupt end against another elbow of grass, and the eastbound slip road.

'Okay,' he said. 'Last one, and we're there.'

'There?'

'Well. The other side of the road.'

On the far side, a short way down the slip road, lay a stretch of hard shoulder. This meant crossing diagonally, a longer route, but one that should see them safe when they got to the other side. Taking a deep breath and holding it, Ibrahim nudged the trolley forward so its front wheels left the kerb. Traffic streamed down onto the slip road from the dizzy chaos of the junction, and Ibrahim watched each passing car, wishing the traffic would just stop. Just for a minute. Not even that. Ten seconds. If it could stop for just ten seconds.

He looked to the other side of the junction, where the traffic came up from the opposite slip road. There was a moment's pause as a truck slowed to allow through the next wave of traffic.

'Now!' shouted Ibrahim, giving the trolley a forceful shove; pushing it off the kerb and out into the road. He cursed under his breath, the same one word over and over, increasing in time with his pace. No time to say or think anything else. Everything was action and movement without thought. Time didn't slow down; it imploded, dragging into itself anything and everything outside that moment.

The trolley veered right, causing its back end to drift, and Reenie almost lost her footing, only keeping herself upright by clinging to the side of the trolley and for a moment taking both feet off the ground and allowing herself to be carried. Without her help the front end twisted sharply another degree to the right, and Ibrahim felt himself being pulled along by its weight and its momentum, so that they were now rushing down the slip road's inside lane. He yanked the trolley's handlebar to the right, hoping this would bring it across to the hard shoulder, but it was no use. Laden with shopping bags, the trolley acted of its own accord; its clumsy caster wheels twisting in every direction, searching for the path of least resistance. Solomon's cage tipped over onto its side, and the bird started fluttering crazily in every direction, waiting for the world to stop shaking.

Ibrahim heard the sharp blare of a horn, and glancing back saw a car bearing down on them, the driver's face scrunched up in rage. He tugged at the trolley again, bringing its back end off the road, and Reenie followed his lead so that they were now on the hard shoulder, out of the path of the cars and lorries, but still moving and with no sign of slowing. The trolley clattered percussively, the birdcage tumbling from the child's seat and down into a gap between their luggage, and Ibrahim dug his heels into the gravel. The trolley slowed, the hiss of gravel faded to a crunch, and they stopped.

'Fucking hell,' said Ibrahim.

'You're telling me,' said Reenie, breathlessly. 'And mind your language.'

She leaned against the front end of the trolley – half for support, half to stop it running away – and peering into it saw the upturned birdcage.

'Solomon,' she gasped.

Ibrahim reached into the trolley and lifted out the cage. Lying at the bottom, among the droppings and the empty shells of birdseed, was Solomon, his beak wide open but his grey eyes puckered shut.

'Is he okay?' asked Reenie.

Ibrahim lowered the cage back into the trolley and shook his head.

'I'm sorry,' he said.

Reenie let out a long shuddering sigh, more one of resignation than grief, and her eyes became glazed and red.

'My stuff,' she said, a little angrily, and she began rummaging through the rest of the trolley.

'What are you looking for?' asked Ibrahim.

'If it's broken,' she said, glowering up at him and shaking her head.

'If what's broken?'

She opened one of the bags and produced what looked like a framed certificate, colourfully illustrated and written out in Hebrew script.

'Thank God,' she said. 'Thank God.' Then, looking down at Solomon's cage again, she sighed. 'We need to bury him.'

It took ten minutes for Ibrahim to dig a small hole, perhaps eight inches deep and four wide, using one of Reenie's spoons. Reenie wrapped the bird in sheets of kitchen towel, and after she'd placed him in the tiny pit, Ibrahim filled it in and patted down the fresh earth with his hands.

When they'd first met, only a few days ago, Ibrahim had wondered what, if anything, Reenie could have that was worth so much she couldn't leave it behind. He could think of nothing he owned that would be worth carrying this distance – nothing that didn't serve a practical purpose – but Reenie, he now understood, had her whole life in those boxes and bags; everything she cared about, everything she loved. The pieces of a life, proof that she had been here. What did he have that wasn't disposable? What permanent mementos did he have but scars?

'You packed it down tight?' said Reenie.

He nodded. 'Yeah. Really tight.'

'So nothing'll get to him?'

'Nothing,' said Ibrahim.

They began moving again, down the sloping hard shoulder of the slip road. At the bottom of this incline the road fed into the motorway's eastbound side, and here the land became flat and the horizons distant; the sky opening out into an immense blue canopy, mostly cloudless but scratched through by a white grid of contrails. The traffic was loud, and they were shaken by the rush of wind from each passing truck and car, but finally it felt as if they were making progress. This was the road that would take them to London.

They were ill-prepared for a whole day of walking. Ibrahim spent much of the time glancing back for approaching vans and trucks, anything that could carry a trolley and two passengers, and when anything large came their way he stuck out his thumb, but no one stopped for them.

If it was foolish of them to come here, they had little choice now but to keep walking. The motorway offered nowhere to stop and rest. Its purpose was relentless. It served only as a sluiceway to an endless flow of traffic, carving the country in two, from one side to the other. The few living creatures that had attempted to cross it now formed dark patches on the tarmac. The entrails of a fox – pink, grey and glistening – stretched out from a smear of red and black, and further along an orange claw clutched at the air from a cake of blood and feathers.

The dead creatures on the road made dangerous pickings for the scavengers that flew above the motorway. A buzzard swooped down, its large expressive eyes given a look of intense concentration by a permanent, dark scowl, but the bird was buffeted back by the turbulence from cars and trucks. It found and rode a spiralling current of warm air, and with every sense it searched for the next, and allowed itself to glide and descend. It headed west, away from the two shambolic figures shuffling along the roadside, and scanned this way and that for signs of movement in the fields and bushes either side of this great river of coloured metal. Further back, one side of the river had stopped flowing altogether, and as it came down from another current the buzzard saw glinting blue lights, and heard human voices crackling and distant. Several blocks of colour were screwed together in a field of broken glass, and clouds of steam rose from the damage. There was blood on the black ground, but not an animal's blood. There was nothing to be scavenged here.

Oblivious to the crash, Ibrahim and Reenie walked on along the motorway, and no one stopped them. Every police car in ten miles was at the scene, so even though they were spotted, in a room full of monitors many, many miles away, there was nobody to move them on or take them back the way they had come.

This was the limit of their luck that afternoon. No van or truck stopped for them, and they walked ten miles along the hard shoulder, on top of the four already walked from the lanes to the motorway. By mid-afternoon the sky had clouded over, and it rained; the rain falling as a fine mist, almost unnoticeable at first but drenching them all the same. It was early evening when they reached the service station, and they were soaked. The sky had darkened to become the kind you only ever see after rain – heavy lilac clouds brushed orange and gold where they faced the sun; the scimitar of a rainbow half-buried in a mess of sunlight and gloom. To the west, splinters of sunlight broke through the clouds, drawing long shadows across the damp, grey car park.

Neither of them had said much in the last two hours, and Reenie breathed in short heavy gasps, and walked with slow, plodding steps, her expression like that of someone grieving. Ibrahim could barely bring himself to look at her, but when he did he felt a wave

181

of guilt and shame at having done this to her. She would have been better off where he left her, however long it would have taken her. At least back in the lanes there were places for her to camp. What did the motorway have but concrete, tarmac and danger?

The service station was hidden from the motorway by a grassy bank, and it was here that Reenie settled, kicking off her boots and letting out a long sigh. Her feet were red raw and blistered in places; the varicose veins on her legs more pronounced. She seemed to have aged ten years in a single afternoon.

'I'll get us some food,' said Ibrahim. 'And something to drink.'

'We've got food,' Reenie snapped, scowling up at him.

'I mean something warm. A proper meal.'

'You said we'd be able to hitchhike.'

He looked away, helpless with remorse, and held his breath. Yes, it was a long walk, too long for a seventy-five year old, or however old she was, and yes her bird had died, but she had agreed to it, hadn't she? And what about the state she was in when they'd found her? Hardly a thing to eat, almost nothing left to drink. She would have starved there if they hadn't turned up. She'd still be there now, resting and starving.

'I know,' he said. 'And okay, it's not exactly going to plan. But we can stay here for the night. How does that sound? We'll get some sleep, and then in the morning we'll try again. There'll be dozens of lorries and vans coming through here. It might be easier than trying on the motorway.'

'And what other choice have we got?' said Reenie. 'I mean, yes, we can stay here and sleep, or *what*? Keep walking? I'm knackered, love. My feet are in bits. And Solomon...' Her lip trembled and she shook her head. 'What other choices have we *got*?'

Ibrahim sighed. 'I'm sorry, okay? Really, I'm sorry. I thought this would work, and it hasn't, and I really hoped it would, and it hasn't. I wanted to make things right...'

'What do you mean, "make things right"?'

He paused, avoiding her gaze.

'When I left you, in Newport,' he said, without conviction.

'*I* left *you* in Newport. What do you mean, make things right? What does that mean?'

'It means…'

This was his chance. If he wanted to tell her everything, this was his opportunity.

'Nothing,' he said. 'It means nothing. I wanted to help you, and it didn't work. But I didn't know what else we could do.'

'We could have kept going the way we was going.'

'And we would still have had to walk. We'd still have been a hundred miles from London, maybe more. I mean, you *are* actually going to London, aren't you? You weren't just saying that to wind me up?'

'Did you think I was doing this for *fun*?'

'Well, I don't know, do I? I mean, I don't even know *why* you're walking to London.'

'And I don't know why *you're* walking to London.'

He said nothing. They'd discussed everything, almost everything, but this. If anything, perhaps their progress so far had been fuelled by not knowing each other's reasons. That made it simpler, somehow. To ask the question would have meant taking a scalpel to something small and delicate, something that wouldn't survive dissection.

'You never asked,' said Ibrahim.

'And you never asked me.'

They looked at one another with narrowing eyes, locked in a stand-off that could end only with the question being asked or by one of them walking away, and after a long and wordless moment of unease, Ibrahim turned around and made his way silently toward the service station.

22

It was possible – no, *certain* – that Vincent had passed his millionth mile years ago, if you included every journey made in the twenty-three years before he began driving for a living. Even if you discounted every journey in which he was the passenger and not the driver, he must have crossed that line much earlier, but the point was unknowable, because only when he became a professional driver did Vincent start counting the miles.

It began with him monitoring distances. Understanding distance, knowing how far he travelled each day, was integral to his job, but in time this was surpassed by his determination to reach that next point when a messy figure was flattened out, regimented by zeros. First ten thousand, then a hundred thousand. Soon enough he began thinking of those distances as trips around the world, and by the age of twenty-six had, by his reasoning, circumnavigated the globe four times. Always counting in miles, rather than kilometres, because miles offered a rounder, neater figure. The earth is 24,000 miles in circumference; a thousand miles for every hour of the day. The moon is 250,000 miles from the earth, give or take. And when his laps of the earth became meaningless he looked to the skies. At twenty-eight he'd been to the moon. At thirty-two he had been to the moon and back. Now, aged thirty-seven, he had almost completed his second return trip.

Only three men had ever done this for real – the astronauts Jim Lovell, Eugene Cernan, and John Young – and of them only Young and Cernan set foot on the moon itself. On his second trip, Lovell captained Apollo 13 and, while passing over the dark side of the moon, reached, along with his crew, a point more distant from the earth than any other men before them. It being his second mission, this made Lovell the farthest travelled person in the history of mankind, meaning he had travelled the farthest *from* earth, rather than *on* it, but Vincent liked to think the point in that night's journey somewhere between Bristol and London would place him in an exclusive group of men, standing shoulder to shoulder with the likes of Lovell, Cernan and Young.

So much of his driving happened at night, and he spent so many hours in his cabin, that he felt a certain affinity with Lovell in particular. Sometimes, when he was between cities, he believed he understood how remote, how disconnected from the world, an astronaut might feel at that halfway point between worlds. People had made good work of naming most places, labelling almost everything down to the square mile, but there were still voids in between, and at night those voids were featureless but for the rhythmic sweep of the lights above, and the smooth Morse code of lines and patterns on the roads.

The emptiness and monotony of the night were hazardous. It was easy for the mind to wander, and a wandering mind was perhaps the most dangerous thing for a long distance driver. How to keep the mind sharp and focused when the world around him was hell bent on hypnosis. In fourteen years he'd tried everything – caffeine, amphetamines, every genre of music the radio could supply. He'd experimented with his diet, with his sleeping habits, even with the décor of his cabin. It took much of those fourteen years for him to find exactly the right combination, the right configuration of lifestyle and environment to keep him alert and in the moment, to stop his mind from wandering.

Drugs no longer played any part in it. Amphetamines had been recommended by a frazzled older driver he met at an all-night café near Frejus. There, this Satanic-looking character – black goatee beard and multiple piercings in his left ear – pushed a small paper wrap of crystal meth across the table they shared, and told Vincent he should try it.

'Pour le voyage.'

He should have known from the dark rings around the man's eyes how the drug might leech the life out of him. Day and night, light and dark, happy and sad, all became meaningless. Amphetamines crashed through the barriers between days and between moods with equal recklessness. Once the initial euphoria passed he was left only with an inability to rest, even when the journey was done and it was time for him to sleep. However much his limbs might ache, however heavy his eyelids might feel, his mind still fizzed with unspent energy, each thought barging past the next, vying for his exhausted attention.

His two years on crystal meth had given him the restless, agitated look of someone hunted. Not twitchy, but never calm. He was a man in perpetual motion, and had been for years, even before he began driving trucks. Taped to his dashboard, next to a yellowed Polaroid of his sister, was a tattered photocopy of an English poem he learned in school. Not the whole poem, only a few lines from it. English was the only subject he'd ever excelled in, and that poem, and those lines in particular, stayed with him. On the longest of nights he would read it aloud, listening to his own voice saying the words of an 'idle king'. He wondered sometimes if he loved that poem because it so perfectly captured the nature of his existence, or if his life had itself been moulded by his memories of studying that poem and its meaning.

The solitude of the road had suited him over the years, but now he found the longer nights left him empty, the voices on the radio sounding more distant, more artificial. When he thought about those three astronauts who travelled a million miles, he realised he was different from them in one important aspect; his isolation. None of them, not even Lovell, travelled alone. The loneliest of the Apollo astronauts were those men in the command modules, orbiting the moon while their colleagues touched down on the surface. Perhaps those six men, from Michael Collins to Ron Evans, experienced the same depths of loneliness and of distance as him. Perhaps they too were the ideal men for the job, drawn to darkness and peace. Or perhaps not. No one ever made the trip twice, so maybe that feeling of remoteness had been a step too far away from the world. And perhaps Vincent had spent too long driving through the night. When driving he now imagined himself out there, beyond the dark side of the moon, with even the earth blotted from the sky, as distant as he could be from everything he'd ever known, and he wondered if he'd ever laugh at another person's joke or flirt with another pretty girl in a bar. When he reached the

186

next city or the next service station, he imagined he was coming in to land, the glow of orange streetlights the fire of re-entry, knowing all the while the people he saw might treat him differently, like someone changed by the distance he'd travelled and the time he spent alone.

In recent months he had begun making plans while he drove. Perhaps one day he would start saving money, and having saved enough would hand in the keys to his truck, and find somewhere he could be still, stationary, a place to live. Not the place where he grew up. Never there. Some place a little further south, perhaps. A postcard villa, next to a vineyard; terracotta roof, azure sky, cypress trees lining the nearest road – a collage of those things he believed made a place beautiful and serene. It was laughable, he knew that, and so he told no one his plans, but he was certain he'd settle in a place like that, and he waited patiently for the day when he could drift off to sleep without the sensation that he was still moving, still in transit, as if his body remembered every bump and every turn of every road.

23

Glass walls and white tiles. Soft muzak piped through speakers, and the rattle and chime of arcade games. A slice of the high street wrenched out and planted far beyond any town or city. The service station was exactly what Ibrahim expected. Here there were coffee shops, amusement arcades, a newsagents, a restaurant. A shop that sold jewellery, another toys, and he found it impossible to imagine who could need jewellery or toys on the motorway. It was as if this place existed solely as a diversion from the road's monotony; taking travellers away from that endless strip of tarmac and road signs and offering them something human, something normal. If anything this concentration of normality, boxed in on all sides by floor-to-ceiling plate glass, only made the place more unsettling; the muzak and the drowsy wandering of customers giving the place an air of forced serenity.

Ibrahim loathed the service station and everyone inside it. He saw it not just as a place where tired drivers and their passengers could stop and rest, but as a microcosm; the country reduced to its basest raw ingredients. Here was the compulsion to eat, the compulsion to shop, the compulsion to gamble. Here people demanded to be fed and entertained. The travellers in the service station were helpless, caught between places. Harassed by screaming children, frustrated by road maps. Shocked speechless by the prices. Assaulted by an impersonation of normality, and confronted everywhere they looked by adverts and primary colours, what else could they do but spend?

And what did any of them really know about travelling? He doubted any of them had been on the road more than a few hours; a few short hours away from their televisions, their computer games, their internet. If they were hungry, it was the kind of hunger that would pass if they had something else to occupy them. If they were tired, they were merely heavy-eyed, not exhausted. If they ached, it was the kind of pain that passes after a quick stretch and a brisk walk, not the kind that keeps you sleepless for nights, no matter how tired you are.

In the restaurant, Ibrahim bought a veggie burger and fries and a large cardboard cup of coke, and he took a table near the window. From here he could see out over the car park, and he saw Reenie, still resting on the embankment and, about halfway between the embankment and the service station, a minibus. Crowded around the bus was a group of men and women – he counted twelve in all – and their roof rack was crammed with luggage; oversized suitcases and backpacks huddled together with bungee cords. Along the side of the bus someone had painted – amateurishly – the words 'King's Temple Rapture Tour 2009'.

One of them, an older man with salt-and-pepper hair and a powder blue cardigan – popped open the bonnet and leaned in, studying the engine. It was getting dark now – the sun had disappeared behind a distant row of trees, dragging in a veil of dark blue from the east – and the older man had to use a torch. After a moment he stood and shook his head, and the others sagged in unison; shoulders drooping, faces glum. After a few minutes more of anxious shrugs and shaking heads, they locked the minibus and made their way toward the service station.

Presently, they entered the restaurant, queuing for food before taking three nearby booths, and keeping his eyes on his own table Ibrahim listened to their conversation.

'Listen,' said the older man. 'This is just a test. If we give up now, He'll know we're not serious.'

'I could phone the AA,' said a young, dark-skinned boy in a brightly patterned shirt. 'I'm a member. I'll be covered for this.'

'No, Zack. It's fine. I don't think there's anything wrong with the engine.'

'But it won't start.'

'I know that, but I don't think it's a problem with the engine. I think it's a test. I mean, for this to happen when we've only just started out? And I only took that thing to be serviced two weeks ago.'

'Yes, but I could still try calling the…'

'Let us pray.'

Those three words were a slammed door on the discussion, and on all three tables the makeshift congregation bowed their heads. With half a burger in one hand, his cup of Coke in the other, and a smudge of ketchup in his beard, Ibrahim stopped chewing and listened.

'Lord,' said the older man. 'Help us through this, the first trial of many we shall face on the long road ahead. We know that Satan will do all he can to stand in our way…'

'Amen,' said the others.

'We know he will try to tempt us from the road and from our pilgrimage, but we promise to you, oh Lord, that we will stay true, and that we will not give in to such temptations.'

'Amen,' said the others.

'And so we pray to you, Lord, that you will heal our bus, as you would one of your own flock, and help us on the road. Amen.'

'Amen,' said the others.

As they opened their eyes once more, the older man looked at Ibrahim and smiled, and Ibrahim looked away, embarrassed, and took another bite of his burger. Chewing, and with his eyes fixed on the table, he sensed the older man getting up and crossing the aisle.

'Hello.'

Ibrahim looked up. He couldn't speak without spitting out a mouthful of half-chewed bread and burger, so he nodded and smiled with puffed-out cheeks and sealed lips.

'Mind if I…?' asked the older man, gesturing to the opposite seat. Ibrahim shook his head, and the older man sat, waiting for him to swallow his food before speaking again. 'Hello, brother,' he said. It sounded strange. To Ibrahim, 'Brother' was a word he associated with Muslims. Brother. *Akhi*. It was what they – he and his friends, back in London – had called each other, called any other man from the *ummah*. This guy wasn't from the *ummah*. He looked like the kind of man you see talking about gardening or antiques on Sunday night television.

'I saw you watching us, just now,' he said. 'While we were

praying. I hope you weren't… *unsettled…* in any way. Some people find praying a little…' and now he moved his head from side to side, as if to shake the right word down from wherever it was kept. 'Well, a little *off-putting.*'

'Not at all,' said Ibrahim.

'That's good,' said the man, reaching across the table with an open hand. 'My name's Graham, by the way.'

Ibrahim shook his hand, and Graham held on with a firm grip, sandwiching Ibrahim's digits between both hands in a way that felt warm and invasive at the same time.

'Ibrahim,' said Ibrahim, pulling his hand away as gently as he could without it seeming like a recoil.

'Ibrahim. Like Abraham?'

'Yeah. Like Abraham.'

He remembered Reenie telling him her father's name was Avram.

'The father of us all,' said Graham. 'Do you follow any faith?'

If Graham's first point had been a segue, it was a clumsy one, but Ibrahim let it pass. 'Kind of,' he said. 'Not as much as I used to…'

'You see, we meet people from all kinds of faiths, and the question we ask them is, do you believe in the immortal soul?'

Ibrahim looked down at what was left of his food – the last orangey, hard-looking fries, the soggy bread, the daubs of ketchup. He looked at the cardboard cup of Coke and the drinking straw sticking out of its plastic lid. He braced himself against the table's edge, wondering if this was a dream. Perhaps everything that had happened in the last forty-eight hours had been a dream. Perhaps he was still lying on a pavement in Gloucester, unconscious and bleeding. Or earlier than that. This whole week, everything that had happened. Because what were the chances, really? Perhaps, having realised the dream for what it was, Ibrahim was on the verge of waking in his flat in Cardiff, the long walk to London still ahead of him.

'The immortal soul,' he said. 'Well, I… I suppose I haven't really thought about it in a while.'

'No, no,' said Graham closing his eyes and nodding

sympathetically. 'And that's the thing, isn't it? I mean, these days, everyone's so busy. So few of us have the time to give it any real thought, but we *should* make the time. We really should.'

'Yes,' said Ibrahim, with too little conviction. 'We should.'

'Now, I don't profess to know a lot about the tenets of your religion, Ibrahim. I'm assuming you *are* a Muslim, is that correct?'

Ibrahim nodded.

'Good, well, I don't know *much* about Islam, but I do know this. I know that you venerate our Lord Jesus Christ almost as much as we Christians, and that you too are the children of Abraham, and that's a really good place to start. You see, by letting Christ into your heart you become a new person. You are almost literally *born* again. Does this make sense?'

'Er, I guess so, I supp...'

'And when I saw you, just now, I thought, "There's a young man who's had a tough time of it. There's a lad who could do with waking up afresh tomorrow morning."'

Ibrahim glanced briefly at the window. With the sky outside almost black, the reflection of the restaurant and everyone in it grew more distinct, and he saw the stitches on his eyebrow and the purple bruises on his face. He saw himself as Graham – Graham, with his salt-and-pepper hair, his powder blue cardigan, his invasive handshake and over-friendly voice – had seen him.

'Really?' he said.

'Yes, really,' said Graham. 'And I thought, "There's a young man who's ready for Christ." Am I right? Are you ready for Christ?'

'Um...'

'You see, a lot of people think you have to *want* to be a Christian to let Christ into your heart, but that's not true. If you open your heart, Christ will find you. Ask any of my friends over there,' he gestured across the aisle toward the three booths, 'and they'll tell you the same thing. We didn't *ask* to be Christians. Some of us didn't even *want* to be Christians. Christ found *us*.'

'Right.'

'But you have to be ready for Him. Are you ready for Christ?'

'Not really.'

'Now you say that,' said Graham. 'But I think you *are*. The heart is deceitful, and your heart is telling you you're not ready, when really you *are*.'

Could Graham really believe he'd found a convert in the making? Was he that deluded? But Ibrahim knew this was what it meant to preach. This was what it had meant to stand in the street, near Stratford tube, handing out flyers. Even when it was raining. Yusuf yelling through the loudhailer, his voice squeaking with feedback. And Ibrahim hated that loudhailer, hated the way it made the *adhan* sound so harsh and tinny. The *muezzin* at his father's mosque sang so sweetly it sounded to Ibrahim like violins, but this noise, this bristling electric noise, was nothing like that. And some people would change direction even when they were fifty feet away; subtly turn a little to the left or the right, working out the best route so they could avoid them, Ibrahim and his friends, *and* the *Big Issue* vendor near the station doors. That was what it meant to preach. The belief that if they kept handing out those little slips of paper ('GOD IS THE WAY!') someone, *anyone*, might take notice. And now this. Another believer, leaning across the table and asking him if he was ready for Christ.

'No,' said Ibrahim, with a forced smile. 'I think I'd know if I was, and I'm not.'

Graham flared his nostrils and his pursed lips shifted over to one side. 'I see,' he said. 'Well, you'll be ready one day, I'm sure. And I'll pray that day comes soon.'

'Maybe,' said Ibrahim, lying. 'So. Where are you guys going?'

Graham smiled. 'Israel,' he said. 'The Holy Land. We're travelling there in preparation for the Rapture.'

'The Rapture?'

'Yes. When all those who have accepted Christ will be taken up into Heaven, before the final conflict between Good and Evil.'

'Right. Of course.'

'It's written in the Book of Revelation that this battle will take place in the Holy Land, when the prophecy of Zion has been fulfilled.'

'The prophecy of Zion?'

'When the Jews have returned to Israel.'

'Right.'

'We're volunteering at a vineyard in Hebron.'

'A vineyard?'

'Yes. There are settlers there, and they grow grapes. We're going to help out, picking grapes.'

He'd heard of Hebron. He'd heard of settlers. Words that had stirred him and his friends into a state of spittle-flecked indignation. Words that were still barbed.

'Jewish settlers?' he said. 'In Hebron.'

'That's right,' said Graham.

'That's a Palestinian town, isn't it?' asked Ibrahim, though it was more a statement than a question.

'Ye-es,' said Graham, splitting the word hesitantly. 'This is true. But there are settlers there, and...'

'Illegal settlers.'

'Well, that depends on your point of view. In the scriptures...'

'I'm not talking about the scriptures. I'm talking about people. I'm talking about the law.'

'The fact remains, before the settlers, before they *settled* there, there was *nothing*. Nothing grew. It was arid, and barren, and lifeless.'

'There were people there. There are still people there. Palestinians.'

'Yes,' said Graham. 'Though, of course, it's important to remember that Palestine hasn't really existed as a country, I mean as a sovereign state, since... when? The seventh century? If ever? The Macedonians, the Romans, Byzantium, the Caliphate, the Ottomans, the British. It's never truly been independent, so who *are* the Palestinians, exactly? What claim have they, if...'

'They were there,' said Ibrahim. 'They were there the whole time. That's what claim they have. Did Britain cease to be Britain under the Normans? Did the people here stop being British?'

'No, of course not. But the subject of Israel... Those people, the Jews, they needed a homeland. There wasn't another country on the face of the earth which they could call their own...'

'So they took someone else's?'

'So we... we being Britain, America, the UN, gave them a plot of land. Not a *big* plot of land, but a plot of land to which they felt historically tied. Now was that the right thing to do? I don't know. What would you do? What's *your* solution?'

Ibrahim threw up his hands and laughed. 'I don't know,' he said. 'I honestly don't know. I don't know if there *is* a solution.' Graham couldn't understand, but for Ibrahim, in that moment, not knowing, admitting that he didn't know, felt like a victory.

'Well, anyway,' said Graham. 'We're not *just* going to Hebron. We'll be visiting Jerusalem, also. The Western Wall, the Church of the Holy Sepulchre…'

'The Dome of the Rock?'

Graham shook his head. 'No,' he said, smiling bitterly. 'Funnily enough, though Muslims and Jews can visit the Holy Sepulchre, and Muslims and Christians can visit the Western Wall, they've made it very difficult for anyone who isn't a Muslim, particularly a group like ours, to visit the Dome of the Rock. We made enquiries.'

Ibrahim laughed again with tired resignation. 'Jerusalem,' he said. 'Why is it always Jerusalem?'

'I don't understand,' said Graham.

'Well, why did He – Allah, God – have to put the Dome of the Rock, the Holy Sepulchre and the Western Wall within the same square mile?'

'Point taken,' said Graham. 'Well, He *does* move in mysterious ways.'

'Mysterious? That's just downright cruel.'

'Perhaps. But I suppose it was men who built those things, wasn't it? The dome, the wall, the tomb. Maybe He's treating us like children.'

'What do you mean?'

'Do you have any? Children, I mean.'

'No.'

Graham nodded. 'Well,' he said. 'If you have two children, or three children, or however many children, and they're squabbling, you sit them down. You make them resolve the argument. You don't let them leave the table until it's resolved. You can try separating them, send them off to different rooms or different naughty corners, but as soon as they're back together, in the same room, they'll just carry on fighting. Am I making sense?'

'Kind of,' said Ibrahim. 'Except two kids arguing aren't packing bombs and missiles.'

'No,' said Graham. 'Quite. And let us be grateful for that small mercy.'

Ibrahim laughed. 'Well,' he said. 'If it was His plan to make Muslims, Jews and Christians sort it out themselves, it kind of backfired, don't you think? We've had, what, fifteen hundred years to sort it out, more or less. And look at us.'

'You have a point.'

'And this Rapture. Happening any time soon?'

'We believe so,' said Graham. 'The signs are all there. The wars, the earthquakes, everything that's happened in the Middle East, all in accordance with prophecy. We believe it'll happen very soon.'

'So maybe we'll never sort it out.'

'Maybe not.'

Ibrahim had nothing more to say. What was left of his food was now cold. He looked out through the window, at the pools of light spread out across the car park in a grid, and at the broken-down minibus with its badly painted logo. 'And you're driving to Israel?' He asked, remembering a time when he had refused to call the country by that name.

'Oh yes,' said Graham. 'First to Dover, taking the ferry to Calais. From there we drive across Europe, Turkey, down through the Middle East. We could have flown to Tel Aviv, but it's quite expensive.'

Ibrahim stifled a laugh. Surely, if Graham and his flock were right, they'd soon have no need for money. 'That's a long way to go in a minibus,' he said, trying not to smirk.

'I suppose it is,' said Graham. 'But it'll be worth it in the end.'

Ibrahim contemplated these last words – 'in the end' – and felt the hair on his arms and on the back of his neck stand up. It wasn't just a throwaway figure of speech, an 'at the end of the day' or a 'when all's said and done'. When Graham spoke about 'the end', he meant the absolute end, and though Ibrahim no longer believed any such end would come, at least not within the lifetime of anyone he knew, a part of him still wondered what that day would be like. Certainly, he had once believed in the idea of it. It was the driving force of his convictions, the central pillar supporting his every furiously held belief. The rhetoric of his friends, and of the books they read in the *halaqah*, was of war and destruction, blood and fury, the end of days, and he often wondered if eschatology was the one true dovetail between the religions. Forget that dusty square mile in Jerusalem, with its dome, its tomb, its wall. Forget the names that appeared in each book – Ibrahim and Abraham, Issa and Jesus. The one thing they all had in common was a fantasy, almost a fetish, of devastation; the fervour of their believers longing for battles and earthquakes like adolescent boys watching big-screen pyrotechnics. What was so terrible, so disappointing about this world that they were willing it to end?

Before he or Graham could say any more, they were joined by the younger man, Zack. He stood next to their table, beaming down at them both.

'I've called the AA,' he said.

'What?' said Graham. 'But I…'

'It's fine,' said Zack. 'The way I see it, it's all part of the plan. These people do their jobs for a reason. So if we need help, it's already been provided for us.'

'Yes, but the AA…?'

'Yes. The AA. They'll be here in quarter of an hour or so.'

'Oh.'

'The guy I spoke to said it sounds like something to do with a gasket. Or something. Vans aren't really my forte.'

'Right.'

'So we should probably eat up and wait outside for them. We may even get to Dover by midnight.'

Ibrahim almost laughed in his face. Dover by midnight? He must be mad. Dover was days, maybe even weeks away. Then he remembered that not everyone was walking. How quickly his perception had changed. It seemed almost incredible to him now that anyone could travel a hundred miles in less than a day.

'Well, I suppose we should be going,' said Graham, getting to his feet. 'Very nice talking to you, Ibrahim. Perhaps we'll see each other again some day.' And he gestured towards the ceiling or the sky beyond it with a playful nod that Ibrahim found both comical and sad.

From the restaurant he watched as the wingless bumblebee of an AA van pulled up beside the minibus; as Graham and his fellow pilgrims gathered around the mechanic who, in just a few minutes, fixed the problem. Each of them shook the mechanic's hand – that same, two-handed handshake that Graham had given Ibrahim – before sending him on his way, and minutes later they drove across the car park and out onto the motorway. Hard to imagine they'd ever make it in that beat-up looking minibus. They hadn't, after all, travelled very far before hitting the first hurdle. Ahead of them were mountain roads, border officials, corrupt police, and all that before they'd even entered the Middle East. And once they were there, what then? What would they do when the world failed to end on time? Perhaps turn their Rapture Tour into a straightforward holiday. Pick grapes and forget about the older residents of Hebron. No room in their prophecy for unrepentant, unconvertible Muslims.

Ibrahim felt an inner snarl of resentment for the Christians – aligning themselves with Jews after centuries of pogroms in an act of collective amnesia – and a prickling contempt for their apocalyptic daydreams. How many before them had set a date on the End, only to find themselves bitterly, embarrassingly disappointed by the dull continuation of everything?

At least they were on the road, and moving, which was more than could be said for Ibrahim. Now that he was alone again, with Reenie still out there, setting up her makeshift camp, he felt defeated by the motorway, and by this nowhere place. The service station had a name, but was it ever the name of anything more substantial than a village? Was there anything here before the arrival of the motorway? No, this place was a vacuum, a whirlpool at the river's edge, an enchanted island luring in passing vessels and dashing them on its rocks.

He wouldn't stand for it. He wouldn't allow himself to be marooned here, in this place between cities. He could call his sister, get her to drive out and pick him up. It would be inconvenient for her, but nothing measured against the days it might otherwise take for him to get there. She'd be grateful, in the long run. And perhaps Reenie would be happier travelling on her own. Perhaps he'd become an inconvenience to her, dragging her on at a pace she couldn't manage. And perhaps she'd never liked him in the first place; seeing him as nothing more than a pair of hands and feet to help her on her way. How much could she really care for him? And what did he owe her?

He searched the few days he and Reenie had spent together for evidence of her duplicity, and a quiet voice beneath this reminded him that she wasn't just any old woman. She was a Jew. Duplicitous. Money-grubbing. Interested only in her gold, she probably cared more about the birdcage than the bird. Was she walking for any other reason than to save her precious pounds and pennies? Graham and his friends, driving all the way to Hebron in a shitty, rusting minibus, and when they got there they'd be working, picking grapes, and for what? For nothing. Slave labour. Because that's what they were like, Jews. Crafty. Very crafty. Good at calling in favours that weren't owed. Look at how she'd got him to do all her hard work for her. Pushing that trolley. Building the fire. And her sleeping in a nice warm tent while he was outside, in the cold. Her inside a nice, warm tent, laughing at him. Stupid Muslim. Stupid Paki. Doing all the hard work for her and getting nothing in return. Because that's what they're like.

He sat back in his chair so violently its feet shrieked against the tiled floor, and he gasped. If he'd said any of that aloud, in front of friends – his university friends, say – he would have blamed his injury, or the time before Cardiff, before his mother got ill, before *everything*, but those thoughts remained unspoken, and they were his. Not Jamal's, not Yusuf's, not Ismail's. Not the Imam's, nor the Sheikh's, nor the authors of the books they read together after prayers.

At the time of the court case, he'd heard a friend of his father's say, 'But they were just reading books. What kind of a country is it where you can be arrested for the books you read, or the *thoughts* you have? Are we living in a police state now?' And his father had mumbled something about them 'knowing better' and being responsible for their actions, but those words stayed with Ibrahim. Were his friends arrested simply for the books they read and the thoughts they had? Were they *only* books and thoughts? For a long time he had selectively forgotten some things, and convinced himself there was nothing more to their crime, that theirs was indeed a 'bedroom *Jihad*', that they'd never once put those thoughts into action, but they had.

And now he remembered what Graham had said.

'The father of us all.'

And those words echoed, and the echo grew louder, and he saw a name he had known for seven years, a name he had never forgotten, and he marvelled at the unlikelihood – no, the *impossibility* – of it all, and he understood what had to be done.

24

An angel staggered towards her through a haze of drizzle and artificial light, and Reenie squinted at it through the glimmer of dusk, her tired thoughts racing to catch up with what she saw. The angel was in stark silhouette, its body the exaggerated outline of a toddler – oversized head and podgy limbs – but framed by translucent pink wings that shimmered with the lights from the service station. She moved with a stumbling lack of grace, tiny feet splatting down into the puddles, and as the angel got nearer, Reenie heard her sobbing.

A little girl, no older than three. Precocious blonde ringlets, lips pursed in an indignant pout, chubby arms flexed as if she had rolled up imaginary sleeves and was raring for a fight.

Reenie looked around, scanning the car park for anxious parents. With a huff and a groan she eased up onto her feet – her sore, blistered, ruined feet – and edged her way down the embankment. A car was coming across the car park, and the tantruming angel was in its path.

'Oy, love,' said Reenie, her voice hard. She'd never quite known how to speak to children, hadn't the time nor the inclination to start improvising maternal, or grand-maternal baby talk. 'Oy. Love. What's the matter?'

The angel scowled at her, hairless eyebrows knotted above tearful eyes.

'Have you lost your mum and dad?' asked Reenie. She was on the tarmac now, the ground cold and wet beneath her bare feet. She couldn't remember what the protocol was these days. Were you even allowed to talk to other people's kids? And all the time the car was getting closer.

Reenie sighed and shuffled towards the angel, feeling every shard of gravel dig into her soles, and picked her up from the ground.

The child was heavier than she had expected, but she wheeled around until they were both out of the car's way. Then, as if she'd lifted something hot or dirty, Reenie put the little girl back down again.

'Where's your mum and dad?' She said, looking not at the child but scanning the car park for her parents. 'Your mummy and daddy?'

Still no answer.

This was ridiculous. She couldn't leave the trolley; someone might nick it. And who leaves their kid to go wandering off at a service station? What kind of parents…

She should have stopped that car, as it passed by. Stopped them and asked them to get help. Every second she stood there, with that frowning little mute, was as good as proof of guilt, of wrongdoing. Doing nothing was as good as kidnap, surely. That's how the law would see it. She was too tired to even think, too tired for this to be real, and that unreality washed over her in waves. Where were all the people? The car park was empty again, the lights of the service station distant. A lorry pulled in on the far side of the tarmac, but too far away for her to get the driver's attention. And the angel was crying again.

'No, it's okay,' said Reenie. 'We'll find your mum and dad.'

But how? Helpless. That was the word. Helpless. And the two of them were quite alone, in the cold and empty car park. But now she saw two people, running toward them from the service station, and Reenie heard a woman's voice shout, 'Tilly! Tilly!'

Reenie's throat was dry, her voice a rasp. If she tried shouting, they wouldn't hear her, so she waved.

The girl's parents reached them seconds later, and the child ran back to them, her arms reaching up in anticipation of a relieved father's embrace. Hoisted into the air and held against his shoulder she began wailing. The parents – mid-thirties, smartly dressed, as if they'd come from a wedding – looked at Reenie with undisguised apprehension.

'She was wandering out here,' said Reenie. 'She was on her own.'

The parents said nothing to her, turning and walking back to the service station, the father muttering a tender telling off, the mother sighing and gasping half-sentences, until Reenie could no longer hear them. No thank you, nothing. Didn't say a word to her. Not so much as a by your leave. Maybe thanking her would have meant admitting a mistake, admitting they just weren't paying attention when the little girl came tottering out here in the first place.

Reenie shook her head and went back to the embankment. Some people. No, not some. Most. You hold a door open; they barge through without saying a word. Give them back their daughter, and they look at you like you were the one who took her in the first place. Like no one can be bothered any more. Everyone walking down the street with those little headphones in. Sitting on the bus, music buzzing away like a swarm of bees. She could remember when strangers said 'good morning' to one another. Wouldn't happen these days. Say good morning to a stranger nowadays and they'd look at you like you were mad. They just didn't want to know. Everyone living in their own little world. And if you dropped down dead right there in the street they'd walk past you, step over you, like you were rubbish. Leave you there for days, most likely. There was only one person you could ever depend upon, and that was yourself. Everyone else goes away, sooner or later. Take Ibrahim. He would probably find himself a lift, while he was in there. Someone with a car, driving to London. He'd slip off when she wasn't looking, she'd never see him again, and that would be the end of it.

She looked to the service station, and sure enough the table where he'd sat a little earlier was now empty; Ibrahim was gone. Halfway to London by now, most likely. Silly of her ever to think he'd do otherwise. Reenie returned to the embankment and sat back down, taking the weight off her aching feet and letting out a very long sigh.

Minutes later she saw him, Ibrahim, leaving the service station. For a moment she expected him to come over, head hung low, a muted, well-rehearsed apology on his lips, but he didn't. Instead he crossed the car park toward the far side, where the articulated lorries were lined up.

She watched as, one by one, he approached the lorries, tapping at their windows, or stopping the drivers as they came down from their cabs. He spoke to each one briefly, and each time the driver shook his head or held up his hands in apology. Ibrahim was growing more desperate, more anxious with each rejection – she could see that, even from this distance – but he kept going, and there were dozens of lorries.

Still, Reenie was sure that as soon as a driver said yes, agreed to drive him, he'd leave and she would never see him again.

Another driver, another rejection, and just as it looked as if he might give up altogether, Ibrahim spotted someone returning to one of the lorries; a tall lad, with short hair, pale skin, a crooked, rugby player's nose. Ibrahim said something and the driver pulled a face, almost a frown, scratched his head and casually lit a cigarette. Awkwardly, and with some difficulty, Ibrahim went down on his knees and clasped his hands together – unbelievable… he was *actually* begging – and Reenie heard their voices, though not their words. It sounded as if the driver was telling Ibrahim to stand up, and as Ibrahim stood the driver nodded, and Ibrahim punched the air and shouted – 'Yes!' – before hobbling across the car park, towards her, the driver following close behind.

'Reenie,' said Ibrahim, short of breath. 'Meet Vincent.'

Reenie rose to her feet a little cautiously, frowning at the driver, and shook his hand.

'Pleased to meet you.'

'Vincent's gonna drive us to London,' said Ibrahim.

'Well, Hammersmith,' Vincent corrected him, pronouncing it *Ammersmeeth*. He sounded French.

'What, *really*?' said Reenie.

'Really,' said Ibrahim.

'I am driving to London anyway,' said Vincent. 'And your friend tells me you are walking, and London, er… *c'est bien loin d'ici*. It is quite far. So I will drive you as far as Hammersmith.'

'You don't want anything for it?' asked Reenie.

'No. Nothing.'

Reenie turned to Ibrahim, still expecting the catch, the clause. Vincent would drive her, but not the trolley, not her things. The framed photographs and her *ketubah* and Solomon's old cage and her books she'd have to leave right here, on the embankment. He wasn't insured. Health and safety. Something like that. But Ibrahim just smiled at her. No catch. And she remembered the way Jonathan had looked at her when he first saw that jagged little scar on her right shoulder, the way he rested his forehead against hers and said, 'I won't let anyone hurt you again', and how, for the first time in years, she had believed the world and all the people in it to be made of something more than cruelty.

'So,' said Ibrahim. 'What do you think?'

'You're on,' said Reenie.

Within minutes Vincent and Ibrahim had loaded her trolley onto the back of the truck, parking it between crates bound for Hammersmith, and as they were about to climb up into the cabin Ibrahim stepped to one side, and Reenie saw him knock back two small, blue pills with a swig of water.

'What was that?' She asked, regretting at once how hard, how much an accusation, it sounded.

'What?'

'Those pills. What were they?'

'Just Valium,' said Ibrahim.

Now everything made sense. Why he was walking. Why, back in Newport, he had turned down the offer of a lift. The way Ibrahim looked at Vincent's lorry, with a weary apprehension, told her everything.

'Can we just wait five minutes?' he said, wiping the water from his lips with his sleeve.

Reenie looked at Vincent, who simply shrugged.

'Makes no difference to me,' said the driver. 'No hurry.'

Ibrahim paced back and fore, his hands shoved into his pockets, walking first in straight lines, then in ever decreasing circles around his backpack. He stood beside Vincent's lorry and rested his forehead against the passenger side door, taking in deep breaths and letting them out slowly.

'Okay,' he said, at last. 'I'm ready.'

Once they were in the cabin, they buckled their seatbelts, and Ibrahim clasped his hands on his knees and closed his eyes. The lorry rumbled to life, the whole thing shuddering around them, and they pulled out from the parking bay and headed for the exit.

'We have lift-off!' Vincent roared, triumphantly, slamming his hand twice on the horn.

Reenie placed her hand over Ibrahim's.

'It's alright, love,' she said. 'We'll get there. We're on our way now.'

Then they were on the motorway, and the lorry's wheels hissed against the wet tarmac, and the broken, dotted lines marking the lanes streamed beneath them, and the motorway lights and the tail-lights of the cars ahead were refracted and amplified by drizzling rain. Reenie rested drowsily against Ibrahim, and he put his arm around her, and they were barely a mile into their journey when she fell asleep.

'What's this?'

Between his forefinger and thumb, Ibrahim held a creased and worn piece of paper; a single page taped to the dashboard.

'That?' said Vincent. 'It's a poem I learned in school.'

'But it looks like it's in English.'

'I know. I learned it in English.'

'What's it about?'

'Read it if you like. It's not the whole poem, only a few lines. Read it.'

'I can't. It's too dark, and my eyesight's rubbish.'

'That's okay,' said Vincent. 'I can remember it.'

'What, the whole poem?'

'Yes. I remembered all of it. Learned it all.'

'Don't believe you.'

'No? The part on that piece of paper says, *"For always roaming with a hungry heart, much have I seen and known; cities of men and manners, climates, councils, governments, myself not least, but honoured of them all, and drunk delight of battle with my peers, far on the ringing plains of windy Troy."'*

Ibrahim said nothing, but peered at the scrap of paper, struggling to make out the words in the irregular flashes of copper light that filled the cabin. What words he made out matched, almost perfectly, those said by Vincent.

'How'd you remember all that?' he asked.

'I told you. I learned it in school.'

'Who's it by?'

'Tennyson. He was a famous English poet.'

'Yeah. I've heard of Tennyson. I just… it's not really my thing, you know? Poetry, I mean. What's it about?'

'Ulysses. It's about Ulysses. Odysseus. He's looking back on his life, as an old man. It is a very good poem, I think.'

'I'll take your word for it.'

He looked again at the piece of paper. They were driving on another dark stretch of motorway, and the printed words were now little more than hieroglyphs.

'So why've you got it in here?' he asked.

'Because I like it,' said Vincent. 'Because it reminds me of my life, maybe. I don't know. We live in these things. Drivers, I mean. They are our homes.'

'And who's this?' said Ibrahim, pointing at a photograph next to the scrap of paper.

'That is my sister,' said Vincent. 'Her name is Zoe.'

'She's pretty.'

Vincent scowled at him. 'She is my sister.'

'Sorry.'

'But yes,' Vincent laughed. 'You are right. She is very pretty. But that photograph, it's quite old now. There, she is maybe twenty, twenty-one. Now, she must be thirty. I haven't seen her in a long time.'

'How long?'

'Seven years, maybe.'

'Does she live far away?'

'No. Not really. In Nanterre. Just outside Paris. Do you know it?'

'No.'

'Well, that is where she lives. But she has a family now, and they don't know me.'

The radio played quietly enough so as not to stir Reenie. Jazz mostly, and sometimes low, ponderous voices talking about the music. The Valium had calmed Ibrahim enough for him to sit in a moving truck, not enough for him to forget everything before that night, but he didn't want to forget.

He had spent years forgetting, had structured much of his life around forgetting, and so while Reenie slept he revisited a single moment over and over, reviewing it as if it were videotaped evidence. He replayed clips that lasted seconds, flashes of unhinged violence; single, blunt moments of barbarism. He heard the dull, stony crack of breaking marble; the rattle of a ball bearing inside a can, the snake's hiss of spray paints. He heard Jamal and the others laughing, cheering, goading him on. Ibrahim, the youngest, was also the quietest in their group. If there was doubt about anyone's conviction, about anyone's courage and nerve, it was his. He was too bookish, too academic, ever to take it seriously. And yet there they were, on that night, with their hammers and their chisels and their paint, and he was more crazed than any of them.

'Check it out,' Jamal squealed with delight. 'Brother's gone *pagal*!'

And again he heard the cold hard smack of hammer against stone; the dry rustle of flaking chips and splinters. Sweat running down his face. Another smack, and another chunk of marble fell away. He enjoyed the weight of the hammer in his hand, the way it gathered its own momentum when he swung it. It felt good, destroying something. The others tried, but he was bigger and stronger than them. At last, his sheer bulk served some purpose, and now his friends saw that beneath him, beneath bookish, awkward, lumbering Ibrahim, was something brutal. They'd mocked him so many times; for the books he read, for his love of history. Told him he was studying lies and propaganda, written by *kuffar* bastards. Believe their lies and you may as well be one of them. But no one ever took to vandalism as enthusiastically as Ibrahim, and this wasn't just vandalism; the scrawling of another declaration of lust or an insult on the inside of some bus shelter. This was absolute destruction. With his hammer and his chisel he was scratching a name from history, chipping away at history itself. As good as killing someone, that was how he rationalised it. Take a man's name and he might never have lived at all. And now a name was broken and chipped and lying in a hundred or more slivers of shattered marble, while the nameless man lay six feet beneath. They'd chosen him at random, for no other reason than that he was buried in *this* cemetery, and Jamal and Yusuf and Ismail made similar attempts on other gravestones, but none were as accomplished, as absolute, as Ibrahim's. He'd gone to town on that inscription, on the Latin and Hebrew letters carved into the marble, until there was almost nothing left of it. For just those few minutes he had hated the dead man, a stranger, more than anyone who'd ever lived.

When they had vandalised perhaps a dozen or more headstones, with spray paint and chisels, they heard the sound of barking dogs from the far side of the cemetery and made a run for it; climbing the far wall, using an old rug to clear the barbed wire, landing painfully and awkwardly in the darkness of Brampton Park before laughing all the way home.

The irony, almost seven years after that night, was that Ibrahim had never forgotten the name carved so elegantly into that headstone. He'd forgotten the names of people he had met and known – old school friends and university acquaintances, friends of his parents – but had never forgotten the name on that headstone, and he saw it now as clearly as he had before taking to it with a hammer and chisel.

They were perhaps halfway between Bristol and London when, out of nowhere, Vincent slammed his hand down on the horn and cheered.

'One million miles!' He said. 'I have travelled a million miles!'

Reenie stirred, but was too tired to wake fully. Ibrahim asked the driver what he meant, and Vincent told him that in his life as a truck driver he had driven a million miles, that they were now driving through his millionth. He smiled at Ibrahim across the cabin, and took in a long, shuddering breath.

'I am glad someone was here to see this,' he said, still smiling.

And just as leaving London had always felt like a take-off, so entering it again from the west was a landing; the road elevated above the suburbs, flying in between oversized billboards and glass-fronted offices. Reenie woke up as they neared Hammersmith; a sudden stop at traffic lights jolting her awake. She sat upright and looked out at the road ahead.

'Where are we?'

'London,' said Ibrahim, as if even he didn't quite believe it.

So many times when he was a student the drive between Cardiff and London had dragged, the silences between father and son painfully acute, but that night, despite the scene he'd revisited, over and over, and the twin drones of nausea and anxiety underlying every moment spent in the truck, the journey seemed to have lasted minutes. It felt as if they had cheated the laws of physics, bent the fabric of time to get here, but now that they were in London he wanted nothing more than to get out and start walking again.

Vincent took them off the carriageway at the Hammersmith flyover, and kept driving until he had found somewhere to pull in. There, he let Ibrahim and Reenie out of the cabin and offloaded the trolley.

'Well, this is it,' he said, smiling. 'I would say *'à bientôt'*, but I think we will not see each other again.'

As the truck drove away and turned a corner, and the sound of it faded into the city's rumble, Reenie turned to Ibrahim and said, 'It's funny. I think I've met more people in the last week than I have in the last ten years.'

And now the unreal city sprawled before them, an immense patchwork of towns and villages stitched together with roads and train tracks, but it was getting late. The Tube stations were closing, the bus services winding down; just a handful of night services carrying the gaunt, the tired and the drunk back to their homes.

Ibrahim would have to cross the city, and possibly on foot. Though he'd conquered, at least in part, his terror of travelling by car, he couldn't face the claustrophobia of the Tube. Newham was more than ten miles away, as suburban as Hammersmith, and between the two suburbs lay the noise and danger of London.

He could always call his sister. Now that he was in London, she couldn't object to coming out, no matter what time it was. He imagined they would drive across the city in near silence, neither of them daring to speak. Perhaps she'd drive him straight to the hospital and he'd see his father for the first time in almost four years. He created and recreated the scene with different emphases. In one version he and his sister argued in a hospital corridor, or rather he stood silent and sullen as his kid sister yelled at him. In another he broke down crying the moment they entered his father's room, as the weight of all human mortality bore down on him in one crushing moment.

Then he thought of Reenie. It was a Saturday night, and the streets of Hammersmith were busy with drunks – incoherent songs sung loudly, the harsh music of glass breaking on concrete, the sirens of police cars and ambulances overlapping to form a single, atonal wail. Even if they found somewhere for her to pitch up for the night, she wouldn't be safe.

He asked her where she was going.

'Mayfair, to start off,' she said. 'I've got to see someone there. Too late to see them now, though. How about you? Where are you going?'

'Newham,' he replied.

'Newham!' said Reenie. 'That's where I grew up. Small world, ain't it?'

And though she was grinning at him with a kind of nostalgia, he didn't smile back, because it was another confirmation of something he already knew, something nauseating and dreadful. He was from Newham, she was from Newham. In Cardiff they had both lived near Roath Park. He wasn't superstitious, but he believed in patterns, in the almost astronomical beauty of chance. There didn't have to be a reason, or some great force behind the coincidences that brought them together like the pieces of a puzzle. All it took was a world of billions to allow those fragments to be carved just right, for two people, two strangers, to be mirrored in that way.

They walked through the night; heels dragging, trolley rattling; their pain and tiredness almost transcendental, as if they had become their agony and exhaustion. It took almost two hours for them to reach St James's Park, and it was a walk neither of them needed. Even so, as they passed Harrods, then Buckingham Palace, he sensed her joy at seeing each landmark, each one a confirmation that they were getting there.

Halfway along The Mall they left the road, and with some difficulty pushed the trolley out across the park until they'd found a point some distance from the roads and paths where they could set up camp. This place, midway between The Mall and the lake, was dark enough to be almost invisible to anyone driving by, but with just enough light from the roads and from the ochre night-time clouds for him to see what he was doing as he unpacked and pitched the tent. Reenie set up her camp stove and the kettle, and in the darkness and the noise of the city they sat on deckchairs drinking tea. Reenie laughed.

'What is it?' he asked 'What you laughing at?'

'Us,' said Reenie. 'Look at us. It's gone midnight and we're having a picnic in the middle of St James's Park, like a couple of tramps.'

Ibrahim peered at her through the dark, and could just make out her face, and her helpless grin, tears glistening in the corners of her eyes. He looked out across the park, at the silhouettes of distant trees, the London Eye lit up like a crescent of gemstones beneath dark, infernal clouds, and the glowing, yellow clock face of Big Ben. He latched on to these as the proof, if it were needed, that they'd made it, that they were *here*, and though his legs were in agony and his bruises and scabs were still sore, he felt the skin along his shoulders and arms rise up in gooseflesh, and that night-time postcard of the city began to blur and sparkle through his tears.

Big Ben was halfway through its hourly rendition of Portsmouth Bell when the shower began; the raindrops whispering on the leaves of nearby trees, the subtle droop of each leaf causing branches to dip and rustle. Reenie began packing away the camp stove, the kettle and the mugs, but as she climbed inside the tent Ibrahim stayed outside, sitting in the rain.

'You staying out here?'

Ibrahim shrugged. 'Not much else I can do.'

'Get in.'

'What? But...'

'Don't be daft. Get in. It's pissing down.'

Were there any more light, she may have noticed the sudden colour in his cheeks; an almost adolescent blushing. Yes, it was raining, and yes he was cold, but he hadn't shared a bed with a woman in over three years, and the idea of sharing a bed was so entangled with the dark morass of sexual desire and guilt that, despite her age and the absence of any physical attraction, he found the prospect daunting and shameful.

'Er, I...'

'Listen, Ibrahim. Stop being a prat. It's raining. Get in. I'll keep my hands to myself, I promise. But shoes off. I'm not having you traipsing mud in here.'

The tent was small, even smaller than he'd imagined, and the two of them lay close together, their thick clothes only adding to their bulk. Every slight movement caused a rustle of man-made fibres, and there were several moments of awkward shuffling and wriggling before they were both comfortable beneath her single blanket; not touching, and all too aware of the person next to them in the dark.

'Goodnight,' said Reenie.

'Goodnight,' said Ibrahim.

Though at first he was unsure he'd be able to sleep, within minutes Ibrahim was unconscious, too exhausted by the day, and by all the days of the week so far, for the sounds of traffic, or of aeroplanes, or of raindrops puttering against the canvas to keep him awake.

25

''Scuse me, sir, but would you mind stepping out of the tent?'

A heavy-set man in a beige coat, and beneath that a grey suit, blue shirt, patterned tie; leaning into the tent. Behind him, another man in a suit. They looked official, important, serious.

His thoughts still muddled by the leftovers of a dream, Ibrahim raised himself up on his elbows, for a moment forgetting where they were, imagining they might still be in some remote place far from any town or city.

'What's happening?' he mumbled, wiping the sleep from his eyes and clearing his throat.

'I'm DCI Garfield, Metropolitan Police. Could I take your name, sir?'

'What? Metropolitan? What?'

London. They were in London. They were driven to London, dropped off in Hammersmith. Walked from Hammersmith to St James's. Pitched Reenie's tent in the park, a short distance from The Mall. In the early hours that tent was invisible against the park's black fields. Now, after sunrise, its orange canvas must have stood out like a beacon against the green.

'Would you mind stepping out of the tent?' The DCI asked, more impatiently than before.

Ibrahim nodded and, after slipping on his trainers, crawled towards the bright morning. Behind him Reenie began to wake, and outside and upright he saw the second plainclothes policeman; taller, younger and red-haired with a moustache and goatee beard.

'Morning,' said Ibrahim.

'This is DI Donovan,' said DCI Garfield. 'Would you mind telling us your name?'

'I'm sorry?'

'Your name, sir? Could you tell us your name?'

'Ibrahim Siddique,' he replied. 'What's happening?'

'Sir… are you aware that you are not permitted to camp in the park without permission?'

'What?'

'You are camping in the park without permission. Did you know this is against the law?'

'What? No, I… really?'

'Yes, sir. Could I ask what you're doing here?'

The flaps of the tent opened, and Reenie poked her head out, scowling at the two detectives, then at Ibrahim. 'Who're they?'

'CID,' said Ibrahim. 'We're camping illegally.'

'Who says? And why've they sent CID?'

'Madam,' said DCI Garfield. 'Do you know this man?'

'I should bloody hope so. I've just shared a tent with him, so I don't know what it would say about me if I didn't.'

'And what relation is… er… he to you?'

'He's my *friend*,' said Reenie. 'Now, alright, okay, maybe we're not allowed to camp here, but we'll be packed up and on our way in…'

'I'm afraid it's a bit more serious than that, madam. Mr Siddique… if you'd care to join me. We'll just go over to the car and go through a few more questions.'

Ibrahim looked at Reenie and shrugged, a small, tired part of him wondering if this was some elaborate prank. One of those TV shows with a hidden camera, and a studio audience laughing at the footage, and the person being pranked standing there on stage, embarrassed and blushing.

'Mr Siddique?'

'Yeah, sure,' said Ibrahim. 'Whatever.'

He followed Garfield across the field, towards The Mall, and heard Reenie's volley of short, irritated questions to the second detective getting quieter with the distance. Garfield spoke into his walkie-talkie; most of it indecipherable gibberish to anyone but a police officer, but the one turn of phrase Ibrahim understood clearly was 'requesting back-up'.

On reaching the car, the DCI had him put his hands on the roof and patted him down, finding only a wallet, a set of keys, and a wad of printouts, which he unfolded one by one, laying them out on the car's roof.

'What're these?' he asked.

'Maps,' said Ibrahim.

'I can see that. What are they for?'

'I've been walking. I needed maps.'

'I see.'

DCI Garfield helped him into the car, a large saloon, and closed the door behind him with a loud clunk before climbing into the driver's seat.

'Mr Siddique. Do you know where you are?'

'What? What kind of a… yes. Yes. I know where I am.'

The DCI said nothing else; he simply raised one eyebrow and nodded, as if to prompt a more elaborate answer. In the closeness of the car's interior, Ibrahim imagined the detective would smell of cigarette smoke laced with aftershave and maybe toothpaste, if only he could still smell. Rather, that smell was half tasted, half imagined.

'I'm in London,' he said. 'St James's Park.'

'That's right,' said the DCI. 'St James's Park. And about three hundred yards down there is…?' He pointed out through the windshield, towards the far end of The Mall.

'Buckingham Palace?' said Ibrahim, with a noncommittal shrug.

'That's right. Buckingham Palace. And about a quarter of a mile over there?' He pointed over Ibrahim's left shoulder, through the car's rear window.

Ibrahim craned his head around, but all he could see was the park and the distant trees. 'I'm not sure,' he said.

'Houses of Parliament,' said DCI Garfield. 'Now, perhaps you could tell me why you were camping in the middle of the park between Buckingham Palace and the Houses of Parliament.'

'What?'

'Who's the old woman, Ibrahim? It *is* Ibrahim, isn't it?'

'Yes… I… what?'

'The old woman. Who's the old woman?'

'Her name's Reenie. Well, Irene. We met in… we've been walking. I've been helping her. Why are…'

'Is she homeless? Is she a homeless person?'

'No. She has a tent. She has a *house*. In Cardiff. I…'

'So what's the deal? You saw her here last night? Figured her tent would be a good place to hide out?'

'No. What?'

'Right, Ibrahim. Here's what's going to happen. We're going to take a trip across town, and we're going to have a little chat about why you were camping in the park. How does that sound?'

'A little chat?'

'Ibrahim Siddique, I am arresting you on suspicion of vagrancy. You do not have to say anything, but it may harm your defence if you do not mention when questioned something which you later rely on in court. Anything you do say may be given in evidence.'

'Vagrancy? What are you talking about, 'vagrancy'? I'm not homeless. And that's not what you were talking about. You were talking about Buckingham Palace, about the Houses of Parliament. Do you think I'm a terrorist? Is that it?'

Ibrahim heard himself say the word, but at the same time couldn't quite believe he had said it. Its three syllables seemed to echo in the car.

'You tell me,' said the DCI.

'This is ridiculous.'

'Really?'

'Yes. We've walked from Cardiff. Both of us. We got here last night, and we needed somewhere to stay. She's got that trolley. I thought…'

'Save it for when we get to the station, Ibrahim. I think we should get this down on tape, don't you?'

There were other police cars now, two of them pulling up in front and behind the saloon, and uniformed officers climbed out. Some crossed the park, to where DI Donovan was still talking to – or rather being talked at by – Reenie. There was a brief exchange between uniformed and plainclothes, and the DI walked back to the car, carrying Ibrahim's bag, and climbed in next to him on the back seat.

'Nothing, sir,' he said. 'She says they've been walking from Cardiff. Got here last night.'

DCI Garfield looked at Ibrahim in the rear-view mirror with a bitter, ironic smile.

'Nice work, Ibrahim,' he said. 'I see you've got her well primed.'

Ibrahim refused to meet the detective's glare, instead looking out across the park at Reenie. She was still talking to the uniformed officers, but looked back at him, and he held her gaze as the car began moving along The Mall. The finality in their exchanged glance told him everything he needed to know. They would never see each other again.

'Where are we going?' said Ibrahim.

'Charing Cross Police Station,' said DCI Garfield.

'This is crazy.'

'Is it?' Said DI Donovan. 'You were camping in the park. That's illegal. That's vagrancy right there. Vagrancy Act. 1824.'

'Well remembered, DI Donovan,' said DCI Garfield. 'You ought to go on *Who Wants To Be A Millionaire?* with a memory like that.'

'Thanks, sir.'

'Yeah, but I'm not a vagrant,' said Ibrahim. 'I've got a flat in Cardiff. I'm visiting family in London.'

'Really?' said the DI. 'Family in London? Is that why you were sleeping in a tent?'

'And then there are your maps,' said DCI Garfield. 'And your location when we found you. Look at it from our perspective, Ibrahim. You can see what it looks like.'

'And what about Reenie? What'll happen to her?'

'She'll be fine. Don't worry about her. Obviously, we'll probably have to contact social services, but she'll be looked after.'

'She doesn't *need* looking after. She has somewhere to go. She has to *be* somewhere.'

'Where, Ibrahim? Where does she have to be?'

'Somewhere in Mayfair.'

'Where, exactly, in Mayfair?'

'I don't know.'

'Thought not.'

Nauseous, his body tingling, Ibrahim couldn't bring himself to believe this had happened; that they could travel so far, and for this to happen now, when he was so close to home. Though it must have lasted minutes, the drive across the West End seemed to take hours, and his nausea was coupled with a sense of alienation, of being foreign here. He no longer recognised his surroundings, and he'd forgotten how each part of the city fitted together. He'd hardly ever made these journeys above ground; always underground. When was the last time he had seen the West End? He couldn't put a name to any of these streets.

The police station was an unfamiliar slab of beige tucked away a few streets from Trafalgar Square. Inside they processed him and placed him in a narrow, high-ceilinged cell with no windows, and from there he heard the sound of other prisoners yelling and shouting in the neighbouring cells, the *slap-slap-slap* of people passing by in the corridor, and the endless ringing of distant telephones.

This was it. They had made it to London, they had actually *got* to London, and now this. He thought of all the things the detectives might find, if they just looked hard enough, if they investigated further. Perhaps they would make a connection they had failed to make six years ago, linking him to Jamal and the others. Maybe then they'd join the dots, tie his being in St James's Park on a Sunday morning to the books he had read as a teenager. Or perhaps they would go further than that, and some bright spark would remember the night of vandalism in an East London graveyard. He imagined the moment when, sitting in a box-like interview room, they'd slam the hammer and chisel down onto the table before him, the chisel's blade still dusty with powdered marble. He laughed desperately at the idea that his journey had never been about seeing his father; but was about this. About being caught. No second chances now. He might as well have walked back into London with a sign around his neck, telling everyone what he had done.

When the time came for him to be questioned, he gave only the most recent of facts. His father was in hospital. He was unable to make the journey by car, bus or train. He began walking. On the road he met Reenie Glickman, and they walked together, for a while, before parting. They were reunited on the outskirts of Bristol, and they took to the motorway.

'You *walked* on the motorway?' said DI Donovan, scratching at his russet beard with his index finger.

Ibrahim nodded.

'You *do* know that's illegal?' said DCI Garfield.

From the station he tried calling his sister, but the call was diverted to her voicemail. He gave the detectives her details. She could verify his story, he told them.

Back in the cell, he found he was unable to focus on any one thought with undivided attention, as if every concern was a brick, and those bricks had built up into an impenetrable wall. He was in a police station and his father was in a hospital. Reenie was... well, Reenie could be anywhere, as could his sister. The police could do anything with him, anything they liked. They had the power now, didn't they? And what sympathy would there be for him? What sympathy was there for anyone arrested like this, when a name like his was as good as proof of guilt? The details were all there, the circumstantial details that would give the papers what they wanted. He was arrested between Buckingham Palace and the Houses of Parliament. There's no smoke without fire. And with him, the fire was there, if only they could find it, and they might.

26

She'd weathered many things in the last few weeks – washing and going to the toilet outdoors, surviving on scraps – but this took the cake. For the uniformed officers who arrived, shortly before they took Ibrahim away, she played dumb. No, worse than that – she played *senile*. Not *incompetently* senile. That would have had them calling social services, the arrival of concerned people with clipboards, and a swift referral to a hospital or care home. No, instead she played *mildly* senile – doddering and bemused, the harmless old bag lady – and it helped that she certainly looked the part, but she hated every second of it. She hated their patronising tenderness, the soft tone of voice they adopted, the way they spoke about Ibrahim. She insisted he'd done nothing wrong, that they'd been together since Cardiff, but here her playact senility backfired on her, and they humoured her, telling her no harm would come to the young man, that they just needed to ask him a few questions. She knew what that meant, understood perfectly the veiled threat those words contained, but there was nothing she could do.

Once they'd left her, one of the officers having pushed her trolley back as far as The Mall, Reenie made her way into Mayfair. Here, she saw the difference between small town folk and Londoners. In the small towns and villages people had stared at her openly; here in London they made a point of *not* staring at her, of looking everywhere but at her.

The address on the letter was a place she'd heard of but never visited; a narrow, cobbled street of Georgian townhouses. Reenie ambled along the pavement, checking each house number in turn, and received a condescending sideways glance from a woman in a fur coat who clipped and clopped past her in stilettos. She got a similar look from a man in a tweed suit who passed by walking an Afghan hound. When she found the house she was looking for,

Reenie parked her trolley next to a bollard, rang the doorbell, and waited.

From within the house she heard muffled voices, footsteps on a staircase, and then the sound of perhaps half-a-dozen locks being turned before the door was opened by a young man, no older than thirty; short blond hair and pale blue eyes, dressed in a bright red jumper and blue jeans. He looked almost Swedish or perhaps Norwegian, and Reenie wondered if she had the wrong house. It was hard enough for her to imagine any relative of hers living in a place like this, let alone looking quite so *goyish*. The young man looked at her askance and said, 'Hello? Can I help you?'

'Lauren Bartlett?' said Reenie, hesitantly. 'I'm here to see Lauren Bartlett.'

'That's my wife. Could I ask who you are?'

'My name's Reenie. I mean Irene. Irene Glickman.'

He took a step back, dazed and blinking as if the morning sun was suddenly blinding, and stuttered half-formed words until calling back into the house: 'Lauren. Could you come here a moment?'

In the darkened hallway, Reenie saw movement, a silhouette making its way from the back of the house toward them, which in turn became a young woman with long dark hair. There were traces in her looks familiar to Reenie; the wide expressive eyes and strong, high cheekbones of Albert, perhaps even a trace of Reenie at that age. The woman stood beside her husband and looked at Reenie with a cautious half-smile.

'Hello?' she said. 'I'm sorry, do I…'

'This is Irene Glickman,' said the young man.

She gasped and covered her mouth with her hand, and her eyes began to glass over with tears.

'You're Irene?' She said, the words catching in her throat.

Reenie nodded.

'Then you'd better… I mean… come in. Please.'

Their house was beautiful. Fresh flowers in vases, fine rugs on polished floors. In the sitting room, arabesque cushions scattered on plump sofas. A real, working fireplace; empty, but waiting for winter. A mantelpiece crowded with family photographs. A homeliness and cosiness Reenie remembered, but that felt distant and foreign to her now.

With her husband still pondering the trolley parked on the street outside Lauren took Reenie through to the kitchen, which backed onto a small, artfully unkempt terrace. Feeling scruffy, and dirty, and smelly, and about as out-of-place as she'd ever felt, Reenie sat at the large, oak kitchen table, while Lauren went about making tea.

'We could have come to Cardiff,' said Lauren, her back to Reenie as the kettle boiled. 'I said in the letter. It wouldn't have been a problem.'

'I wanted to come here,' said Reenie. 'I thought it for the best.'

'Right. And how did you get here? I mean… the trolley. Is it yours?'

'Yeah. We walked. Well, part of the way.'

'You *walked*?' Lauren turned, frowning and blinking in disbelief.

'Yeah. Only *part* of the way. A Frenchman drove us most of the M4.'

'A French… who's "we"?'

'A friend I met when I was walking.'

'Do you take sugar?'

'No thanks, love. Just milk.'

'And this friend…?'

'He's been picked up by the police. We camped out on St James's Park last night and they picked us up this morning.'

'You camped out on… I'm sorry. Did you say he's been picked up?'

'Yes. He's Paki*stan*i, see? I think they thought he was up to no good. And the thing is, he wasn't. He's a good lad. Bit shy, but he's a good lad. I don't even know where they took him.'

'Okay,' said Lauren. 'Well, listen. My husband. Paul. He works with the Home Office. Perhaps we could, I mean… he must have contacts. I… I mean, it's Sunday, so, you know… but still…'

'Oh, if there's anything you could do that would be lovely,' said Reenie. 'Poor boy wouldn't say boo to a goose, so he must be worrying himself sick if they've got him in the cells.'

Lauren nodded distractedly, holding a cup of tea in both hands.

She leaned back against the granite work surface, considering her next words, her mouth opening and closing silently with each abortive attempt.

'You *walked* here?' she said at last, though Reenie was fairly certain she had already answered that question.

'Yeah, like I said, but we hitchhiked most of it.'

'Right.'

The door opened slowly with a creak and Lauren's husband appeared in the doorway.

'Uh... I've chained your trolley to the bollard with one of my bike locks,' he said. 'It should be... you know... it should be fine. It's quite a nice, uh... neighbourhood. Not much... you know...'

'This is my husband, Paul,' said Lauren.

With a still-distracted expression, Paul waved at Reenie from the doorway.

'Listen,' said Lauren. 'Paul. Um. Irene has a friend. She was walking with him. Apparently he's been picked up by the police.'

'The *police*? What? Arrested?'

'Yes,' said Lauren. 'And, well, I was just wondering if you could maybe, I don't know, find out where he is, where they've taken him. It all sounds like a misunderstanding, isn't that right?'

Reenie nodded.

'Right,' said Paul. 'And where was this? Where was he arrested?'

'The Mall,' said Reenie.

'Okay,' said Paul. 'Well, they'll probably have taken him to Charing Cross. But, you know, it's the *police*. I work for the Home Office...'

'*Paul*,' said Lauren, opening her eyes wide and leaning forward, as if nudging him into action.

'But... I suppose I *could* make a few calls...'

'Thank you,' said Reenie. 'That's very kind of you.'

Nodding, but still dazed, Paul stepped back into the hallway, closing the door behind him.

'I'm sorry,' said Lauren. 'We weren't... I mean... this is all such a surprise. We didn't think you'd actually... I don't know. The children... they're with Paul's parents in Ham for the weekend, otherwise they'd be... and... It's just. It's a surprise, that's all.'

'Did you have plans? 'Cause I can come back later if you're going out somewhere, or...'

'No, not at all. No. It's fine. Really. It's just a surprise.'

Lauren looked away, having run out of things to say, and Reenie placed down her mug.

'So,' she said. 'How did you find me? You never said. In your letter, I mean.'

'Well,' said Lauren, sitting at the far end of the table. 'It wasn't easy. Granddad, I mean *your* dad, Albert... he spent years looking, asking around, but, well... this was a *long* time ago. I think he thought you'd stayed in London, maybe gone south of the river or something. London's certainly big enough to just lose someone, I guess.'

Reenie nodded. After leaving Upton Park she'd stayed in London another three years, and hadn't once seen anyone who knew her from before.

'And when did my dad pass away?' she asked.

'That was in '82,' said Lauren. 'I was only little at the time, so I don't really remember much about him. My brother remembers him better. He's three years older than me. Lives in Hong Kong.'

'And Vera? I mean your Grandma?'

'Oh, she died last year,' said Lauren. 'She was ninety-two. A right old battleaxe.'

'And your mum?'

'Mum passed away three years ago. She'd been diagnosed, first diagnosed back when Dominic, my brother, and I were kids. She beat it that time, went into remission, but it came back.'

Reenie looked down. The letter had explained some of it. Lauren's mother was born Dorothy Lieberman, three years after Reenie ran away. She was the only child of Albert and Vera, and in time married and had two children of her own. Dorothy Lieberman was Reenie's sister, nineteen years younger than her, and they had never met.

'After Granddad died, Grandma, I mean Vera, carried on looking for you,' said Lauren.

'Really?'

'Yes. There were things she wanted to give you, things Granddad had kept. I think Grandma blamed herself for, well, for what you did. She even hired a private detective at one point.'

Reenie laughed bitterly.

'Seriously,' said Lauren. 'About twenty years ago. She hired a private detective. Bit of a con, if you ask me. He wasn't very good. Found nothing. Charged her a *lot*. Kind of put her off trying another, I think.'

'Okay,' said Reenie. 'So how did *you* find me?'

Lauren smiled. 'Well, as I said, Paul works with the Home Office.' She closed her eyes and shook her head bashfully. 'Obviously, don't go telling anyone I said that. Paul would get in a *lot* of trouble. I mean, it's not like we broke the law, not really. It was just electoral roll information. And one or two other bits and pieces. We found something from the early '60s saying that an Irene Lieberman had married a Jonathan… that's his name, right?'

'It was,' said Reenie.

'Oh, I'm sorry.'

'It's fine, love.'

'Well. We found something saying an Irene Lieberman had married a Jonathan Glickman in Cardiff, and then we checked the electoral roll, found Irene Glickman, wrote to you, and now you're here.'

'And now I'm here.'

A human silence fell between them; the only sound in the room the faraway drone of a descending aeroplane.

'You said my dad kept stuff by for me,' said Reenie.

'That's right. Just a few bits and pieces. They weren't particularly wealthy, Albert and Vera. It's just a box full of things. There was no inheritance or anything like that…'

'I never thought there would be.'

'I'll just go and get it for you,' said Lauren, rising from the table and leaving Reenie alone in the kitchen. She heard Lauren climb the stairs, and the sound of her footsteps on the landing, then murmured words between Lauren and her husband, a cupboard door opening and closing, more footsteps on the stairs, and Lauren came back carrying a small, crumpled shoebox, placing it down on the table.

'That's it,' she said. 'That's everything, I'm afraid. Like I said, we could have brought it to you, or posted it…'

'No,' said Reenie. 'That's fine. I'm glad I came here.'

She lifted the lid off the box, releasing at once the dry, smoky scent of old paper and dust. Inside were trinkets, nothing of any worth. A pin cushion with rusting pins still embedded between its embroidered flowers. A small, yellowing copy of the *Lambs' Tales From Shakespeare*. A handkerchief monogrammed with Reenie's childhood initials; *IL*. A black and white photograph of Reenie and her father, taken on a sunny afternoon in Margate. Few of the objects held any significance for her. Some stirred vague memories, none of them momentous, but finally she came to the picture frame, face down, at the bottom of the box. She knew it immediately, without having to turn it over, recognising the marbled pattern of its backing, and its creased support made of thick card. She knew, almost by touch alone, the single brass tack holding that support in place, and recognised the chip in the frame's corner where, as a child, she'd once knocked it down from the mantelpiece during a game, sending her father into a rage that terrified her. Fortunately the glass hadn't broken, and the frame – and its picture – was placed back on the mantelpiece, where it stayed until the day her father remarried.

Reenie lifted the frame from the box, turned it over, and looked down at a face she hadn't seen in sixty years. As a child the picture hadn't looked to her like an antique. All photographs were black and white or sepia then, and there was nothing, in the subject's clothes or the way her hair was styled or in the little make-up that she wore, that made it feel like a relic. It had been easy enough for Reenie to imagine this woman laughing, or smiling, or greeting her when she came home from school. In the years that had since passed, Reenie had forgotten almost everything about the portrait, to the point where she could no longer quite picture her mother's face. It was sepia; that was all she knew. And now the photograph looked old, so old, and the woman in it was a fraction of Reenie's age, little more than a girl.

'He kept this,' said Reenie, her voice breaking until the last word was barely a whisper.

'Yes,' said Lauren. 'He kept all these things. For his sake, as much as anything, I think.' Lauren reached across the table and closed her hand around Reenie's. 'He missed you so much.'

Reenie nodded without looking up at her. She couldn't take her eyes off the photograph, but neither could she forgive herself for the years she had lost and the family she would never know. Many years ago she had resigned herself to the idea that fate would have its way; that in leaving her family she had, in turn, met Jonathan, and that this was her happy ending, that it was meant to be, but there had always been regret. Of course she hadn't expected her father to be alive, still, or for even Vera to have lasted as long as she had, but without knowing for certain, neither were they dead. Rather, they were preserved, never ageing or changing with time. Now that the photograph of her mother looked like an antique, and this young woman was without grandparents or a mother, the past was definite, the outlines of that vague but constant sense of grief Reenie had felt brought into a clearer definition.

'And where is he now?' she asked, wiping tears from her eyes with the back of her hand. 'My dad, I mean. Where did they bury him? Was he buried?'

Lauren nodded. 'East London,' she said. 'Near where they lived. He chose the cemetery. I think later on in life he regretted some of the choices he'd made, and... well... he wanted to be buried there. We can take you there. I mean, if you'd like, we could...'

'No, thanks,' said Reenie, standing and placing the framed photograph back in the box. 'It's fine. Thanks, anyway. I've made it this far. Another couple of miles on the Tube won't make any difference.'

'Fair enough,' said Lauren. 'But before you go to his grave, there's something you should know.'

27

Aisha was waiting for him in the police station's reception, her handbag in her lap, knees close together, distracted and impatient. On seeing him, she stood and he paused, trying to take in – to accept – the sight of her as a woman. When he last saw her she was still a teenager, still girlish, but now her posture, the way she looked at him, everything about her was grown up.

DCI Garfield offered a mealy-mouthed apology for the inconvenience, qualifying it with several 'Of-Course-You-Understands', and of course, he understood. He understood perfectly how the details tied in with their chosen narrative; the young man with his maps, found sleeping between the palace and parliament. He almost felt sorry for them, as the different pieces of the puzzle fell away, as the elements of his – Ibrahim's – version of events came together and made sense. They called his sister, checked with the hospital. They did *not* make any connection to arrests now seven years old or to the damage done at a cemetery out east, and why should they?

When he was out from behind the wall of glass separating the waiting area and the duty officer's small office, Aisha ran to him and hugged him, standing up on tiptoes to get her arms around his shoulders and his neck.

'What were you *thinking*?' she said. 'Camping? Near the Mall? Are you mental?'

'I got here, sis,' he said. 'Alright? I got here.'

Aisha's car – she passed her test two years ago; Ibrahim had forgotten to send a card – was parked several streets from the station, in Covent Garden, and for a moment Ibrahim stood on the kerb, looking down at the car with apprehension. He would happily have walked to Newham, sure that he could navigate his way there through a kind of blind instinct, but he knew this would be the final straw, and would piss her off more than anything he'd done this last nine days, and so he climbed into the front passenger seat, and they drove out of Covent Garden and headed east.

'So… you okay?' said Aisha.

'Yeah. I'm okay.'

'What happened to your face?'

'My what?' He flapped down the sun visor and saw his reflection in its small mirror. 'Right. Yeah. My face. I had a bit of trouble. In Gloucester.'

'Right. And that's where you were two days ago, yeah?'

'Yeah.'

A minute or so of silence passed between them. He looked out through the windows, waiting for a familiar street, a landmark, something he might remember, something to reassure him that he *could* have found his own way to Newham, if he'd wanted to. Eventually, when that silence became uncomfortable, he asked, 'How's Dad?'

He was ashamed he hadn't asked earlier, but had known what her response would be.

'How do you fucking think? He's had a stroke. He can't speak properly. He can't walk. Oh, he's dandy, Ib. Fine and fucking dandy.'

'Aish, please, don't swear.'

She looked at him across the car, appalled, and let out a short, desperate laugh.

'Don't swear? Don't *swear*? You've got a fucking nerve.'

'I didn't mean it like… I just mean it sounds wrong. You swearing.'

'Right. Because I'm your little sister, yeah?'

'Yes.'

'Well, I know you have trouble thinking about anyone outside your little world, Ib, but I'm actually twenty-one now, so I'll say what the fuck I like, *thankyouverymuch*.'

'Aish…'

'Ib, don't. Alright? Just don't. I'm not… I'm not *mad* at you. I'm just having a bit of a hard time of it right now, okay? I've been the one staying at the hospital. I've been the one phoning everyone, giving them updates, and a fat lot of good they've been. The family,

I mean. Oh, don't get me wrong, they've got a billion remedies for every illness under the sun. Except a stroke. If he'd had a heart attack they'd say' – she adopted a strong, sing-song Punjabi accent – 'he was eating too many sweets, or that he shouldn't fry everything, or that he should cut down on *ghee*, or that we should call a *hakeem...*' She let out a short, ironic laugh; almost a gasp. 'But a stroke? They just don't know. None of us do. I look at him, and he looks so *small*, Ib. It's like he's shrunk, or something. And it's like half the life has been sucked out of him, like he's lost the will to live. I can't...' she paused as they neared a junction, the only sound in the car the rhythmic tapping of the indicator. 'Sometimes I can't even look at him. It's just too much. And I really could have done with you being around this week.'

Ibrahim craned his head back and sighed. 'I'm sorry,' he said. 'It's just, it's difficult. Even getting here. Even *thinking* about getting here. And with me in Cardiff...'

'I know, Ib. And I know *why* you had to go to Cardiff.'

'What do you mean?'

'Yeah. Dad told me. After the bombings. Not long after your accident. We were watching the news, and they were talking about extremists, and he said you once got yourself mixed up with those nutters at the mosque that got raided. Is that true?'

His inability to answer her was all the answer she needed.

'Ha!' She laughed. 'My brother the terrorist.'

'Aish. It's not funny.'

'Oh, I don't know. I mean, look at you! It all makes sense now. Remember that time you tried getting us to wear the *niqab*, and me and my friends just laughed at you? Remember that?'

'Aish...'

'We were *thirteen*. And you and your mates thought we should go around dressed like ninjas?'

'Aish, please. It's not funny.'

'Yes. It is.' She gave him a sideways glance, smiling, expecting him to smile back, but he didn't. 'Someone's had a sense-of-humour bypass, I see.'

Little more was said for the remainder of their journey, though it took almost an hour and a half to reach the hospital. It was midday, and from Holborn to Limehouse the traffic moved at a listless, grinding pace. When Aisha spoke, it was to the traffic lights or the drivers of other cars, yelling insults and curses at the top of her voice.

Ibrahim, meanwhile, kept his hands on his knees and took slow, deep breaths. He had left his Valium behind some place, perhaps in Reenie's tent – wherever it was, it was in neither his bag nor his wallet when he left the police station – and though only a Sunday afternoon central London was still busy. So many cars, so many people. Cyclists weaving in and out of lanes. Motorbikes tearing between cars and buses and trucks. Armies of pedestrians pouring out into the road at every crossing. Thudding, almost industrial-sounding music blaring out of every souped-up, two-door cabriolet that passed them. This was London at its worst; a vortex of people and noise, the traffic smells of exhaust fumes and hot tarmac, the warm, damp air and stern sky promising rainstorms.

At the hospital in Newham they walked through vanishing-point corridors and the cloying stench of bleach and illness until they came to their father's ward. The man lying in a bed that looked more like a machine was small, but more than that he was *old*. His hairline had receded further in the years since Ibrahim last saw him, and what hair remained was streaked through with white. The colour had drained from his skin, leaving him a bloodless grey, like something carved from stone. Ibrahim wondered, for a moment, if they had entered the wrong ward, if Aisha had made some mistake. The man in the bed was barely recognisable as his father.

Aisha walked around the bed, taking up the chair at its side, and gestured to Ibrahim that he should do the same, but he could only stand and look down at the shrunken, grey old man beneath the blanket. His father was sleeping, and silent, and Ibrahim felt a jarring moment of resentment for him, an emotion he'd never give voice to.

He wanted to grab his father by the shoulders, shake him until he woke, and say, *'I came all this way, and you're asleep? Do you even care that I'm here?'*

Ibrahim thought of all the wasted hours without words that had passed between them, in all their journeys from London to Cardiff and back again; journeys that seemed long at the time but that were now dwarfed by the last week. He thought of all the bristling silences they had endured in the weeks and months after his friends were arrested: the accusatory glances and his father's frequent looks of disappointment and dejection. He thought of the years that had passed since they last spoke to – let alone saw – one another. He thought of all the things he would repair, if only he could go back; the choices he'd make and the words he'd place in those silences.

Aisha was on her feet again and at his side, holding his hand and taking him to the blue plastic chair, one arm reaching up to cradle his broad shoulders. She helped him into the chair beside their father's bed, and stroked the top of his head, leaving her hand there. He leaned in to her, his head against her side, and she held him close.

'It's okay,' she sighed. 'He's gonna be okay.'

Ibrahim nodded, though he didn't believe her, and he cried without sobbing, crying for the time and the people he'd lost and for the things he would never say.

Presently, they were joined by a doctor who greeted Ibrahim with surprise, as if he hadn't known there were a son as well as a daughter, and he talked Ibrahim through each detail of his father's condition. In a way, their father was lucky, the doctor said. If he had suffered such a stroke just ten years later he would almost certainly have died instantly. Even so, it might be months before Nazir Siddique would have any kind of mobility, and longer still for him to recover basic speech. He'd need round-the-clock care. Being the age that he was, it was unlikely he'd ever work again.

Through all this Ibrahim looked at his father and with each new detail watched him disappear, replaced by a helpless sketch of the man he once was. The man who had an opinion on everything was gone. The man who, if not working, became restless and agitated, who was always working, always busy: gone. The man who hated relying on others, who would happily struggle alone rather than ask for help, gone. When this doctor, with his cool, impassive voice – neither unsympathetic nor comforting – had finished tearing each facet of his father away, Ibrahim wondered if there was anything left except the grey husk now asleep in the bed.

The doctor left them, and Ibrahim reached out and held his father by the hand, something he hadn't done since childhood. Then, his father had insisted on holding his hand each time they crossed the road, and it was embarrassing (what if a school friend should see them?) and his father's grip was vice-like, almost painful, his skin rough and calloused, but beneath all that it made Ibrahim feel safe, as if nothing bad could ever happen to him while his father held his hand. Now his father's hand was limp – there was no grip in it, no strength – and even his skin felt softer, as if it wasn't the calluses that had given them their texture, but rather the life and the irascibility of the man himself that roughened and coarsened them.

And how irascible he'd been. When angry, Nazir Siddique's silences were keen, his words thunderous and terrifying. Though he'd lived his whole life in London, and spoke with an accent that was more East End than Punjab, his command of the language always felt stilted, unpolished. He spoke directly, never mincing his words. Five years ago they'd been in a situation much like this, Nazir and his son, only then their places were switched, with Ibrahim in the bed and his father at the bedside. It was only the second time Ibrahim had ever seen his father cry.

'Why these things?' he had asked, mopping the tears from his face with a handkerchief. 'Why do these things happen to *us?* What did *we* do that was so terrible?' He looked at his son and shook his head. 'Perhaps this is a sign. Those other boys, they faced justice. And at the time, I said to your mother, I said we should have called the police. It didn't seem fair, those other boys, and their mothers crying at the court, and you still at home, then going to university. Perhaps I *should* have called the police, told them what I knew, but I didn't, because you're my son. And so you went away, and we thought you were safe, but no. You find yourself a girlfriend. A *kafir*. If your mother was here… Do you think this is what she'd want? Because we didn't want you going to that mosque, with *those* people, you think this? You think we want you to marry a *kafir*, to have *kuffar* children. And then this happens. And it happens for a reason. *Ittaqullah*, Ibrahim. Justice will find you. Always.'

It started with those words, the fissure that opened up between them. The weeks, months and years when they didn't speak. Amanda's leaving him did nothing to remedy this, if anything making it worse. Suddenly he could blame his father for not only saying something so vile, but for causing the very process by which he stopped loving her, stopped loving *anyone*. But now, sitting at his father's bedside, holding his hand, Ibrahim wanted to tell him that if his accident was a part of some divine plan, that plan was more crafted and more brilliant in scale than anything Nazir Siddique ever imagined; a vast mechanism of meaningful coincidences, crossing paths, and lives brought together with precision timing. He would tell his father that life, when viewed in close-up, is chaos and noise. He would tell him that only when you draw back, retreat from the world, step outside it, do the patterns become visible, their meanings apparent. He would tell his father that he had never forgotten the name on the headstone he attacked with a hammer and chisel, that he remembered it even now, and that there must be a reason for this, because if there were no reason what was the point in anything?

Ibrahim and Aisha were in the ward almost two hours before their father woke. His eyes opened, and there was a moment's hesitation when he peered at his son as if trying to remember him. Then came the glint of recognition, and he tried to form a word, his mouth opening and closing silently on just a fragment of the nickname he had given his newborn son, and Ibrahim shook his head. It didn't matter. He didn't have to say a thing.

'It's Prakash, Dad,' said Ibrahim. 'I'm right here.'

And he held his father's hand a little tighter than before.

28

It was the first time she had been there – Upton Park, not London – in almost sixty years, and Reenie climbed familiar steps with much less vigour than she had the last time, and passed through the well-remembered, low, dark station before stepping out onto Green Street.

Across from the station, where there had once been a chemists, there was now a shabby currency exchange with too many brightly coloured notices in its windows. Next to that a former café, now boarded up and the wooden boards plastered with tattered posters. The chip shop was still there, but now nestled between a shop selling saris and another offering 'CASH FOR GOLD'. She stepped back against the station's brown-brick façade to make way for the crowd – Asian women in headscarves; colourfully dressed Africans; statuesque, track-suited Slavs – and her ears struggled against so many dialects to pick out a single word in English.

Bracing herself against all this movement and noise she considered turning left and left again, down onto Harold Road. From here it was just a short walk to the house where she and her father had lived, an even shorter one to the house where she had lived with Mr and Mrs Ostroff. She could walk the pavements where she and her friends carved their hopscotch grids with chalk, find the low brick walls where they would congregate before an elderly neighbour moved them on, or the crooked side streets where they smoked their first, clandestine cigarettes, but this would achieve nothing. Reenie wasn't nostalgic. Leaving this place had been almost too easy. By the time she ran away she felt she had little attachment to it. Perhaps it would have been more difficult if she'd thought she had roots, a real past here; if she could feel history's pulse beneath her feet.

From the moment her father arrived, and told her how

impermanent and unsafe Vienna had been, she could no longer think of Harold Road, or Upton Park, or even London as anything but temporary. All places, she came to believe, and carried on believing, are temporary. There was no such place as home, at least not in the past tense. Walk down Harold Road and all she would see were houses she hardly recognised, lived in by strangers. Different coloured front doors, different curtains in the windows. Different kids playing in the street. Best to ignore Harold Road altogether, turn right, and keep going along Green Street.

She passed through the almost chewably thick smells of the market, where crates of iced fish sat between barrows of bright fruit and intricately patterned rugs. Reggae music strolled beneath the banter and haggling of the stallholders, a polyglot cacophony of East End, Urdu, Slavic and sub-Saharan. This part of London was always noisy, and had been just as noisy – if not more so – in her childhood, when there were still factories nearby, but she was out of practice, no longer used to the bustle and the pace of it, to the clash of it happening all around her. She scanned the face of every white person she passed, looking for a trace of something – anything – Jewish, and she came up short. Even in the '50s there were few Orthodox Jews in this part of town, but she could still look at other people, other kids, and know they were like her. Where had they all gone?

She knew the answer. They had moved elsewhere. Some, like the Ostroffs, took the age-old sentiment – 'Next year in Jerusalem!' – as an order. Others drifted out into the suburbs and the counties, and it occurred to Reenie that the city's eastern reaches had always been the home of new arrivals. Chapels and churches became synagogues; synagogues became mosques.

Further along Green Street she saw nothing but posters and signs. Takeaways, letting agents, minicabs and Western Union. These were houses once. All these shops and takeaways had been people's living rooms. And opposite the shops-that-were-once-houses, West Ham's stadium; bigger and uglier than it ever was when she lived here, like a fortress, its fake turrets glowering down at the street.

That was London. Everything built on top of something else.

Turrets on a stadium. Terraced houses all dressed up with pebble dashing, mock Tudor, stone cladding. Dormer windows jutting like afterthoughts from rooftops. Everyone trying to find a little more space in all the nooks and crannies; just a bit more room to breathe.

The end result was a city that was different every time she saw it. Always shifting, always changing. On the train here, as soon as they were above ground she had looked for places she knew, but her only real moment of recognition came when she saw the rusting, drum-shaped skeletons of the gasworks near Bow Creek. Everything else was new or changed.

To her father the city had been forever foreign. He arrived months after the war's end looking hungry, but with a kind of hunger that could never be sated, and he'd never lose that lost and distant look, even after he remarried, as if he was forever in a different season to those around him.

Once reunited, there was no chance of them returning to Austria. Reenie was to all intents and purposes English, and what could Vienna offer them but disruption for her, and bitter remembrance for him? Besides, so much of the old city was gone now. It hadn't suffered the same obliteration as other cities – Hamburg, Dresden – but it had changed. And its people would have changed also. If they could have walked Vienna's streets, would others know their story just by looking at them? Would they feel shame for their complicity, or the unspoken consent their apathy had given to such crimes? If Albert Lieberman's old neighbours still lived there, could they have faced him, knowing how they'd watched impassively or even cheered as doctors and lawyers and schoolteachers were dragged from their homes and made to scrub the pavements on hand and knee, or as Albert and his wife were evicted and made to walk the streets, carrying a bare fraction of everything they owned?

'They made a bonfire of our belongings,' he once told her.

Vienna had nothing for them, and so they stayed in London. There, Albert Lieberman and his daughter tried to undo and repair seven years of damage and loss, and eventually they failed. Or rather, as Reenie saw it now, she had failed. Her father had witnessed things she could scarcely imagine, even when she had seen monochrome images of men and women rendered sexless by hunger, their corpses heaped up like so much refuse. A little maturity might have allowed her to forgive him for his quiet, insular moments, his occasional ill-tempered outbursts, his second marriage, or even his half-hearted move from *shul* to church, but she was just a girl, and a girl who didn't understand the depth and texture of real grief. She understood death, and the finality of death. What she couldn't understand, what took her years to understand, was loss and the vacuum it creates in a life. Her first glimpse of that kind of grief – immediate and raw – came when, thirteen years old, she attended her first funeral.

A neighbour of theirs, Eli Lipmann, was run over and killed in the street. He was a year younger than Reenie, but she knew him from school, knew his sister and the family well. It rained on the day of his funeral, she still remembered that. Though it was summer the sky was bruised, and as Eli's father recited *Kaddish* at his graveside, the rain began to fall. She wondered then if it rains at every funeral, no matter what the season, as if the sky was paying its respects, but more than that she remembered Mr Lipmann's expression; tired, no colour to him, as if he'd aged a decade in just three days. Staring at his son's too-small coffin in disbelief.

Eli was buried here, somewhere in this graveyard; a sprawling cemetery, well-hidden behind surrounding streets, its entrance tucked away in a gap between the terraces on Sandford Road.

What struck her there, more than at any other cemetery she had visited, was the density of the graves – so packed together, side by side, barely room to stand between so many of them – and the vastness of the sky. So much grey and so much stone, as if the place was camouflaging itself against the clouds. There could be few places in London this flat and open.

Above the cemetery, aeroplanes descended with agonising slowness, emerging from the clouds with all the urgency of gondolas, and beyond the graves and the synagogue the skyscrapers of Canary Wharf were hazy silhouettes on the horizon. Closer to the cemetery's edge, Reenie saw blocks of flats and the rooftops of houses; balconies garlanded with laundry, satellite dishes and aerials tilting at the sky.

She wondered if many people attended her father's funeral. She wondered if he had many friends when he died. Even in marriage Albert Lieberman had been a solitary man, preferring his own company, or the company of a book, to that of a large group. Could he have changed much in the years after she left? She doubted it. The box Lauren gave her, filled with forgotten trinkets and the framed photograph of Reenie's mother, suggested he hadn't. Other than the photograph, the items in it weren't so much things precious to Reenie – she'd taken anything with sentimental value with her when she left – as they were things that must have reminded him of her; the last remaining evidence that she'd been there, that they'd been together, however briefly. And now she saw her leaving him in another light again; this time as her denying him a victory that was already pyrrhic. He'd survived for her, after his home was taken from him, after every other member of his family, even his wife, was butchered, he'd survived, and had done so in the hope that he would see his daughter again. But reunited in East London she hadn't recognised him. She'd never seen a photograph of him, and Mr and Mrs Ostroff were strangers, volunteer foster parents. They'd never met the man official documents named as Avram Lieberman, knew nothing about him, and so could never describe him to his daughter.

How crushing it must have been for him to face that single truth; that his daughter had become a stranger, that to her he was as intangible as an imaginary friend – powerful when invisible and silent, but bound to disappoint in the flesh. She'd created an image of him as the conquering hero, fighting his way across Europe in a one-man struggle against the Nazis (she imagined him as Clark Gable or perhaps Gary Cooper, socking Hitler in the jaw with an impressive right hook), but when he arrived he was gaunt and frail, and spoke a language she didn't understand. Whole afternoons he would spend in their sitting room, listening to a recording of Bach's Cantata 159, and when he was in there, listening to that piece of music, he would say nothing, and could not be spoken to. He didn't look or sound like a hero, and so his daughter never thought of him as one, but perhaps seeing her again, and having her with him, was enough for him to taste a kind of victory, if only for a short while.

The shoebox full of trinkets became a trophy, then, of sorts. A small, shambolic memento of that brief time when Albert Lieberman, the conquering hero of his daughter's imagination, was winning, when it looked as if they might make it, that they might not lose everything.

His grave lay only a few blocks from the gates, a short distance from the attendant's house and the small shelter where visitors could wash their hands. Luckily for her, his grave faced out onto one of the wider paths – it wasn't tucked in tight behind another row of graves – but on both sides of him were the graves of strangers, and every headstone told a story.

To his left, the wide resting place of a couple who had lived into their nineties, dying within a month of each other. To his right, twin boys who died the day they were born. All strangers.

Her father's headstone was of plain, black marble; the Star of David, a line of Hebrew, his name, his real name, Avram, and the dates he was born and died written out in gold script. Below that, the inscription:

Father of Irene and Dorothy.
Beloved husband of
Irina (née Epstein) (1912-1943)
who perished in the Shoah
And Vera (née Brown)

Perished. Such an old-fashioned word. So polite. Nobody would say 'perished' these days. And it wasn't the word she would use. That bitterness almost blinded her to the sight of her own name, carved into the marble as if it belonged to someone else, but there it was: *Father of Irene and Dorothy.* As if she and Dorothy had grown up together, known each other.

Reenie reached into her bag and took out the pebble – palm-sized, smooth, a bluish grey – which she had brought from her garden in Cardiff, and she placed it at the base of the headstone. Something to say she was there, that someone had visited him, that he wasn't always alone.

His gravestone was practically new, the marble gleaming and the lettering unblemished, just as Lauren had said it would be. A replacement. But Reenie was too tired for anger. Those emotions required a strength she simply didn't have. It was easier for her to be relieved. Relieved that she had got there, relieved to find the headstone was replaced, relieved she would never have to see it in whatever state those bastards left it.

There were donations from strangers, Lauren told her. Some as far away as America. People who heard about the vandalism and gave money when Reenie hadn't even known, hadn't even heard or read about it. On her way across the cemetery she passed headstones that had subsided, and a workman toiling at levelling one out by hammering slabs of stone beneath one of its corners. The dull smack of the mallet still echoed across the cemetery. Other headstones were worn and weathered, wind and rain bleeding the colour from their inscriptions, but her father's grave looked bold and new, and if it didn't bear the date of his death in both calendars, she may have thought he'd passed recently.

She looked at those dates and tried to remember where she had been and what she had done that day; tried to recall if there had been a moment, however brief, when she had felt his passing. She wondered if she thought of him at all that day. She had heard friends talk about times when they felt such pangs of sadness, synchronised invariably with remote incidents of injury or death. In these stories a relative of theirs had died, and at that very moment and before hearing the news they smelled that loved one's perfume, suffered a migraine, or were seized by melancholy. Why, if these things were possible, hadn't this happened to her that day?

She had felt nothing. In time it became almost inevitable he must have died, but the uncertainty of it, the lack of proof, and of a date, something to pinpoint the moment of his death, meant she never truly grieved. Had anyone sat *shiva* for him? Did anyone recite *Kaddish* at his graveside? There were no sons, no brothers who survived. No man other than the rabbi. And so, alone and sitting on the hard ground beside his grave, Reenie began reciting the prayer; a prayer she had last said aloud for Jonathan.

'*Yitgadal viyitkadash shimay rabbah…*'

Magnified and sanctified be His great name in the world…

The words, from a language all but dead, came easily to her, and she wondered if only this prayer, with its harsh, foreign sounds, could properly mine the seam of loss inside her. It didn't matter that the deceased aren't mentioned once, that the prayer is about everything other than death. 'May his great name be blessed forever and into eternity' is what she said ('*Yehe shimay rabbah mevorakh le alam ul alme almaya*') and *These are the words we say when we're grieving* was what she thought. These are the words we say when we're grieving, just as 'I love you' are the words we say when there are too many words, and 'I'm sorry' when there are too few. And she kept thinking this until, unfalteringly, she had reached the prayer's end.

'*Vimru: Amein.*'

And let us say: Amen.

At 4pm she heard the crunch of footsteps on gravel, and glanced up to see the attendant, middle-aged with a grey beard and thick-framed glasses, walking towards her. When he was nearby he stopped for a moment, blinking at the grave, then Reenie.

'Are you a relative?' he asked, cheerily.

'I was,' said Reenie. 'I am.' She looked at the solitary grey pebble resting beside the headstone, then up at the attendant. 'Do me a favour, love,' she said. 'Sitting down's easy. Getting up again's the hard part.'

The attendant helped her to her feet and walked her back across the cemetery to the gates. 'Feel free to visit us again,' he said, with a warm smile, but Reenie left the cemetery knowing she would never come back.

At the junction of Green Street and Barking Road she thought she saw Ibrahim, just fleetingly, in a car that passed by as she waited for the lights to change. For a moment she was convinced it was him, but the young man in the car didn't notice her. His eyes were focused on the road ahead, his expression faraway. Looked just like him. She almost waved, but thought better of it. Couldn't be him, London was too big, and she no longer trusted her eyesight. Had to be someone else, a coincidence. Someone who looked like him. But whoever that young man in the car was, she hoped Ibrahim was safe, that he had reached his destination, found whatever it was he was walking to.

Reenie was so very tired, the pain in her feet and legs so constant, she struggled to remember a time when she hadn't felt it.

At Upton Park, on a crowded platform, she waited. A pair of teenage girls listened to music through shared headphones. A heavyset black man in luminous labourer's jacket and woolly hat rubbed his eyes with the palms of his hands. Three lads, tall and wiry and clad in tracksuits, stared lustfully at the headphone-sharing girls, but looked the other way the moment the girls noticed them. A white man in an ill-fitting grey suit, one of the few white men on the platform, checked his wristwatch and leaned out from the crowd to scan the tracks for an incoming train. Then the rails began to jangle, and with a metallic sigh the train came sweeping in. The doors opened, passengers got off, passengers got on, and Reenie began her journey back across the city.

Back, but to where? She was too exhausted to give it much thought. Her hands tingled with the cold and her feet throbbed inside her very damp and very old hiking boots. Perhaps she could shut her eyes and sleep a while.

She rested her head wearily against the window and looked out at a shifting horizon of skyscrapers where there had once been warehouses and cranes. Beyond the towers of Canary Wharf the sky was darkening like a frown. The clouds swallowed half the sky, and they resembled geological formations, high ridges and canyons bruised pink and purple by the setting sun; a world above the world. They looked hard, unmoveable, as if carved from something much more solid, more constant than vapour, and Reenie remembered her father telling her that in Vienna, when she could have been no older than three, she had once mistaken such clouds for snow-covered mountains. She had only the vaguest memories of that day, but her father remembered it clearly.

'We were travelling home from the zoo at Schöenbrunn,' he said. 'It was late winter, February, I think. Just the three of us. That month was quiet. What is it they say, in English? *The calm before the storm.* Things were becoming very bad for us. We didn't leave our neighbourhood very often, it wasn't safe. But that day we went from one side of Vienna to the other. And we looked like any other family. It was cold. Crisp, and beautiful, and sunny. But by the time we left Schöenbrunn there were large clouds in the sky.

'I was carrying you on my shoulders, like piggyback, yes? And you pointed at the clouds, and you shouted at the top of your voice, *"Berge! Berge!"* Mountains! Mountains!

'And I said to you, *"Nein, meine Liebling. Sie sind keine Berge. Sie sind Wolken…"* I said, They're not mountains, darling, they're clouds, but you did not believe me. No matter how hard I tried to tell you, you wouldn't believe me. You were so stubborn at that age. Well. How could I convince you? So I said, You shall see, darling. They may look like mountains now, but when you wake up in the morning, each and every one of them will be gone.'

Acknowledgments

A number of books helped furnish *Ibrahim & Reenie* with detail, in particular Bernard Wasserstein's *On the Eve: The Jews of Europe before the Second World War*, *Balti Britain* by Ziauddin Sardar, *The Islamist* by Ed Husain, *Radical* by Maajid Nawaz, Abdelwahab Meddeb's *Islam and Its Discontents*, *The Mystery of the Kaddish* by Leon Charney and Saul Mayzlish, *The Great Partition* by Yasmin Khan, and *Kerry's Children* by Ellen Davis. Any factual errors or misunderstandings are mine, and not the authors'.

Where I've quoted from works of Sufi poetry those translations are taken from Penguin Books' *Islamic Mystical Poetry: Sufi Verse from the Early Mystics to Rumi*, edited by Mahmood Jamal, and Farid Attar's *The Conference of the Birds*, translated by Afkham Darbandi and Dick Davis.

The insights into brain injury provided by Tim Williamson and Dave Hampson couldn't have been gleaned from any book, and were very much appreciated, as was the input of Tim Wells, Zahra Ullah and Jeni Williams.

Finally, I would like to thank Christine and Brian Stone for telling me the story that inspired this novel and Dan Edwards for providing me with the garden, table and chair – not to mention the hope – to begin writing it.

About the Author

David Llewellyn was born in Pontypool in 1978. His novels include *Eleven* and *Everything is Sinister*. He lives with his partner in Cardiff.